When she stepped inside her apartment, Caroline entered the bedroom and took off her shirt and slacks. Eight o'clock on a Saturday night and she could think of nothing better to do than go to bed. Alone, too.

She checked her answering machine.

No messages.

Nothing from The Caller.

She picked up the telephone and dialed Daniel Romero's room number, but there was still no answer.

She took off her bra and panties and stared at her reflection in the mirror. A sensation of vulnerability went through her, as if her nakedness were a target focused through the sights of some sniper's rifle—

Which was when she realized that she wasn't alone in the apartment.

Cold terror. A chilly instinct—

Somebody was here—

She listened, holding her breath, then moved toward the bathroom door, thinking that if she locked it she'd be safe.

As she reached for the handle, the plastic shower curtain shivered and crackled and the small curtain hooks rattled together and a shadow moved toward her . . .

**THE INTRUDER**

Bantam Books by Thomas Altman
Ask your bookseller for the books you have missed

DARK PLACES
THE INTRUDER
KISS DADDY GOODBYE

# THE INTRUDER

*Thomas Altman*

BANTAM BOOKS
TORONTO • NEW YORK • LONDON • SYDNEY • AUCKLAND

THE INTRUDER
*A Bantam Book / October 1985*


*For information address: Bantam Books, Inc.*

ISBN 0-553-24113-3

*Published simultaneously in the United States and Canada*

---

*Bantam Books are published by Bantam Books, Inc. Its trademark, consisting of the words "Bantam Books" and the portrayal of a rooster, is Registered in U.S. Patent and Trademark Office and in other countries. Marca Registrada. Bantam Books, Inc., 666 Fifth Avenue, New York, New York 10103.*

---

PRINTED IN THE UNITED STATES OF AMERICA

H 0 9 8 7 6 5 4 3 2 1

*To Nessa Rapoport,*
*who did some heartfelt*
*editing.*

# 1

Caroline Cassidy struggled out of a dream she hadn't enjoyed, one of those faintly menacing dreams she assumed had its origin in a feeling of guilt. Although nothing had actually happened, there had been the nameless sensation that something was about to. Something darkly unpleasant.

Frightening.

She opened her eyes and for a moment couldn't remember the name of the man who lay sleeping beside her. She smoothed her yellowy hair away from her face and gazed at her companion. He had thick gray hair the color of steel and a firm face that hadn't slackened in sleep. His broad arms lay outside the covers. A tattoo on his upper left arm had been cut in the shape of a tulip. His whole body was taut, solid, stomach flat, muscles hard.

Caroline sat upright.

Whore, she thought.

You meet a guy at four in the afternoon, you never saw him before in your life, then at eight o'clock you're in bed with him and he's making love to you in ways you never knew existed.

She tilted her head back, stared upward at the ceiling.

She smiled.

Daniel Romero, that was his name. She touched his tattoo lightly.

He had made love with a strange mixture of roughness and delicacy, exploring her entire body with his lips and hands, making her feel perfectly tuned. Rough and delicate.

Something else too.

An edge of danger.

She shook her head and thought: I couldn't have done what I did, I couldn't have played that kind of game with him.

But you did, Caroline.

He opened his eyes and stared at her. There was something just a little cold in the gray eyes, she wasn't sure what. They were the color of recently dead ashes.

"I know this is going to sound like a line," she said. "But I don't exactly make a habit of this."

"I figured that." He had a deep voice. "You were a little shy."

"Shy?"

He smiled. She couldn't tell how old he was. Mid-forties maybe. It was hard to know. Shy, she thought. How could he even say a thing like that after what had happened? She's never felt so . . . uninhibited.

"Maybe you don't see a lot of action around this place," Romero said.

Caroline reached for the relic of a joint in the bedside ashtray and lit it, inhaling slowly. There was a sensation of warm water gliding toward her brain, relaxing nerves and muscles. A lot of action, she thought. Las Cosimas wasn't exactly Vegas, for sure, but it wasn't altogether a morgue either. She watched smoke rise from her fingers to the bedside lamp.

"You shouldn't smoke that stuff," he said. "It's bad for you."

"It makes me feel okay." And she smiled at him. She moved her eyes a little, gazing toward the half-open curtains. It was almost dawn: you could see little stitches of pale gray light embroidered through the darkness. Daniel Romero yawned, reached for her hand, held it lightly. Then he took the joint from her fingers and crushed it in the ashtray.

"I don't like to see a pretty young woman ruining her health," he said. He lowered his face and pressed his mouth against her knuckles as she slid back against the pillow, closing her eyes. She lay without moving, listening to the sound of his breath against her skin. A moment out of time. A suspension of clocks. She could feel herself begin to drift. What did she know about this Daniel Romero in any case? He had come, he said, from somewhere in Wisconsin; he was thinking of relocating in California and had selected Las Cosimas as a likely prospect. He had stepped into her office and she'd liked him immediately—there was a decisive quality about him, someone in control of himself, a man who seemed to move and think with a fixed purpose. She couldn't imagine Daniel Romero ever being caught in two minds about anything.

She liked that kind of man.

Now she opened her eyes and rolled away from him, rising from the bed with a sheet twisted around her body. Romero gripped the corner of it and stripped it away from her.

"You look better naked," he said.

She put her hands on her hips and tossed her hair back from her shoulders, conscious of the way she was coming across as provocative.

He makes me behave like a whore, she thought.

After a moment, she turned and went inside the bathroom. She closed the door, moved past the mirror, paused at the window. Below, there was a square of stores and boutiques, an expanse of red cobbles neatly landscaped with trees that grew from huge wooden tubs. The beating heart of Las Cosimas. Its nerve center. She could see the little stores that had been endowed with cute names. Re-Threads, which sold expensive used clothing. Tubby's, where you went if you wanted to buy yourself a sauna. The Green Valet, an emporium that specialized in selling and maintaining plants.

Caroline Cassidy closed her eyes a moment. She could sense Las Cosimas all at once, the houses built on the gentle hills that stretched away beyond the square. Large redwood homes with sundecks and swimming pools and exotic plants that cluttered the front yards or masked the invariable two-car garages. Stained-glass windows, solar panels on the shingled rooftops, open-plan spaces with concealed stereo speakers and kitchens in which you knew there were scrubbed pine counters and whole-wheat muffins in refrigerators and unwrapped tofu. Las Cosimas, a planned community, a dormitory for executives who made their living in the computer industry, whose lives were filled with a strange argot that included words like semiconductors and integrated circuits and microchips.

Las Cosimas, with its plush country club and well-lighted tennis courts and health spas and its smattering of expensive restaurants that specialized in nouvelle cuisine: tiny portions of frog legs in raspberry and kiwi sauce. . . .

Caroline washed her face, brushed her teeth quickly. She liked her own appearance, the high cheekbones and the unusual blue of her eyes. She looked like she had spent her college years lying on Californian beaches, surrounded by surf-bums and muscular young men who always seemed to be searching for a drowning victim they could rescue at the last possible moment.

In fact, Caroline had been born and raised in the East, had spent a year at Wellesley, a place she'd hated. Her father, a man who had made a reasonable fortune on Wall Street by dealing in such boring commodities as rubber and soybeans, had sent her to Rutgers, where she'd dropped out after a year of history. A family shame—why couldn't she be like her brother, Roy, who lived a smugly expensive life in Miami, where he ran a lucrative chain of clam-chowder joints? Why did Caroline have to be so different?

After Rutgers she'd spent a year in Washington, rising to a junior-executive position with a company that dealt in tax shelters and investments and pension plans for a wealthy clientele composed mainly of persons too senile to understand the time of day, let alone the intricacies of financial management. Then, somewhere along the way, she had run into a certain J M Dunbar, the man who had developed the community of Las Cosimas. Dunbar was a Man with a Dream. Computers were the Coming Thing. People who designed computers were the New Rich. They needed nice homes to live in. And J M Dunbar would fill that need by creating the town of Las Cosimas (named after an obscure Mexican village where he'd apparently spent his honeymoon).

Caroline went to work for J M Dunbar and his Dream in a capacity that was not exactly well-defined. She wrote publicity brochures, she handled public relations for the Las Cosimas Development Company, and she dabbled occasionally in real estate. For this nebulous employment she was well-paid and lived in a rent-free apartment on the fashionable Hermosillo Square. (In pursuit of his long-ago Mexican romance, J M Dunbar had named all the streets of Las Cosimas after Mexican towns and villages.)

Las Cosimas, Caroline thought. A place where nothing much ever seemed to happen. J M Dunbar's Paradise for Executives, gorgeous and safe. Safe because Dunbar was a man who believed in the gospel of security, which, for the residents of Las Cosimas, came with a high price tag. They could afford it: people who lived in Las Cosimas didn't have to worry where the next Perrier or the next Mercedes was coming from. Or the next gram of cocaine, for that matter.

And she turned her thoughts to Daniel Romero because she couldn't imagine him living in this community. For one thing, what kind of work did he do? She couldn't quite see him hunched over a circuit board or developing some innovative piece of software.

A little mystery here: was that why she felt so drawn to him?

Romero was sitting up in bed and smoking a cigarette. His gold cigarette case lay open on the bedside table. Tobacco's okay, reefer's taboo. Well, well.

"So," he said. "You think I should buy a home in this burg of yours?"

She shrugged. "If it's what you want, Daniel." She paused a moment. "You never said what kind of work you do."

"You're right. I never said."

"Meaning you don't intend to?"

"Meaning nothing. Maybe I just want to find a little peace and quiet. Maybe that's all I want these days."

A slight shadow moved in her mind. He was concealing something. She went slowly toward the bed and looked down at him. He reached up and stroked her breasts, pinching the nipples gently. Then a little more severely as she lowered her body against him. She wanted to say that he was hurting her but she didn't talk—somehow she understood that the pleasure she experienced with him had its origins somewhere along the taut wire which separates the gentle from the violent. That thin, terrible dividing line.

She felt his hands slide between her legs and she held her breath.

There. On the rug beside the bed.

The strips of white bandage he'd fetched from the bathroom earlier, which he'd held out toward her, puzzling her until she understood what it was he wanted to do. At first, the notion had repelled her. She'd never been interested in anything like this before. It was a concept she relegated to the pages of weird magazines. But to her own surprise, she hadn't reacted, hadn't fought him off when he'd gathered her hands behind her back and bound them.

"A game," he said. "Just a game."

"I never played it before." A stranger, God, a man I don't know anything about, a man I never saw before, and he makes me do things I never did in my whole life. . . .

Now she thrust her body toward him, hoping, actually hoping he'd tie her hands again, but this time he didn't, he moved slowly on top of her, entered her, and she lost herself against him.

When she started to scream later, she felt Daniel Romero cover her mouth with his hand.

# 2

Tobias knew the names of all the plants and trees and shrubbery that grew along the streets of Las Cosimas. He had learned to recognize nandina and jacaranda and eucalyptus and he had come to tell one scent from the others that blew through the dark streets during his nightly patrols. He even understood that when the soft breezes blew in from the Pacific the air was filled with a quality for which a man was supposed to feel grateful. Something clean and good and pure. As he paused on the corner of Guaymas Drive, he took his cap from his head, scratched his scalp, and wondered why—despite the obvious beauty and tranquillity of Las Cosimas—he had come to the irrevocable decision that what he really wanted was lead in the air, gas fumes and glorious pollution, the kind of clogged city air that was a high all of its own.

He stuck his hands in the pockets of his stiff brown pants, conscious of the gold stripe that ran from his hip to his cuffs: it was a ridiculous uniform and he felt clownlike in it.

Nandina and jacaranda and eucalyptus.

The very names of these plants made him feel he was an alien moving through a very strange land indeed. Now, as he walked past the orderly houses, he could hear the hum of air-conditioning units or the hissing of sprinkler systems or the swish of water that suggested some nocturnal activity in a hot tub. When he reached the corner of Guaymas, he found himself on Monterrey Drive, darkened by huge trees at this silent hour of the dawn. Las Cosimas, he thought.

Lost Cosimas.

Lost Causes.

He remembered other times, other streets. He remembered a city that never closed. He remembered the mixed smells of roasting chestnuts, hot dogs, and garbage. Wild broken-down neighborhoods, where the only bath anybody ever got was from a busted fire hydrant, where there were punks who thought they owned the streets and corpses were fished out of the East River, where there were handguns and muggings and old ladies stabbed for a few nickels, where old men beyond the reaches of welfare sustained themselves on cans of catfood on good days, where the streets of Manhattan were wild and glorious like a sadistic mistress that kept whipping you—and you, driven by the whims of your poor foolish heart, went back time and again for more of the same punishing love.

The way he missed the city was like a tiny hole in his heart, a place he couldn't plug.

Now here he was in the Garden of Eden and a long way removed from the city of dreams and decent pretzels.

Tobias crossed Monterrey and started up the hill. When he reached the crest, he stopped once again. He took a small leather tobacco pouch from his jacket and began to roll himself a cigarette. The pouch carried his initials in faded gilt. TM. A gift from his son. Long ago now—but how could you measure the seasons of grief? There was a slow ticking in your heart, something you knew wasn't ever going to stop.

A boy dies.

You could reduce it to three easy words, but it didn't make a bit of difference. It was past, the way his beloved New York City had receded. His own wake, his jetstream.

Manhattan. A dead son. He rolled the cigarette, lit it, closed his eyes a moment. Behind the smell of smoke, he could catch a hint of the distant tide. He flipped the butt away (such a small mischief: littering these pristine streets) and wondered what his old partner Art Frye was doing right this minute in Manhattan. Art Frye. A dead boy. A lost city. Everything was tethered together, like a knotted length of string that was the total sum of your history.

Sighing, he started downhill, seeing faint lights on the water below, thin reflections of dying bulbs that had been strung out along the short stretch of the old pier.

Here was the underbelly of Las Cosimas. The snake in the Garden. The shadowy places. The Mexican Quarter that had been here when Las Cosimas had been nothing but a twinkle in the eyes of J M Dunbar.

It was the only part of Las Cosimas Tobias liked. And J M Dunbar, despite his millions, hadn't been able to buy the Mexican Quarter because there were deep family roots there, traditions, things Dunbar could never understand. Three or four blocks of run-down buildings and decrepit stores. Sooner or later, the executives who lived in Las Cosimas with their pretty little bimbo wives would turn the Quarter into a tourist ghetto and the Mexican pots would come from North Korea and the wrought-iron gateways would be fresh from foundries in Taiwan. The taco stands would yield to such fast-food concoctions as burritos stuffed with bean sprouts and touted as Tijuana Eggrolls.

When he reached Libertad Street, the place was deserted. A single weak light burned in the window of Enrico's Taverna, a bar that observed a curious chronology all its own.

He stepped into the taverna and moved toward the

counter. Three guys sat at a table in the corner. Although Tobias recognized them, he knew only one by name, a good-looking kid called Carlos who sometimes made extra pin money tending the greens at the country-club golf course. The other two were farmworkers who stopped to shoot tequila before they rode in their broken-down old truck some twenty miles to pick apricots. And Enrico always kept his place open for them. Some kind of tradition. Tobias put his elbows on the bar, glanced toward the dusty window in which a neon tequila sign hung. Beat-up trucks and surreal lowriders were parked all over the Quarter: you wouldn't get any of the Mercedeses or the Porsches down there.

"Tobias." Enrico approached him. He was old and small and his flesh hung loosely on his bones, but there was a bright quality to his eyes, as if some essential part of him inside had refused to age. He opened a Dos Equis and slid it toward Tobias.

"How's business?" Tobias asked.

"Quiet," and Enrico shrugged. "It's always quiet in Las Cosimas."

Yeah, Tobias thought. What this place needs is some good old-fashioned mugger, or maybe a team of bad-check artists, or some mysterious nighttime prowler scaring the well-dressed wives of the computer execs. He smiled at Enrico and glanced at the three guys in the corner. They wore plaid shirts and blue jeans and they looked as if they breathed dust and dirt instead of oxygen. He sipped his beer, then set the bottle down.

Enrico said, "I tell you what I don't understand, Tobias. I don't understand a cop who don't have a patrol car. You tell me: what kinda cop is it that walks everywhere, eh?"

Tobias wiped his lip with the back of his hand. That little mustache he'd taken to wearing recently would have to go. It was always trapping liquids. "Our good sheriff believes in public relations, Enrico. He believes a cop can only be a cop if he wears out a pair of boots every month. Personal contact with the neighborhood. A cop in a car doesn't cut it. So I walk."

Enrico smiled, glancing at Tobias's beer a moment. "Makes sense," he said. Tobias wasn't sure if the old guy was being sarcastic.

Tobias was silent. The Good Sheriff, one Karl Rezabek, formerly a colonel in the United States Marines, had stepped into civilian life as if the world were nothing but an extension of army disciplines, rules and tired regulations that had to be obeyed no matter what.

The Book, that's what Rezabek called it.

Live by the Book. Die by the Book.

A holy manuscript, illuminated by monks like Rezabek and all the countless monks that had gone before him.

Tobias drained his beer, and as he did so his walkie-talkie crackled into life. For a moment he was tempted to ignore the damn thing. It hung on his hip like some kind of tumorous growth to be surgically removed. Someone pass the scalpel, please.

Enrico seemed amused by the gadget. "You gonna answer that, Tobias?"

Tobias plucked the device from his belt, pressed a button, and said, "Manning here," embarrassed by the way the three Mexicans at the corner table turned to smile at him.

Rezabek's voice came through loud and clear and clipped. "Manning? Where are you?"

Tobias wanted to say that he was getting drunk in a Mexican bar, but that kind of activity wasn't included in the Good Sheriff's immaculate schedules. "I'm just leaving the Quarter," was how he answered.

Crackle crackle. Sometimes Tobias had the odd impression that the airwaves were filled with the sounds of breakfast cereals popping in bowls of milk.

Rezabek came back through: "We've got a missing-persons report, Manning."

Tobias said nothing, wondering how somebody could contrive to go missing in Las Cosimas. All those nice well-marked, well-lighted streets. It wasn't exactly a ghetto, a maze of alleys where you needed a compass to find your way around.

"You better get back here," Rezabek said.

"Right," Tobias answered.

"Over and out at 0523 hours," said the sheriff.

Tobias strapped the gizmo back on his belt and gazed a moment at his empty beer bottle. Missing persons. What was it? Some loony computer engineer whisked off in a flying saucer to have his brain probed? Tobias closed his eyes, rubbed the lids: Your trouble is, Tobe, you do not take this place seriously. You do not give it any credence. You see it all as California Fake, the houses nothing more than movie-set fronts, the people extras from Central Casting. Even the Mexicans might have been imported from south of the border to add a little local color.

Smiling, he raised one hand in the direction of Enrico; then he stepped out into a dark that was dissolving rapidly now, faint lights on the water and streaks of yellow sun trapped in the sails of small boats.

0523 hours, he thought.

You couldn't be a real cop in Las Cosimas.

You could only be a kind of glorified security guard, under the generalship of a man who dreamed nights of planting flags on Iwo Jima and other colonial outposts.

* * *

Tobias crossed Hermosillo Square, trying to ignore the boutiques, whose window contents were now becoming apparent in the rising sunlight. He listened to the echo of his own footsteps and, despite himself, glanced every now and than at the little shops. He saw mannequins contorted into positions that suggested St. Vitus' dance. Ostrich feathers. Dangling furs. Outrageous hats. Rattan furniture that had not been designed to hold human beings.

Halfway across the square, he paused.

There was a light in one of the apartment windows over the stores. And the brief movement of a figure against glass. Tobias held his breath, watched a moment, then moved on.

A figure against glass, he thought.

The figure of a young woman.

He pushed the image from his mind as he left the square and walked toward Mascota Street, where the Police Department offices were located. (HQ, as Rezabek called the place.) Halfway along the street a large black Lincoln was parked. He stopped, studied the expensive vehicle a moment, observed the Wisconsin plates; then he continued toward the Department.

A strange car on Mascota Street.

And the report of a missing person.

The joint was jumping tonight.

He stepped beneath the lamp that hung above the office doorway, and the image of Caroline Cassidy came back at him, thrusting itself into his mind.

Making him feel the clawing of an old hunger.

Not far from Enrico's tavern, the tide slithered against the rotted wood piles of the old pier, ferrying scraps of wood and clumps of seaweed and the occasional carcass of a dead fish. As it shoved these things back and forward in its relentless movement toward the beach, it created a certain repetitive music, as if it meant the debris to dance to its monotonous tune. Quick white flecks caught the meager pier lights, then changed, then died.

Apart from the usual flotsam, the sea carried something else tonight.

Something that would inevitably find its lifeless way up onto the sands and lie there, exposed to daylight like a stranded sea beast.

# 3

Karl Rezabek wore his hair cut so close into his scalp that his head had a faintly blue tint. His fingernails were immaculately clipped and his hands, perhaps incongruously, were those of a pianist or surgeon. Delicate, sensitive things that might have been used to perform either sonatas or lobotomies. Apart from his hands, he resembled nothing so much as a bullet. He had stumbled into his present position as sheriff of Las Cosimas through the good offices of the Old Military Boys' network. His name had been whispered into J M Dunbar's ear by someone who owed Rezabek a favor dating back to those halcyon days at boot camp. And Karl, pensioned, honorably discharged, seized the opportunity to continue upholding the laws of the land. That he saw no difference between civilian and military law hardly mattered to him. A regulation was a regulation, a uniform a uniform. And this morning, just after dawn, he had a missing person to deal with. (It was only a slight inconvenience that there was a difference between a missing person and someone who had gone AWOL.)

He studied his hands for a moment, in the manner of someone examining his most prized possessions, and then he raised his blunt face and looked at Tobias Manning, who had come in only a few moments before. He always found a certain sullen, insubordinate quality about Manning, a certain insolence that implied a lack of respect. He understood Manning's problem, of course: the guy was a fish out of water, nothing more. He was a transplanted New York cop, somebody accustomed to taking the rules and regulations with more than a pinch of the old proverbial salt—bending things here, twisting them there, whenever it suited his purpose. Such bendings and twistings were not considerations in the sheriff's scheme of things.

There had to be a little envy also—after all, Manning had street experience and here he was, after fifteen years pounding the streets of Manhattan, subordinate to a former colonel in the U.S. Marines.

Karl Rezabek liked to think he took everything into account in his assessment of other people. Their emotional strengths, their failings, their personal sorrows, their grievances: he enjoyed the notion that he was, above all else, a fair man. And as he looked at Manning, who was leaning against the wall, he knew that the man had had enough tragedy in his life to explain a whole lot of things about his attitudes.

Rezabek stroked the palms of his hands together.

To lose a son was bad enough, he thought. (He himself was unmarried and childless, but he had imagination.) And then to have your wife die on you—salt in the old wounds, for God's sake. Things like that left deep furrows in a person's heart. The young man, David, had died of some congenital heart disease back in New York City. After which, Tobias Manning had fetched his wife out to Las Cosimas, a fresh start, a new life . . . and Edith Manning had expired after only a few months. The same withering heart disease, Rezabek understood.

Some families carried curses, like fault lines just beneath their emotional surfaces.

Rezabek rose from his chair, cleared his throat. There was another son, a kid called Paul, off at college somewhere. At least Manning had somebody left. At least there was that.

The sheriff looked at the digital wall clock.

0555 hours.

He cleared his throat again and tried to dismiss from his mind the suspicion that Officer Manning was given to the habit of sipping a couple of beers in the Quarter during his patrols. He looked at Manning again. There was a crumpled quality to the man's uniform, an untidiness that rankled the sheriff, but he chose not to say anything.

The missing person, he thought. AWOL.

"Sharp," he said.

Manning pushed himself away from the wall. "Sharp?"

"Isadora Sharp," the sheriff said. "Wife of Henry Sharp."

Manning nodded. He folded his arms a moment; then he took out his tobacco pouch and began to roll one of those foul cylinders he constantly inhaled.

"Henry Sharp. Big wheel at Sharp MicroSystems."

"I know the name, Sheriff."

"Last saw his wife at supper. Said she wasn't feeling good. Went up to bed. Sharp worked on some papers. At two hundred hours he went to bed. Wife gone. Two hours later he calls me."

Tobias Manning listened to the clipped way Rezabek talked. He had the odd feeling he was being sprayed by tiny pellets. Maybe this was the efficient military mode of communication. Waste not, want not. Make yourself understood. No frills.

"Maybe she went for a walk. Maybe she's got a nocturnal lover."

Rezabek shrugged, returned to his chair. "If she went for a walk, she did it barefoot."

"Henry counted her shoes, did he?"

It crossed Rezabek's mind that Tobias was being sarcastic, but he ignored the possibility. "People walk barefoot, Manning. It's not exactly unknown."

Tobias nodded. "How old is Mrs. Sharp?"

Rezabek consulted a sheet of paper on his desk. "Full description right here. Late thirties. Five-seven. Black hair worn in curls. Was apparently wearing bottle-green negligee when she went to bed."

Bottle green, Tobias thought. I like that one. Not Lincoln, not pea, not avocado. Bottle. "Maybe she's a romantic. Maybe she likes strolling around at dawn. She could be at that time of life when she's bored with Henry, bored with the way he sits up working on papers while she's tossing restlessly around in the marital bed. So. She gets up and goes off into the darkness."

Rezabek smiled suddenly, a secretive little look that meant some item of important information had been strategically withheld. "I hardly think so, Manning. I hardly think she was prone to late-night rambling."

"Why?"

"Henry Sharp says she's sick. A sick woman. Regular medication. Not very strong."

Tobias was silent a moment.

Medication. Sick. Not very strong.

Old echoes, tiny reverberations, little sounds of his history he didn't want to hear. He gazed at the tobacco pouch in his fist and he thought of the empty apartment here in Las Cosimas that he would go back to, as he went back to it every damn day of his life, empty apartment, empty bed, silent rooms . . . And all the ghosts everywhere, as if they—not he—were in possession of the property.

"So, we've got a sick woman who's vanished into the night," he heard himself saying in a voice so flat he hardly recognized it as his own. "And if she's that sick, she couldn't get very far, could she?" He paused; then: "Did Henry Sharp say what was wrong with her?"

"He wasn't specific," Rezabek answered.

Tobias shut his eyes. Caroline Cassidy in the window. Why the hell was that always coming back to him? He had talked to the young woman twenty, thirty times on the street. He'd noticed her walk toward her pale blue Datsun with a high-kicking grace that made him feel a tightness inside his chest. A chiffon scarf fluttering behind her, her long hair billowing, her black cord pantsuit clinging to her body.

Enough already, he told himself. Go find yourself this missing woman. Go find the errant wife of Henry Sharp.

As if it were relevant, Rezabek was droning on about the life and career of Henry Sharp, who, it seemed, was some kind of revered pioneer in the field of computers. And it was this same Henry Sharp who was turning his attention to the future applications of holograms—you might think H Sharp was some kind of high-tech saint, if you were to judge from the tone of Rezabek's voice. Suddenly it occurred to Tobias that the only reason Rezabek wanted to find the missing wife was less any concern for her safety and more the sycophantic urge to please one of the hotshots of Las Cosimas. Big house up on Esmeralda Canyon Drive, the sheriff was saying. Big place with the TV dish. You must have noticed it.

Tobias tried to pay attention. "Big house. Big dish. Yeah, I know it." No, the verb "to know" was too strong here. He'd seen the joint, spread like some modern castle against the sky. Henry had wired the whole place to run by computers. Computers turned on thermostats and greeted you at the door and a whole bunch of other stuff. The guy probably had electronic German shepherds roaming the grounds.

Rezabek was silent a moment. A vague look of sadness crossed his face. He said, "Three years, Manning. Three years sheriff of Las Cosimas. First missing person yet."

Tobias stifled a yawn. A sick woman takes a hike.

Simple things like that had complex consequences, such as preventing one weary officer from tumbling into his big empty bed. And the big empty spaces in his own heart.

"We'll take my car," Rezabek said.

Outside, Tobias noticed that the sleek black Lincoln with the Wisconsin plates had gone, leaving a strange, indefinable vacancy, an absence emphasized by the strong yellow sunlight.

Like a hole in the fabric of things.

When Caroline Cassidy woke, she lazily stretched one hand across the bed, finding it empty. Blinded by slats of sun, she forced her eyes open. Her mysterious lover was gone—and yet she had a strange sense that he was nearby. One of those fine spidery intuitions unrelated to reason, the kind of nebulous feeling you couldn't quite locate. Licking her dry lips, she pushed the bedsheet aside and stepped onto the rug.

Come out, come out, wherever you are.

She tiptoed toward the bathroom door and yanked it open, expecting to see Danny Romero in front of the mirror, shaving himself with her dainty little pink-handled razor.

But there was no Daniel in the small room.

Very quietly she called out his name.

An echo chamber.

She crossed the bedroom and stepped inside the living room.

No Danny. No Mr. Wisconsin.

She sat down on the sofa, crossed her bare legs, gazed

at the closed slats of the venetian blinds. Maybe it had been one of those One-Nighter Affairs. Slam and thankyou and gone with the wind. It wasn't her custom to indulge in these casual encounters, because she'd always found them in the past to be unsatisfactory. A collision of strangers. The quick wet passage of flesh. What did you say your name was again?

Mr. Romero, who had come into her office talking real estate, who said he'd rented a room at the Las Cosimas Country Club and Resort, who said he was staking out the territory. Who said, who said.

Why did she suddenly feel that she was the territory that had just been staked?

She rose and wandered around the room.

Still the feeling persisted that he was close.

A figure in a closet. Breathing heavily. Hiding behind a sofa or a drape, trying not to giggle.

A practical joker.

She moved out into the hallway.

It was a dim space, far removed from the reaches of the sun.

The sensation she had was of somebody disappearing out of the corner of her eye. Nothing definite, nothing she could get a fix on. But when she swung her head around she saw that the front door was halfway open, and even though she called out his name a couple of times she heard nothing by way of an answer.

She had never liked jokers much—she'd never cared for those pranksters who, at the lower end of the joke scale, placed plastic dog droppings on rugs, or those others, somewhat more ambitious, who hid in secret places to scare you or made telephone calls and did nothing except breathe heavily, as if they might be calling direct from a sauna. Like the call she'd received yesterday at her office when there hadn't been anyone on the other end of the line except for a Breather. What she'd imagined then was a spindly little guy with a skinny face and a greasy gabardine standing inside a phone booth, one hand tucked down inside his baggy pants and dirty fingernails playing with his puny member.

She stepped inside the living-room and felt a strange little sense of expectation—a kind of intuition that Daniel Romero was going to spring up from behind the sofa or that the phone was going to scream at her suddenly.

But neither of these things took place.

Just the same, her absurd uneasiness didn't go away as quickly as she would have liked.

# 4

Rezabek drove the gray-and-black Honda Accord with the LCPD insignia on the door panels. This shield, said to have been dreamed up by J M Dunbar on the Sunday following the scant weeks it had taken him to construct Las Cosimas, consisted of two angry-looking eagles perched atop what appeared to be the arched gateway to a hacienda. If this symbol had any significance, it was known only to the old man himself. (There were those in the Quarter who referred to the twin eagles as Los Estreñidos, the Constipated Ones.)

Rezabek drove carefully, as if he were welded to the rim of the steering wheel. The curving driveways and gentle canyons of Las Cosimas assumed a diversity of textured shadows in the morning light. Houses appeared to float on the calm air or at least on invisible stilts. Tobias, drowsy, saw the rambling structure of the Las Cosimas Country Club and Resort, the eighteen-hole golf course float off into a pink-tinted mist that rose from the ocean. Even at this godforsaken hour a solitary loony could be seen in the distance pursuing a golf ball.

The sheriff, eyes epoxied to the road ahead, cleared his throat. "I figure you must have had some experience, Manning. This kind of thing."

Tobias drummed his fingers on the dash. "What kind of thing?" he asked.

"You know. Missing persons." Was it a trick of the light

or did some slight flush of awkwardness go across the sheriff's face?

"Now and again," Tobias said. Then fell silent. Sometimes Rezabek's presence plunged him into a mean, taciturn mood, a place where he didn't particularly want to be helpful. Let the guy ask me outright for my expertise and not go pussyfooting around like this.

"They turn up, I guess," Rezabek said.

"Sometimes. Sometimes they don't."

"Tell me the percentages, Manning."

"Hard to say. Some guys walk right off the face of the earth. Mortgages. Debts. Can't hack the kids. Can't stand the wife. Then again, you get it the other way around. It's the wife can't take it anymore and so she splits. Now and again somebody spots them in North Dakota or New Mexico and you're off on a wild-goose chase. Mainly, though, they go the way of Judge Crater."

As if satisfied, Rezabek nodded. It never pleased the sheriff to ask questions of Tobias Manning, and he always tried to skirt the edges of inquiry. In his own mind, there was a definite pecking order, a hierarchy, and an ex-colonel of the Marines was some way higher up the ladder than a cop out of New York City.

In the rising sun more houses became visible behind thick stands of trees. Here and there figures could be seen serving breakfasts on redwood sundecks. On the balcony of one house a red-skinned guy with a barrel chest strained over a pair of expanders.

"Expect Mrs. Sharp'll be home by the time we get there," Rezabek said, and smiled for some reason. He had this odd little smile that seemed to twist his lips out of their natural shape, making the upper lip a kind of tributary to the lower.

Tobias said nothing. He gazed into the sun. Fatigue

coursed through him. He rolled a cigarette and closed his eyes. And his fingers curled around the soft old leather of his pouch and what he remembered was the day David had given him the thing all wrapped up nicely in this colorful paper that said "Father's Day" across it. But the memory was a candle and when he got too near he felt he'd burned himself and had to pull away.

Too many deaths.

A man couldn't carry too many deaths in his heart.

And suddenly he felt a quick twist in the cold center of his chest because he was thinking of the other son, Paul, the younger kid, and the thought was fragile in his mind, like the dried wing of a butterfly and just as easily broken. Sometimes when he thought of Paul he felt an exhilarating gladness that at least one person had been left to him, at least one had been spared. But there were darker moments too, times when he struggled with the black wish that they'd all gone together, the whole family at once, because then there wouldn't be these terrible splinters and cinders to deal with, these quick cuts that crisscrossed his soul like a deft rapier.

And on certain mornings, when he opened his eyes and realized his own heart was still beating and his pulses ticking inside him, he was angry that he hadn't died in the night, gone out on the backwash of some beatific dream, that he had still another day of emptiness to get himself through.

Now the car was passing a small home perched halfway up a grassy hill. Tobias glanced at this house, which had the appearance of a place abandoned to the elements. Weathered barnlike wood and enormous clumps of shrubbery and a long sloping yard choked with weeds of all kinds. Ragwort and hardhead and curled dock—an embarrassing richness of weeds. The windows of the house were dark, almost as if the sun bypassed them.

It was a house Tobias knew quite well, and not just because he'd passed it regularly on his nightly patrols.

It was where he'd taken Edith when the physicians of Las Cosimas General Hospital hadn't been able to help, when all their salves and injections and panaceas hadn't made an inch of difference to her dying. It was the home of Dr. Andrew Conturas.

Tobias turned his face to the side.

"Sometimes I think that guy will die," Rezabek said, looking up a moment at the dismal little house. "And nobody's going to discover his body for months."

"He keeps to himself," Tobias said, but he didn't want to discuss the physician or the house and he was glad when it had passed out of sight and the small Honda was beginning the climb up Esmeralda Canyon Drive, up up and up where the air was richer and the homes more pretentious and the ostentations of wealth more ludicrously visible. The absurd tower that housed the telescope of Charlie McMartin, for example, a structure that reached skyward like some medieval offering to the deity. Or the enormous aviary that belonged to the Walenskis: you could see exotic birds—macaws and toucans and hornbills created their own private rainbows behind the fine mesh fence. Or the horrendous Tudor spread that had been built by Jacob L. Schwartz of Schwartz Electronics, all white plaster and old dark beams that had reputedly been imported from Stratford-on-Avon at a cost that would have fed half of Nicaragua for two weeks. When you wanted Shakespearean real estate, you had to dig deep in your pocket to get it.

This was it, Tobias thought.

That wonderful, grotesque edge where California—without

the natural help of any San Andreas Fault—toppled over another kind of abyss into lunacy.

And then there was Henry Sharp's big satellite dish, hanging in the sky like something designed to communicate with any passing extraterrestrials. Metallic, gray, ugly, it seemed to deflect the rays of the sun as if solar pulses were of no concern to it.

"This is the place," Rezabek said.

You certainly couldn't mistake it for any other.

Henry Sharp wore a Rado DiaStar watch that he had purchased at Petochi & Gorevic during his last business trip to New York City. His scarlet robe was of a silk so fine, so reflective of light, that to Tobias it seemed made of mirrors. His silvery hair was manicured rather than cut and his hands were soft and white, the little half-moons of the nails as perfect as anything ever seen in the night sky. As he sat and talked on the terrace of his house (a large wooden deck half-shadowed by the TV dish), he poured small glasses of something called Chambord, which he sipped carefully.

"Black raspberries," he said. "They agree with me. Don't ask me why," and he smiled a somewhat determined smile, as if it were not a wife who might be missing but the deep dark taste of the raspberry liqueur. Tobias studied the man a moment, then glanced at Rezabek, who seemed awed by the environment. Who seemed, in effect, about to genuflect, as if Henry Sharp were a five-star general and not just a Captain of Industry. Sharp rose from his soft leather deck chair and strolled to the edge of the balcony. He gazed out over the canyon for a while.

Tobias ran one weary hand across his forehead. Already the early-morning sun was bringing with it a molten, forceful heat. In the distance, the Pacific was little more than a haze, a suggestion of water.

"It just isn't like her," Sharp said. "It isn't like her at all."

Tobias turned briefly, looked through the sliding glass doors to an inner room. He wondered why the rich at times affected a Spartan life-style—those white walls with a few splashy prints, a couple of scattered white rugs, off-white sofas with mauve cushions.

Mauve yet, Tobias thought.

Some interior decorator had gone through this house in a trance inspired by lysergic acid. Tobias had already glanced inside other rooms when he'd first come in; some were cluttered beyond understanding, stuffed with gigantic cushions and potted plants and hanging tapestries; others looked as if no human being ever had, or ever would, draw a breath inside them. At the end of the deck, the statutory hot tub swished and whirled inside the security of its own tiled gazebo. Fine Italian tile. Colored umbrellas. Wrought-iron chairs and tables.

"She ever sleepwalk?" Rezabek asked.

God spare me, Tobias thought. Rezabek knew how to plummet to the gorges of his own imagination and dredge the silt down there for the real zingers. She ever sleepwalk?

Even Sharp seemed to find the question naive. He shook his silver head, studied his hands, said nothing. Into the crystal goblet went another drop of Chambord. Tobias stuffed his hands into his pockets. There were needs here, he thought. The need to see the bedroom. Study the grounds. Check her calendar (if she kept one). The need—oh, the pointed need—to ask personal questions. There was no such thing as an investigation that was not also a trespass. You gate-crashed on the privacy of lives. And on the sanctity of deaths. You arrived—always, always—without a calling card.

"You said she'd been sick, Mr. Sharp," Tobias said.

"She was on medication," Sharp replied. In the depths of this unfathomable house a telephone started to ring. Somebody, somewhere, answered it. Tobias imagined houseboys, valets, maids, an assortment of hired help congregating belowstairs.

"What kind?"

"You'll find all that stuff in her bathroom, Officer."

Her bathroom. Her private bathroom.

Probably separate bedrooms. Separate beds, as in old Hollywood movies. Tobias shifted his feet uncomfortably: wealth had always made him uneasy—not because he desired it, not because he envied it, but because he was never sure how to behave around it. It made him feel both clumsy and uncertain. He knew the streets, whether in New York City or the Quarter in Las Cosimas, but he couldn't get a grip on wealth. Something about the air. The richness of the oxygen. Wealth put him in a state of suspended animation.

"Where's her bathroom, Mr. Sharp?" Tobias asked.

"I'll show you up there."

There was a spiral staircase rising out of a gleaming glacier of white tiles. Delicately shaped iron, suggestive of bird's heads, wings, all manner of flying things. Then a landing stretching away on both sides, the walls hung with oils and acrylics. Simple, naturalistic things, landscapes, still lifes with olives and Chianti bottles. Tobias paused to look at them.

"Isadora had her own tastes," Sharp said.

Tobias turned to the man, wondering at the use of the past tense. Nothing. A turn of phrase, was all. Had her own tastes. He looked at Sharp's face. It was handsomely flabby, as if some time ago he might have turned more than a few female heads. Even now, given the right cut of tux and a decent cummerbund, he could pass for attractive. The age was difficult to estimate. Late forties, maybe. But with that silver hair, who could really say?

"Here," and Sharp was opening a door that led into a large bedroom with a vast picture window overlooking the canyon. He placed his hands in the pockets of his robe as if without his goblet of Chambord he wasn't sure what to do with himself.

Tobias stared at the unmade bed, which was dominated by a canopy. The bedsheets were navy-blue silk, the pillows coral or whatever the current decorator catalogs were calling that sickly shade of off-pink. More still lifes on the walls, a regular art gallery.

In the center of the floor, like something plundered from a country auction, an antique spinning wheel. Rezabek strolled around this object like a time-traveler baffled by an artifact from a forgotten past.

"Don't ask me about that," said Henry Sharp. "I believe the word in current use is 'collectible.' Isadora was into collectibles. That spinning wheel was the start of her collection. . . ."

Tobias could suddenly envisage Isadora Sharp, dressed in something spiffy, lace-gloved, big floppy hat, trying not to perspire in some backwater barn while the auctioneer rattled on in a language incomprehensible to her.

He moved toward the bathroom, pushing the door open. Another tiled room. A large shower stall with a skylight. Pink vanity mirrors designed to disguise the advent of crow's-feet and scrawny necks and tight little lines around the lips. A lying mirror. In reflection, he saw Rezabek and Sharp both staring at him. Plunder, he thought. Going through the personal effects. Like a death had already occurred. Tobias shrugged and opened the medicine cabinet.

Rows of little brown prescription bottles. All the props and crutches of the era, all the little supports against the stresses of the times and the glazes that pushed you back one gentle step from reality.

The Valium. The Equavil. The Librium.

Legal dope.

And, lo and behold, a roach clip that contained the charred remains of one joint.

Isadora went to some lengths to lobotomize herself, for sure. Her days had to be like swimming through sealed tanks of lovely tepid water.

Tobias massaged his eyes a second.

Then he stared at the upper row of the cabinet.

Here there were more brown bottles, only these were different kinds of drugs.

Seeing them, reading the small typewritten labels, he was sucked backward to another time, drawn down and down into a place where he had no desire to go, a place he had already visited and one he knew was overflowing with anguish.

Dizzy a moment, he clutched the edge of the basin and steadied himself and then he closed the door of the medicine cabinet a little more loudly than he intended, seeing his own reflection flash past as the mirror moved in a silver streak away from him.

When he turned to look at both Rezabek and Sharp, it was obvious they hadn't noticed anything; they hadn't seen the way color must have drained out of his face or the tightness of his knuckles on the rim of the washbasin. He had a longing to plunge his face under the cold-water faucet to refresh himself.

Those familiar little script bottles, he thought.

Those deadly familiar things.

The creases of pain on Edie's face.

He rubbed his eyes softly.

Sharp was saying something about the balcony that led out of Isadora's bedroom and Rezabek was following him out of the bathroom in the direction of the sliding glass doors. After a moment, Tobias joined them. Outside, the air was still and the sun seemed lifelessly hot. Tobias could feel sweat trickle beneath his shirt collar and run through the hairs on his chest.

A flight of steps led down from the balcony and ended in the gardens below. Planned gardens, Tobias noticed, geometrically placed trees. Pines mostly—western whites, jelecotes, a stand of spruces. He gazed at the trees for a while, then he looked down at the steps. Isadora could have come this way, stepping out of her silk bedroom and her little world of dope and traipsing out across the gardens.

"Did you hear anything?" he asked of Sharp. "Hear any movement, anything like that?"

Sharp thought a moment, then shook his head. "Nothing."

Tobias took off his cap, scratched his head, observed the meticulous grass that grew between the trees. It was a fair bet that an army of landscape specialists had planned this joint. And he had a sudden vision of all manner of specialists going through this house, painting walls, pruning shrubs, hanging prints, shifting furniture around. It was as if Henry and Isadora were not anchored in their own world, but rather afloat in a universe that had been manufactured for them. Strangers in their own overlarge house.

Specialists.

Including the one who'd written scripts for Isadora Sharp.

He stepped to the edge of the balcony, looked down.

Here was the awkward one. Here was the Biggie. Without looking at Henry Sharp, he asked: "Was she seeing somebody?"

"Seeing somebody?" Henry Sharp looked as if a quick small mallet had rudely cracked his skull on the inside. "What do you mean, seeing somebody?"

"A man," Tobias said.

"Are you serious—"

Rezabek had produced a handkerchief and was blowing his nose into it and his face was red.

"I need to ask," Tobias said. "I'm sorry."

"You're exploring the possibility that she might have run away with somebody?" Sharp said.

"Exploring is right." Tobias replaced his cap. "Things like that happen."

Sharp looked at his expensive watch for a second, almost as if his mind were elsewhere, perhaps rummaging the pages of an appointment book and wondering about the inconvenience of cancellations. Can't do lunch today, old man, wife up and vanished in the middle of the night. Then, with a slight smile on his face, he stared at Tobias. "She wasn't seeing anyone, Officer."

A Captain of Industry had spoken and that was the end of the matter. There was no room for the possibility of infidelity. Agenda closed.

Tobias peered into the sun, narrowing his eyes. Maybe Isadora had run away. Maybe it was a classic case of throwing her heart, like a badly lobbed ball, at the tennis pro at the country club.

But when he thought about the pills on the upper shelf of the medicine cabinet, when he turned these around and around in his mind, he experienced strong doubts.

Mrs. Isadora Sharp wasn't healthy enough to wander

around having clandestine affairs. Not if Andrew Conturas had been writing prescriptions for her.

The way he had done for Edith.

When she had stepped from the shower, still a little annoyed at the way Romero had disappeared (and, in truth, more than a little annoyed at herself for having been lured into a one-night stand when she'd sworn off such adventures: it wasn't as if she were a nineteen-year-old back at Rutgers and letting some knucklehead lure her to the bleachers by moonlight), Caroline Cassidy wrapped herself in a bathrobe and went inside the living room. She opened the slats of the blind a little and looked down into Hermosillo Square. The shops were just opening up for business. Sunlight screamed from the striped awnings and the sidewalk umbrellas outside the Stolen Quiche café were suggestive of bright orange flame. She let the blind fall from her fingers and ran her hands through her damp hair.

Inside the bedroom, she picked up the strips of bandages and dumped them in the wastebasket as if destroying the evidence of some strange private shame. The bedside clock read 9:32. And last night was already assuming the swirling forms of a foggy dream. She dressed—a white cotton skirt and blouse in the style some Mad Avenue drone had endowed with the description "peasant." (Though not at peasant prices, she thought.)

She transferred the contents of her purse into another that was better suited to her clothes and she left her apartment. She walked across the square to her office, which had already been opened by her assistant, a pleasant if dim-witted girl called Cindi. (Cindi with an i.) Caroline sat down behind her desk, looked a moment at the wall calendar, noted that it was the first day of July and realized that she was due a visit from On High, for J M Dunbar never failed to turn up on the first day of every month (save December, when he toured remote areas of Mexico in search of the wife who had abandoned him on the third night of their honeymoon).

Well, the office was tidy. The water in the cooler was at the precise temperature the Old Man enjoyed. There was a decent supply of Dixie cups. The pens and pencils around the place were USA-made and the two typewriters were not Japanese. Even the computer had been built in America. Or so the label claimed. There was nothing obviously Nippon to annoy J M.

She studied a chart in front of her. Two sales had been made in the past month. And another house was making its way through the tortuous process known as escrow. Such little victories pleased Dunbar, who had plans to expand Las Cosimas. He lusted after the Quarter, for one thing, the way a libertine might go mad in his quest to possess what lay between a certain pair of thighs, but so far the Hispanic community leaders down there had taken great delight in resisting his overtures. Capitalism would destroy their tightly knit habitat, was what they said—although sometimes Caroline had the suspicion that they were merely holding out for a better price.

She drew some water from the cooler. It had the taste of mild bleach. She pored over some brochures she'd prepared during the past weeks, scratching out a word here, a phrase there. J M Dunbar liked the soft sell. For Christ's sake, he'd say, these computer guys are using the hard sell every day of their goddamn lives, they don't want it used against them, do they? Tread quiet, catch the monkey.

Catch the monkey, Caroline thought.

She finished editing the draft brochures, then she looked at the huge wall map of Las Cosimas. In pale red were those areas that Dunbar had not been able to purchase so far. Farmlands mainly, old families, wineries, places that might succumb only under the force of a nuclear device and perhaps not even then.

Ten o'clock.

The Old Man never appeared until after lunch.

She watched Cindi for a time, understanding that a vital part of the girl's brain was constantly underemployed. She was given to quirks during idle moments, like making enormous chains out of linked paperclips.

Caroline reread her brochures, made a few more changes, gave the sheets to Cindi for typing, then picked up the telephone and dialed the number of the Country Club and Resort. The unctuous voice that answered might have belonged to some erudite receptionist at Harvard Library. One always expected the voice to spew forth statistics. Fifteen hundred acres. A professional-standard golf course with resident professional. Six tennis courts. Three restaurants. Two bars. One hundred well-appointed rooms and a penthouse.

All I want, Caroline thought, is Daniel Romero's room.

When she was finally connected to Room 78, the telephone rang unanswered. Caroline hung up. Maybe he'd checked out already. She shrugged and strolled to the window and looked into the square. The Croissant Set, nibbling with the same kind of attention that must have marked the behavior of nineteenth-century Lotus Eaters, were already sitting under the parasols of the Stolen Quiche café.

Cindi said, "For you," and held the telephone out toward Caroline.

"Who is it?"

"Man's voice. No name."

Romero, she thought. And, perhaps a little too quickly, she took the receiver from her assistant's hand.

She spoke her name into it. And waited.

And waited some more.

She heard nothing save for the quiet, insistent breathing of whoever stood at the other end of the connection.

A nerve of tension beat against the side of her head. A picture, she thought. If I could just get a picture of this guy, I could deal with it easily. But faceless like this, the whole thing's sinister. She couldn't get a handle on the image she'd had the day before—the greasy overcoat and the blackened fingernails and the sharp, sleazy face in a phone booth.

"Look," she heard herself say. "I have better things to do than stand around listening to a moron like you—"

The caller spoke.

Whispered.

A low voice that suggested a slight wind shifting over cinders.

"Caroline," it said. "Caroline, you're sick."

She slammed the receiver down and was conscious of Cindi watching her just as simultaneously she heard the caller's voice creep through her brain like a weird echo she didn't need. You're sick. . . .

What the hell was that supposed to mean? She sat down behind her desk and pressed the palms of her hands flat against the big blotter. She had a sudden perception of somebody, a shadow, a specter out there, who, armed with high-powered binoculars, had watched as Daniel Romero bound her wrists together with strips of bandage, someone who had spied on the whole passionate business, and now, driven by his own vicarious lusts, had called her on the phone.

Who's the sick one around here, buster? Me for doing it

or you for spying?—but then she understood that the thought of a watcher was ridiculous, the very idea of an espionage agent into fornication belonged in some other reality.

She tugged at her desk drawer and removed two aspirin and she swallowed them dryly. But that voice—that raspy, coarse voice: she shivered, conscious of Cindi still gawking at her.

"Something wrong?" asked the secretary.

Caroline shrugged.

Cindi said, "I just asked because you hung up like the telephone was on fire."

On fire, Caroline thought.

She rose from her desk and looked out on the square, absently observing the women who went from boutique to boutique like lemmings who'd heard about a bargain-rate suicide deal. Out there, somewhere in glorious Las Cosimas, somewhere in J M Dunbar's Paradise, there's an oddball, curled like a maggot at the heart of a gorgeous red apple.

And the thought touched her like cold quicksilver running in her blood.

# 5

If there was a Sad Case in all Las Cosimas, it was Benny Wozzek. At the age of thirty-four, he had burned himself out on both computers and cocaine. Three, four years ago he had been something of a wunderkind in the industry, responsible for certain advances in circuitry that were used in medical prosthetics. It was even rumored that, prior to his breakdown, his fizzling-out, he was designing a practical artificial heart. Given the stresses of the business, the inhuman hours he forced himself to work, and the cocaine he inhaled to keep himself alert during those hours, the collapse of his nervous system was perhaps inevitable and unavoidable. Although unemployed, he was not by any means a poor man, because he collected royalties on certain video games he had invented when his mood had been frivolous.

Benny Wozzek lived alone in a large house on Cordoba Drive, which was situated below Esmeralda Canyon. A casualty of the high-tech world, Benny these days tended a huge vegetable patch and, when not busy in the garden, wandered frequently through the Mexican Quarter, snorted a couple of tequilas at Enrico's and, his head covered by a large sombrero, strolled the beach, where he would attempt to engage any casual bypasser in the virtues of legumes, carrot juices, and raw beets. He was a lentil freak. A caldron of lentil soup was always simmering in his kitchen and, according to local rumor, it had been so simmering ever since Benny's breakdown.

Sometimes he would wander under the rotted wooden pier, and, hunched at the edge of the beach, would cast his unbaited rod into the shallow waters. It was generally acknowledged that Benny Wozzek was a harmless character. He had undergone psychiatric treatment for a while, a process that came to an end when his doctor decided that his brain was as burned as the membrane of his nose. Benny was left thereafter to his own devices, which no longer included computers or cocaine.

On the morning of July 1, he strolled through the Quarter shortly before eleven, stopping at Enrico's for his usual shots of tequila. Through some mysterious chemical reaction, tequila produced certain lucid moments inside Benny's brain, when he would hold meaningful conversations with Enrico that might last for five or so minutes. At these times, there was also a jolt of sorts inside Benny and he would wonder what he was doing in a bar in the Quarter instead of being at his office. Lucidity passed. Benny wandered down Libertad Street, passing the small Mexican shopfronts, sometimes looking in windows, studying colorful pots, woven blankets, leather goods, or watching the cigar-maker at work. (At times, he might even make a purchase, and the storekeepers would send their bills to Benny's attorney for payment.)

By noon, he had reached the beach, passing under the flimsy struts that supported the pier. He liked the darkness and dampness of this place and wondered what, if anything, might take root down here. He moved along the sands, gazing now and again at the sailboats anchored on the slight swell. Expensive boats that belonged to the inhabitants of Las Cosimas.

Benny stuck his hands in his pockets and studied a variety of shells that lay underfoot. Mussels, whelks, broken scallops—all the debris cast up by the ocean. Then he let the edge of the tide run over his threadbare sneakers as he considered an experiment he intended to make in hydroponics. The problem was a temperature-controlled environment, which led logically to the construction of a decent greenhouse—except for one thing; Benny disliked glass for the simple reason that anybody could see through the panes. And when he had resurgent moments of paranoia, flashbacks to his days in the clouds of cocaine, he was given to the profound sensation he was being watched.

He continued to stroll. His thoughts were suddenly interrupted and scattered by the violent hawking of birds further down the beach. Momentarily the sun was eclipsed by a flock of the blackheaded creatures that wheeled and dived and darted like demented things. Benny paused, and when he moved forward again the gulls rose upward and their wings sounded like drumbeats created by invisible tympanists in the sky. Scavenging gulls, the vultures of the sea.

Something had aroused them, for sure.

Something had riveted their attention.

Now they were crying overhead as if his presence had annoyed them.

Benny Wozzek walked a little further.

Then he stopped.

He could see it now. He could see what it was.

Beyond the driftwood and the mazes of dark green seaweed.

He shook his head, astonished by what the tides threw up so carelessly at times.

As Tobias lowered himself slowly onto his bed and kicked off his boots, he thought: Let us now praise this famous apartment. At which he didn't want to look. Or smell or feel. Into whose kitchen he had no desire to go.

He turned his face to the wall. The silences of the place beat at him. Assailed him. It all comes down to this, Tobe. It all comes down to your being a lonely man. You weren't born lonely. You had a mother and a father and two sisters. Later, you had friends in school and Art Frye was your partner in New York City. Then you had a wife and two sons. No, indeed, you weren't born lonely, you just had loneliness thrust upon you.

He sat up, punched his pillow, struggled against self-pity.

Maybe all the loves and friendships of a life were preparations for the ultimate loneliness.

He went inside the kitchen and took a beer from the refrigerator and popped it abruptly. The cold liquid spilled over his chin and onto the front of his shirt and he thought how apt it seemed to be both lonesome and have beer stains on your clothes. He stood at the window. There was a closet five feet away from him and behind that closed door was the folded-up wheelchair that Edith had been obliged to use during the last three months of her life.

After David's death, something had gone out of New York City. A spark, a vital essence. The streets had taken on dead colors. Even the fall of that year had been monochromatic.

We'll go somewhere new, Edith had said.

We'll go West.

And Tobias had nodded.

You can find a job out there.

We'll put it all behind us.

And Tobias had nodded.

He crumpled the beer can and went back inside the bedroom, where he sat on the edge of the bed and looked at the battered aluminum in his fist. There were photographs all around the room. That bright wedding between himself and Edith. Young faces. Rice. The rustle of a bridal gown. Smells of flowers. Those frozen smiles of young love and that first apartment on the Upper West Side. The broken-down brownstone, top floor, two tiny rooms. After David had been born, they'd moved to Queens, where Tobias had felt more than a little adrift. Then, later, Paul had come along.

One photograph showed all four of them together.

Now there were only two. And even Paul was absent, off at school in Los Angeles.

Tobias shut his eyes. Why can't they return, even for a day? Why can't the dead come back for one last moment out of all eternity? A final touch, a last embrace? But they were gone and that most impenetrable blackness of all had swallowed them. No matter if you lived one thousand years, you'd never see them or hear them or touch them again.

He shook his head, opened his eyes.

On his return from Henry Sharp's house he'd seen Caroline Cassidy go across the square and he'd wanted to talk to her but she hadn't seen him and now what moved through his mind was the idea of calling her on the telephone, a notion he dismissed as the folly of a lonely middle-aged man tired of the walls of his life, weary of the absences in his heart. Even the vague lust he felt toward Caroline Cassidy seemed to him an intrinsically lonely thing, a masturbation.

He rose, moved around the room, remembering...

Remembering a hospital bed. Green walls. Instruments.

Remembering how he'd held David's dead hand in his own.

Cold dead flesh. The nightmare of nurses, grim-faced physicians, curtains drawn around a bed that wouldn't be needed anymore by this particular occupant, voices on the intercom systems.

His head felt tight, his brain stretched like taut canvas.

Paint your memories on that canvas, fishing trips to the Adirondacks and camping holidays up in Vermont and Sunday drives out to Jersey or Fire Island, four happy people, count them.

Don't go. Don't leave me. Don't slip away from me like this.

He'd begged like this twice in his life. Begged and prayed.

Both times he'd lost.

Sweet Christ. Thoughts like these were unruly mobs inside his own head. He had no control over them. They went berserk, wild, indifferent to his pleading for order.

He paused at the window.

He would think of Isadora Sharp.

That's the direction he'd take.

Isadora Sharp and her prescription bottles.

The Missing Lady. The mystery of Las Cosimas.

A genuine mystery, something he could ponder, something he might sink his teeth into. And, out of nowhere, he had an old sensation, a tingling feeling that he hadn't had since back in New York when he and Art would go nosing around asking questions that would ultimately bring terrible answers, reveal terrible crimes. Okay, maybe a missing person was small potatoes compared to a weighted-down corpse in a cement mixer, but it was something. . . .

It beat the hell out of misery and loneliness and the drift into that self-pity he so despised.

He walked back into the kitchen and helped himself to another beer, which he sat drinking at the small Formica table.

And then he heard it.

He heard it intrude on his brain.

The squeak of Edith's wheelchair as it rolled from room

to room. And the sound of her voice saying: Toby, you promised to oil this contraption, didn't you?

Didn't you?

Yeah, I did.

Only I never got around to it and then it was too late.

He drained his beer and he thought about how large the claim was that the dead still had on the living, a debt that could never be paid.

Like the squeaking of a wheelchair that didn't need an application of oil anymore.

Like a thousand unkept promises.

The way he missed his wife was a cavity inside him no emotion could ever fill up, a dead place where nothing could possibly grow again. His eyes watered and he hated himself for his own weakness, hated the way he saw his life stretch ahead of him as though it were a desert without the slightest likelihood of an oasis or even a mirage. Even that.

Paul, he thought. If he could see Paul now, that would take the cruel edge off. If he could just see the boy and hold him in his arms and kiss his face, if he could just allow his love to overflow into his son—

The rattle of his telephone shook him and he rose slowly, going toward the living room, hesitating before he picked up the instrument.

It was going to be Caroline Cassidy telling him that she thought he looked sad and lonesome, in need of some affection.

A snowball in hell.

It might even be Paul, calling from L.A.

More likely, it was going to be Henry Sharp or Karl Rezabek telling him that the wandering Isadora had found her way home, safe and sound and none the worse for her misadventure.

Surf had made lanks of the hair and sand covered the eyelashes and the mouth was open wide, containing a single strand of seaweed that had somehow adhered to the upper teeth. Water had pressed the pale gown against the flesh and the tips of the fingers were wrinkled, like those of a person who has stayed too long in a bathtub. Confused by the small crowd of people that had gathered around the body at the edge of the beach, a little bewildered by the presence of uniformed officers, Benny Wozzek was thinking of a mermaid, a sea creature tossed up casually from the waves. He observed one of the uniformed guys bend over the body, and then suddenly the beach was even more crowded, kids wandering down from the Quarter, shopkeepers hurrying to sightsee the sand-covered corpse with the solitary gash in the center of her chest.

Karl Rezabek was making futile attempts to shoo the crowd away, waving his arms like a traffic cop in the center of a jam. Charlie Nicholson—a big guy with a beefy face who'd once been a private eye in Chicago and who worked the day patrol in Las Cosimas—stood alongside Tobias and studied the dead woman.

"Knife wound," he said. "I'd say one single thrust. Bull's-eye in the old central pump, Toby."

"Looks that way," Tobias said. A cop's way of talking about murder victims was a factual thing, as if he were trying to erect a fence all around the harsh reality of the event. Cold words strung together in terse sentences. Tobias rolled a cigarette and glanced away from the dead woman. The sky was alive with screaming gulls. For a second, he stared at the bewildered Benny Wozzek, the thin, frazzled face beneath the big sombrero. Benny had dark eyes that suggested an intelligence of some twisted kind. One day, so they said, Benny had gone off on a trip and he'd never quite made it back. He was more than a little interplanetary.

Tobias edged toward him. "You found her just like this, huh? Lying there that way."

Benny nodded.

"You see anybody else around, Benny?"

Benny Wozzek took off his sombrero, and for a reason known only to himself (if that), stared inside the thing. "There were gulls all around. I was thinking about this hydroponic scheme. It's the idea of greenhouses, though, that depresses me. All that glass. I was thinking maybe one-way glass; then I saw the woman here."

You don't ramble much, do you Benny? Tobias thought.

A guy needed a special kind of compass to plot his route through Benny's sentences. Greenhouses and one-way glass and hydroponics. The dead woman was only tangentially connected to Benny's reality. Tobias dug his feet into the sand. Then he looked once more at the corpse. There was a large ruby ring on her left hand and a slender silvery necklace at her throat.

Somebody stabs her, doesn't steal her jewelry.

Somebody with no interest in robbery.

The end of Isadora Sharp.

He looked out toward the sea; the incoming tide was lapping lightly against the dead woman's feet.

"A looker," Charlie Nicholson said.

Tobias nodded. Thirty-seven, thirty-eight perhaps. And, like Charlie had said, a looker. Tobias gazed at the closed eyes. He'd seen corpses before, more than he cared to remember, and it always bothered him when they had their eyes open. That queer myopic look of death as if the corpse was scrutinizing something just beyond the normal range of vision. He was glad Isadora had her eyes shut.

He turned in the direction of Rezabek, who was still

pushing the crowd away. He was red-faced, sweating, moving his arms like a man who has lost all coordination of limbs. In the distance now could be heard the whine of an ambulance. Rezabek strolled toward Tobias, took off his cap, pursed his lips and sighed. He glanced quickly at the body and what went through his mind was the uneasy notion that nowhere in his Book was there a section on solving murders.

The ambulance was slugging across the sand, lights flashing.

"A stab wound, obviously," Rezabek said.

Tobias turned his face up toward the sky. A stab wound. Maybe a dolphin bite or the playful snap of a passing porpoise. Rezabek, Rezabek, you wouldn't have lasted twenty-eight seconds in Manhattan. The city would have chewed you up and spat you out and left you utterly hollow.

Tobias watched the ambulance attendants lift the body of Isadora Sharp and stuff it, a little crudely, into the back of the vehicle. And then the ambulance was gone again, back across the sands, and the little crowd drifted listlessly away.

"I don't believe it," Karl Rezabek said. "Here in Las Cosimas. I just don't believe it." And he was conscious of the street-bitten faces of Manning and Nicholson watching him, though their expressions were hard to define. Looking down on him, maybe. He cleared his throat and he thought how it was okay for them, they were guys used to murder in all its appearances, but he was new to this, moonwalking and struggling with a lack of gravity.

"Happens everywhere," Charlie Nicholson said. "Rich. Poor. Don't make a damn bit of difference. I seen corpses in the ghetto and I seen them in penthouses. Happens everywhere."

A strange feeling of uselessness went through the sheriff a moment. It wouldn't do. It wouldn't give him any respect, any credibility, if he appeared indecisive.

"Wozzek found the body, right?" he said.

Tobias nodded his head. He stared the length of the beach, seeing Benny Wozzek wander beneath the ramshackle pier, lost in his own little universe.

"You don't suppose . . ." The sheriff let his question fade away.

"Who? Benny Wozzek?" Tobias asked. Was Rezabek trying to suggest that Crazy Benny had had something to do with this killing? "The guy hardly knows the time of day, Sheriff. He's not playing with a full fifty-two—"

Rezabek made a gesture with his hand, as if he were dismissing his own speculation. He shrugged his shoulders lightly, turning his face away from Tobias.

Tobias hitched up the belt of his pants and looked at the impression the corpse had made in the sand, a hollow beginning to fill with threads of the incoming tide. In a few moments the place of death would be smoothed over, washed clean as glass.

Almost as if there were no mystery at all.

But Tobias knew better.

The mystery had only just began.

And something warm flowed through him, a sense of vitality he hadn't experienced in a long time, like a small bright flame dancing in the center of his mind.

A tantalizing light.

An entrance to a maze—and the only thing missing was his old partner, Art Frye.

# 6

In J M Dunbar's mind there existed the notion that if anything went wrong in Las Cosimas, it could always be traced directly to the Quarter. A broken fire hydrant, a clogged sewage pipe, seasonal humidity, brown grass on the golf course, acts of God and nature, it didn't matter—the source of any and all iniquities lay somewhere at the heart of the Quarter. In his imagination, this squalid hive of Mexicans consisted of something more than four blocks of run-down buildings: he was convinced of the existence of hidden alleys and concealed passageways and basements where conclaves of illegal aliens met to plan a dark strategy too nefarious for J M to guess at. He believed there were secret courtyards and small windowless back rooms where all manner of irreligious events took place.

A clogged sewage pipe was one thing, though.

The murder of Isadora Sharp was quite another.

He tapped his silver-tipped cane on the floor of Karl Rezabek's office and glowered at the sheriff, a man who was very low in Dunbar's esteem. And someone he would never have employed had it not been for some form of freemasonry, a network of old favors. He raised the cane in the air, a pose suggestive of someone about to strike, and then he twirled it between his fingers like a drum major.

"Henry Sharp is a personal friend of mine. A close friend, Rezabek. I personally convinced Henry Sharp that Las Cosimas would be a worthy living experience for a man of his stature." Dunbar paused. He considered his pacemaker a moment, the way an old soldier might ponder a scrap of ancient shrapnel in his buttock. Every now and then, it concerned him that the battery would turn out to be faulty (although he was secure in the knowledge that the battery was, at least, not Japanese). He went on: "I did not sell Henry Sharp a prime piece of real estate with the understanding that his wife would be killed. This is not how I sell property, Rezabek. I do not produce brochures that say 'Come to Las Cosimas and Be Murdered.'"

There was a profound quietness in the room. Dunbar looked at Rezabek's two officers. One was a plump man with a face like the side of a ham; the other, who had a rather secretive look, wore a small mustache and had a sorrowful, down-turned mouth. Then he turned his attention to Caroline Cassidy, who had accompanied him to the police office, and he stretched one hand out to lightly touch her rump. Fine, good-looking girl, he thought. And he wished he were fifty again. At seventy-three, looking and wishing and sneaking the occasional feel was the best he could do. He longed to run his hand up under her wide white skirt and touch her nooky and feel her wetness on the tip of his finger. He dropped his hand to his side. The girl hadn't budged. She had come to expect an odd grope or two from the old man.

"This killing," he went on. "This outrage could set our unit sales back drastically. Homes may be vacated. Residents may leave. Prices might drop. Where would we all be then, Rezabek? Do you think the Air Force would take you back, Sheriff? Do you?"

Nobody took the trouble to correct Dunbar. Nobody, least of all the sheriff, wanted to say he had been in the Marines, actually, sir. . . .

J M Dunbar gazed at the silver handle of his cane. At

seventy-three, he weighed the same one-fifty he'd been at thirty. There wasn't an ounce of fat on him anywhere. The only things that troubled him were the odd twinges of arthritis, the occasional wandering of his mind, and an extinct dick. (His own private dodo, he called it.) He was a religious man in his own way, paid handsome tithes to certain Baptist churches in his native Missouri, and he was convinced—beyond any argument, beyond any philosophical sophistry, any nonsense about Prime Movers and First Causes—that God was a red-blooded American.

And here was Isadora Sharp dead.

Found down on the beach like a goddamn flounder.

A murder in Las Cosimas.

"The Quarter," J M Dunbar said suddenly. "You mark my words, Rezabek. You want to find your killer? Go to the Quarter. Hovel-to-hovel search. Damn warrants and that sort of shit. Look in basements. Attics. Make arrests. Fill up the cells. The Quarter."

Tobias, who had been half-listening to the old man, fascinated by something that hung from his lower lip—a scrap of parsley maybe, something that flapped with every word—glanced surreptitiously at Caroline Cassidy. She caught his eye, smiled in a pale way, flicked a strand of hair from her forehead. A yearning, Tobias thought. A yearning he shouldn't be feeling right now, not with God holding forth in the office. J M Dunbar might be a moron of the most rabid kind, but he was a rich old ass and he called the shots around Las Cosimas and you couldn't do anything but listen. He hadn't missed the old guy's hand on Caroline's butt either, but maybe that kind of copping a feel just came with the territory of wealth. Tobias, folding his arms, stared up at the ceiling.

The Quarter. Old J M had the fucking Quarter on his brain.

There's a killer out there and we have to sit listening to this old baboon.

J M Dunbar stopped talking and, leaning on his cane, stood up.

"I have to go pay my respects to Henry now," he said, and he gestured for Caroline to follow him. In the doorway, he paused. He looked at Rezabek and smiled, a wide mouth of yellow teeth and dark receding gums. It was the strangest smile Tobias had ever seen; it suggested a kind of mirthful malice. "Results, Rezabek. Bring me results. Make heads roll. Fast."

And the old guy was gone, Caroline trailing after him expressionlessly. Tobias listened to her white skirt rustle against the wall. What he wondered was whether she ever let old J M screw her, but this was a thought he found so worthless that he felt ashamed.

In white, Caroline Cassidy looked lovely and pure.

Virginal.

A concept Tobias liked.

Because in his imagination he would be the first man to ever have her.

It was late in the afternoon by the time Caroline managed to get rid of the old man, bundling him into his limo and waving him off on the road to San Diego, where he lived surrounded by photographs of his runaway wife. Drained, as she always was by J M's visits, and her ass smarting from where she'd been pinched, she drove out to the country club for a drink she badly needed. Las Cosimas always seemed at its best just before twilight, the landscape made pink by the mellowing sun, the shadows in the canyons deep and impenetrable.

But what she kept imagining was Isadora Sharp's body lying on the beach. And although she hadn't seen it herself, she'd heard the descriptions and she could create her own awful pictures. She shuddered: nobody had been killed in Las Cosimas before. If she ran a list of crimes through her mind, the worst she could come up with was drunken driving, a couple of domestic assaults, and some stolen cars.

Isadora Sharp. A whole other ballgame.

She hadn't known the woman personally, but that hardly mattered.

Up ahead, where the highway twisted, she could see the Country Club and Resort. She wondered if Daniel Romero was in the place. Nursing a drink at the bar, say, or entertaining a new conquest in his room. This last thought irked her more than just a little.

She parked among the Jaguars and the Porsches and the Mercedes convertibles and the Cadillacs. Halfway to the entrance, she paused. Her mind still echoed with old J M's rantings. It was like a locomotive rattling through her brain, screaming now and then down dark tunnels. She stepped inside the air-conditioned foyer, crossing the tiled floor, passing the reception desk, and heading for the Piano Bar, a room so dimly lit that for a moment she was blinded. The guy at the piano was playing "As Time Goes By," peering astigmatically at the keys beneath his plump fingers.

Caroline sat down at the bar, ordered a Polynesian drink that came with a small forest of mini leaves, and drank from it quickly. Then she looked around the place, making out one or two couples tucked here and there in the room. She lit a cigarette and saw her own reflection in the bar mirror.

She looked, in a word, ragged.

Dunbar's presence, the wilting heat of the day, the death of Isadora Sharp—these elements had conspired to spoil her appearance. And she felt, well, yucky—as if she needed a cool shower and a shampoo.

And the Caller, she thought. Let us not forget the Caller. For a moment, a split second, she made a tenuous connection between the Caller and the person who had murdered Isadora Sharp, and she could somehow imagine the owner of that gritty whisper shoving a blade into Isadora's ribs and letting the tide take her flesh. In this same moment, as if her line of speculation here was a spotlight thrown on her face, she felt ruthlessly exposed and vulnerable, her own thoughts and fears visible to anybody nearby.

No, no, no, she told herself. Those perverts who made weird phone calls used up all their courage in dialing numbers—they didn't have whatever it takes to commit grisly murders, did they?

Did they?

She dismissed the possibility of any connection. It was a product of an imagination that had been hyperactive through her entire life. Hadn't she, as a child, imagined gargoyles in gloomy closets and someone who looked quite like Boris Karloff inhabiting the old elm tree outside her bedroom window? Clouds scudding across moons and caped figures with designs on her larynx, and the latticed patterns of dark branches that took on resemblances to an assortment of vultures and vampire bats.

She gazed around the room again.

You're looking for Daniel.

You're hoping he's going to appear before your very eyes.

Carry you off to his room and bind your hands, maybe even your ankles this time—

Christ, what am I turning into?

She finished her drink, ordered another.

Maude Logan materialized at her side, wearing a leotard and a yellow skirt, her hair held up from her brow by an Indian headband. Maude did aerobics. She always looked like she'd just come from an exhausting session of limb-twisting and rope-skipping and a grueling hammering at the hands of the club's masseur. Her skin had the kind of sheen that was associated with either good health or an expensive face lift. She eats only walnuts and almonds, Caroline thought. For kicks, she probably manages to screw in the lotus position.

"You look wasted," was what Maude said.

Caroline nodded, lit a cigarette, blew smoke in Maude's eyes. "Sorry," she said. "Didn't mean that."

Maude's husband worked for Schwartz Electronics. At parties, Abe Logan always drunkenly claimed that he had invented the phrase "Silicon Valley." (Caroline knew for a fact that the phrase had first been written by a man called Don Hoefler, but Abe had a boorishly arrogant way of altering history to suit his own ends.)

"You should come to the aerobics class," Maude said.

And look like you? Caroline thought. Like a brand-new penny? "I'll try to find the time, Maude."

Maude Logan ordered a banana-and-yogurt shake and, reaching out with one finger, poked Caroline in the stomach. "You're okay for now, Caro. But you can't be too careful beyond a certain age."

"I'll have to take your word for it."

Both women were silent for a time. And then Maude slid up on the stool next to Caroline, her brand-new Adidas sneakers positively gleaming. The pianist had changed tunes. "It's a Sin to Tell a Lie."

Maude listened a moment, then said, "Is it true about Isabel Sharp?"

"Isadora," Caroline said. "And it's true."

"The poor woman. Do the police have any suspects?"

Caroline shook her head. "I haven't heard anything," she said. She glanced at Maude. By nightfall, the late Isadora Sharp would have been Maude's best friend, her dearest friend, and the telephone wires of Las Cosimas would be hot as a furnace.

"Was it a gunshot?" Maude asked.

"I understand a knife wound."

"Heavens," said Maude, dipping her face into her frothy shake, a supplicant at the fountain of good health. Maude was perhaps thirty-eight, but she managed to look twenty-five. Caroline, years younger than the other woman, felt suddenly old and weary. And she hated Maude Logan for the way she glowed like something made from phosphorus. Go away, she thought. Go away and leave me with my Polynesian beverage.

Caroline swung around on her stool and surveyed the bar again.

A few more couples had come in, but there was still no sign of Romero. She smoked another cigarette.

The air-conditioning clicked into action and there was a sudden draft of chill air. Maude Logan finished her drink and slid down from her stool and smiled, raising a hand in the air.

"Must be off and running," she said.

"So soon?" Caroline asked.

"Party at the Hamletts' tonight. Aren't you going?"

Caroline shook her head. A party at Dale Hamlett's home was, at the best of times, an ordeal she compared in her mind to running a gauntlet. Snide little invitations to step out on the patio for the quick lift of a drug. Tonight, though, wasn't exactly the best of times for a party of any kind. This was a night made for wakes, for fears of dark places.

And Maude went across the Piano Bar, skipping like some silly schoolgirl. Caroline watched her go: actually, Maude would have been quite a nice person if she'd had a brain and a personality. Skip skip, out of the bar, across the foyer, and into the lengthening shadows of Las Cosimas.

Caroline looked into her empty drink and was about to order a third because she could feel the edge of a buzz coming on—and a good solid buzz was what she needed at a time like this—when she felt someone press his lips against the back of her neck.

Turning, she found herself facing Daniel Romero.

"How did you know I was here?" she asked.

"Second sight," was all he said. With an index finger he tapped the side of his nose secretively.

Second sight, she thought. She tilted her face up toward him, a little surprised by the intimacy of her own behavior in public, and she kissed him full on the lips.

As she did so, the vague suspicion crossed her mind that it had been this man, this same Daniel Romero, who had made the anonymous phone calls. It was a thought that came out of left field, but she didn't dismiss it altogether.

It could be another of his games, maybe.

Another of his strange games. After all, what did she really know about him?

But then the thought dissolved inside her just as quickly as it had formed because he was leading her away from the bar and toward the elevator and the ultimate destination of his room. And she couldn't think of anything save the relentless way her heart beat in anticipation of what lay ahead.

The kid parked his dirty VW on the road that ran through Esmeralda Canyon. He got out, stretched his legs, then leaned against the fender of the car. The scattered lights of Las Cosimas lay beneath him, and there, in the distance, was the pale white fringe of the Pacific. He ran one hand through his untidy hair, took off his glasses, rubbed them against the sleeve of his shirt. Below, he could see the illuminated tennis courts of the country club and a couple of white figures hurrying across the clay. They looked frantic, funny, in pursuit of a ball that was invisible to him at this distance. Figures involved in some strange tribal ritual.

He studied the scene a few minutes longer before he stepped back inside his Bug and twisted the key in the ignition.

Las Cosimas, he thought. Dreamland by the Sea. The amber lights spread below him suggested a necklace worn at the throat of a woman of high fashion.

As he listened to the ticking of the VW, he experienced a small ache at the back of his head, a secret little pocket of pain buried deep in his skull. He closed his eyes a moment, took air into his lungs and held it for a while before expelling it slowly. He did this several times: a means to relaxation, a way of unwinding.

He edged the car forward, moving through the canyon.

He didn't have very far to go now.

He didn't have far at all.

And then it would be surprise time.

# 7

Tobias wandered through the Quarter, pausing every now and then to look inside a store window. Although the night was calm, there was a nervy edge to the sound of the tide as it crossed the beach. Out there, on a far horizon, a storm might be gathering. He walked down Libertad Street, stopping at Manuel's Grotto, which sold religious artifacts. There were plaster Virgin Marys, blue-eyed Madonnas hand-painted as if by someone with palsy. The blue paint tended to run into the whites of the eyeballs, with the result that the Madonnas looked like candidates for cataract operations.

Crucifixes, garish prints of Christ, rosary beads, books about saints, cures at Lourdes. The Shroud of Turin was big right now. You could buy hankies imprinted with the figure on the Shroud. Boxes of six, fine linen. Tobias passed on down the street.

Isadora had come this way. Dead or alive, she had come through the Quarter to her final resting-place on the sands. The forensic report was everything he'd expected it to be: a single knife wound through the heart. The question was whether she'd been killed elsewhere and transported to the beach or whether she'd met her killer on the sands. A nocturnal tryst, say. But she wouldn't walk the six or seven miles or whatever it was from Esmeralda Canyon Drive to the beach, would she?

Possibly, if she'd been loaded up with dope, if she'd smoked too much reefer; then he could imagine her tripping lightly through grassy canyons, lost in a doper's solitary dream. Except that in this case somebody had been stalking her. Somebody had been tracking her to her place of death.

He could hear mariachi music floating out through an apartment window. From the open doorway of a shop there came another kind of music, a popular rock tune rendered in Spanish. Clusters of noise, human voices, TV's, people arguing in their apartments. That's what he liked about the Quarter. Its sense of life. Its crude vitality. The splashes of neon that hung in the air. But there was something else he could feel in the night, something as tangible as a bright thread woven through the entire fabric of Las Cosimas, brighter than any tubes of neon that might glimmer around him.

It was violence and murder, it was the consciousness of death, it was the zigzagging electrical charge of a killing that underlay the night and transformed it. You saw the same surfaces you always did but you were aware of subterranean currents swirling beneath appearances. A woman dies and her killer—free, wherever he might be—takes on mythic proportions. A dark alley, a face in a doorway, a face pressed against a window, a guy walking the sands. This killer could be anybody.

He went inside Enrico's. Two guys were shooting pool and a couple of farm workers were studying dominoes like ancient men on a park bench. The kid, Carlos, sat alone at the other end of the bar. Looking sharp tonight, Tobias thought. Red silky shirt, tight white pants, gleaming loafers, hair recently scissored and shaped. The young stud planning his Friday activity.

Enrico brought the usual bottle of Dos Equis. He shrugged as he studied Tobias—it was a fatalistic gesture but, like so many of those characteristic Hispanic movements, it could have meant almost anything. Tonight it read: *Too bad about the poor lady on the beach*. . . .

Tobias sipped his beer.

Enrico leaned across the counter. "Find out anything, Tobias?"

Tobias shook his head. "Did you ever see the woman down here? She ever come into the Quarter?"

"If she did, she didn't come to Enrico's," the old guy said.

"Yeah." The beer was tasteless tonight. Metallic, it seemed to cling to the roof of his mouth. Tobias pushed the bottle away.

"Terrible thing," Enrico said.

Tobias studied the pool shooters for a moment.

Consider the scenarios, he thought.

For some reason, Isadora takes a hike in the dark.

Had it been a casual thing? Let's say, for the sake of argument, she couldn't sleep, needed some night air, ran into her killer. Somebody with a sharp weapon.

Consider. He kills Isadora, stuffs her inside his car, dumps her on the beach.

No struggle had taken place inside Isadora's bedroom other than the struggle for sleep, if all those bottles of downers meant anything.

She meets somebody.

Or somebody is lying in wait for her.

Isadora wasn't a well woman.

Those prescription bottles from Conturas. Cerebid. Quinora.

Drugs that had also been issued to Edith . . . on scripts made out by the same physician.

Tobias sipped his beer, but he'd had enough.

He glanced at Carlos, who was knocking back a shot of tequila.

From the street, there was a loud report of a vehicle backfiring, followed by the sound of raucous laughter.

No, he thought. A woman on Cerebid or Quinora wasn't likely to be wandering the darkness to indulge in the strenuous activity of screwing somebody in the shrubbery. These were drugs used in the treatment of heart diseases, something he knew from his own bitter history.

He said to Enrico, "You hear anything, you let me know."

"Sure," and Enrico shrugged again because he understood that he wasn't likely to hear anything of value to the cop. So far as he was concerned, the Las Cosimas where all the hotshot businessmen lived was another world, an inaccessible place you didn't enter. It was like you needed a special visa to make a trip to that gringo place. Only gardeners and housemaids went up there, or tradesmen making deliveries. Or, if you were like young Carlos at the end of the bar—so the rumor had it—you sometimes went into this other world because certain ladies required certain, ahem, favors, which Carlos was said to provide in return for gifts. He had the cojones, this kid. Maybe nothing much in the brain department, but the ladies in the big houses of Las Cosimas weren't exactly looking for stimulating conversation.

Tobias stepped out onto the street. He walked as far as the beach, stared across the sands, listened to the breeze rattle the surface of water and knock against the tired struts of the old pier. A mystery, he thought. A mystery carved in the sand. And what he longed for right then was his old partner, Art Frye; what burned through him was the need to sit down and shoot the bull with Art.

Art, what do you make of it?

What do you think happened?

Who killed the woman and for what motive?

Art Frye would look up from his box of cold Chinese food and wipe a morsel of bean sprout from his lower lip. "Tell you something, Tobe, my man. Somebody hated this broad. Somebody hated her guts." And he'd shovel a forkful of chop suey into his mouth and go on muttering. Art always talked with a full mouth.

Why? Who'd hate her that much, Art? Her husband, maybe?

But Art Frye's ghost was already receding as if it were being sucked back by the tide, and the night was suddenly a lonely place. Even the ocean, like a voice struck dumb, was quiet now.

Tobias turned away from the sands and moved toward Libertad, where he saw Carlos come out of Enrico's and go along the block, then inside a phone booth to make a call.

The young stud arranging his Friday-night score, Tobias thought.

He checked his watch. It was eight-thirty exactly.

2030 hours.

Karl Rezabek had the feeling of sinking into a quagmire. Old J M Dunbar had shaken him that afternoon to the core of his being: it was as if the old man was holding him, the sheriff, personally responsible for the death of Isadora Sharp. And nobody had ever talked to Colonel Rezabek like that. Nobody. He thought: I have been hauled unfairly over some very hot coals.

The quicksand into which he was sinking was composed of both anger and an uncomfortable sense of inadequacy. Plus he was very tired because he hadn't slept in what seemed a long time. He rubbed the palm of his hand over his forehead and stared from the sundeck of Henry Sharp's house out across the canyons of Las Cosimas.

Henry Sharp, dressed in the same silk robe he'd worn that morning, had given up his black-raspberry liqueur and had worked his way through a half bottle of Tanqueray, which he slugged straight and quickly. He was leaning against the deck rail, smoking one cigarette after another. As he watched him, Rezabek was very conscious of the intense silence that had grown up between the two of them. What he wished for was Manning's presence right now, because Manning understood these situations—an admission that increased Karl's sense of misery.

"No enemies," Henry Sharp said in a slurry way. "A good woman. No enemies."

Rezabek turned his cap over and over in his hands. He had an awareness here of fragile surfaces, glassy ice that could break quickly underfoot. He wiped perspiration from his forehead. Henry Sharp indeterminately waved the hand that held his glass and a rainbow of gin slithered off the edge of the deck.

Rezabek wanted to reach out and lay one hand sympathetically on the man's shoulder, but he didn't move. "I have to ask certain questions, Mr. Sharp. I know it's a bad time."

"You know when it might be a good time?" Sharp asked. He drained his gin and looked around at the sheriff. "Let me anticipate your questions, Rezabek. No, she didn't have a lover. No, she wasn't unhappy with me. No, she wasn't unpopular in this delightful community of ours. No and no again. No no no," and with each negative he shook his head drunkenly.

Rezabek sighed quietly. That he had been denied the chance to ask his questions made him feel even more useless.

"What was wrong with her?" Rezabek asked. This question popped out in a way he hadn't quite intended. He had meant to ask about the late woman's health; instead he had made it sound as if he suspected something darker and deeper, mental illness maybe, or some deranged suicidal tendency. "I mean, what was the problem with her health . . . ?"

"She consulted with Conturas," Sharp answered. "He prescribed for her. You'd have to ask him. Something to do with the heart. My wife wasn't the kind of woman who talked about her health problems. She was a private person. She never wanted me to know she was seeing the physician. I only found out by accident a few days ago." Henry Sharp paused for a long time. "Very private. Didn't complain. Popular with her friends. She'd go out of her way. The kind of woman who'd bring home stray cats, birds with broken wings. She was a member of the Audubon Society."

Rezabek looked at the Tanqueray bottle. Drink and grief would make anybody ramble, he thought.

"And the Sierra Club," Henry Sharp added, as if he'd just thought about it. "Into preservation, you understand. If she'd taken some more interest in her own preservation . . ." And then, horribly, the man was weeping, leaning against the deck rail and sobbing, and Rezabek was appalled because it was nowhere written in his personal lexicon of the emotions that a grown man might cry. He stuck his cap on his head and turned away, embarrassed. He had never married, he had never formed emotional attachments with women, and his only sexual experiences had been in the beds of hookers—and so Sharp's outbreak was like a sound rumbling from some strange unmapped terrain.

He walked quietly to the stairs, possessed by the strange sensation that so far as Henry Sharp was concerned, he had ceased to exist.

As he stepped softly toward the stairway, the telephone was ringing in the depths of this house of the dead, a sound that pursued Karl Rezabek out into the night like the hawking cry of some predatory bird.

"It was you, wasn't it?"

Daniel Romero shook his head. "I swear."

"It had to be you."

His strong hand lay flat against her bare stomach, the palm covering the navel. She looked into his eyes, which were the color of slate, but she couldn't see anything there except a guarded moment, something hooded. She raised a finger and pressed the tip to his lips. She ached, positively ached. There were muscular pains in her calves, places where she'd never suspected the existence of muscles.

"Who else would make calls and just hang up after doing some heavy breathing and making an inane comment?" she asked. And she had the feeling she was just whistling in the wind here. She'd fallen into a warm, empty space that followed recent passion, and her thoughts had returned, like weary pilgrims, toward the subject of the Caller.

"I'm too old for silly games," Romero said.

"I'm not sure I believe you," Caroline said. She traced the line of his jaw with her fingertip. Then she shut her eyes, feeling sleepy, drained. Counting orgasms instead of sheep, she thought. Time and time again Romero had taken her, almost as if he had an inexhaustible source of sexual energy, like an overdraft on the First National Bank of Erections.

"I like other kinds of games," he said. "You know what I like."

"Yes," and her voice was dreamy, almost girlish in its

breathless way. Could all this become something more than simple uncomplicated lust?

She felt Romero move his hand between her legs. He had a special trick, a touch, a knack—he was like a conjuror pulling excitement out of a hat she had considered empty. She moaned a little and twisted her body to the side, her knees upraised, and then his mouth was pressed against her pubic hair and she thought she was going to explode, vanish in deliciously thin air, take off and zoom upward like some riotous firework on the Fourth of July.

She opened her eyes, looked at his face, saw a strange distance in his eyes—it was as if he had, beneath his hands, an experimental subject whose responses interested him, whose reactions he wanted to record. But Caroline didn't care. She didn't care at all, not about his identity, not about his background, not about the strange calls she'd been receiving.

She had both feet on the roller coaster and the rails were just about to dip violently ahead. Romero. Romeo.

"Do it do it, Jesus, do it, please, now," and the voice that issued from her throat wasn't her own.

She might have been, in the fashion of some cheap thriller flick, possessed by a strange demon. She wanted to say: Who are you, Daniel Romero, who are you and why are you doing these dreadful things to me?—but even though her mouth was open her faculty of speech had become redundant and the only sounds she made could never have been transcribed in any known language.

Just as she closed her eyes and felt him fill her, she had a queer disjointed image of Isadora Sharp being lapped at by the lascivious motions of the tide.

* * *

The Chablis and fondue party at the home of Dale and Emma Hamlett was operating in second gear because the death of Isadora Sharp and the way the news had spread through Las Cosimas like a brushfire had clogged the social throttle. Dale Hamlett, a man in his late thirties who had gone to fat like a soufflé rising in a hot oven, was doing his best. He always did his best. Made sure everybody had enough drinks. Made certain that there were no wallflowers. Pressed strangers into intimate introductions with a laugh and a handshake and backslap and a wink suggestive of extracurricular activity. Dale Hamlett, who had introduced the world to a user-friendly home computer called the Mirabile, threw the worst parties in all Las Cosimas, a fact commonly acknowledged throughout the community. They were forced affairs filled with forced conversations and forced acquaintanceships. Had it been socially acceptable to employ devices of torture to make parties successful—such as bringing together perfect strangers inside an iron maiden—there was little doubt that Dale, an otherwise good-hearted fellow, would have used them.

Tonight, though, was somewhat different than usual. And as Dale, a false beam on his round features, gazed across the crowded room, he knew that all the scattered knots of guests in the place were discussing the recent killing. Various diversions entered his mind, all of them dismissed as being in poor taste. A juggler, say. Or a ventriloquist with a wall-eyed dummy. A stripper streaking out of a big cake. A little depressed, he went to the drinks table and poured himself a glass of California Chablis (a Mondavi), which he topped up, surreptitiously, with a sizable jigger of a concealed malt Scotch. There is no way, he told himself, of injecting gaiety into this congregation. Even the conversations that he heard around him lacked any true enthusiasm.

"I'd say the technology of the chip has far outstripped our present capacity to realize its potential . . ."

"I keep hearing about some phenomenal new developments in VisiCorp software . . ."

He spotted his wife, Emma, on the other side of the big room. She was holding forth in her usual animated fashion on a topic Dale guessed had something to do with the late Isadora. Too much crime, she was probably saying, and too little punishment. In another corner, Abe Logan was drunkenly talking about how the Japanese were more than a little involved in computer espionage. The Boze stereo system was issuing Coleman Hawkins.

Dale Hamlett wandered amply through the throng, touching here, prodding somebody there, backslapping elsewhere. He sipped his drink, noticed John Rickenbacker—a twenty-two-year-old upstart who'd recently been appointed executive director of Schwartz Electronics—turn his face to the wall and nefariously spoon a substance into his nostrils.

"Hi there."

Dale Hamlett turned around and looked at Maude Logan. Something about this attractive woman always put Hamlett in mind of a latter-day flapper, he wasn't sure what. She had about her a look of flighty good health. Sexual activity and the Charleston had somehow become welded together in his mind from old matinee films on Saturday afternoons.

"Dear Maude," Hamlett said. "Not a good night for a soiree, is it? I should have canceled, I knew it."

Maude Logan fingered beads at her handsome throat. "My husband appears not to mind," and she nodded in the direction of the inebriated Abe, an intense man with a bulbous head perched on a matchstick of neck. Maude laid her hand on Dale Hamlett's wrist. "Chips. All I ever hear is chips."

"Chips pay our way," said Dale.

"I don't expect to hear chips in the privacy of my bedroom," said Maude, who appeared to have imbibed too many glasses of spiked punch. She giggled into the palm of her hand a moment. "Too many chips, not enough fish."

The joke, whatever it was, eluded Dale Hamlett. He sipped his drink and laid the palm of one plump hand on Maude's shoulder. The touch of her skin was appealing to him. Maude flapped her eyelashes and pressed herself against him—a slight touch, a vague pressure, nothing more. Dale Hamlett sweated.

"Would it offend you if I split?" Maude asked.

"You have somewhere else to go?"

"I have an engagement," Maude said in the artificially precise way of someone drunk. "And I hardly think Abe will miss me, do you?"

Chips, Dale Hamlett thought.

Too many of these wives looked down on microchips, ignoring the fact that were it not for the application of such slivers of silicon they would not have expense accounts in the better boutiques of Rodeo Drive. He gazed at Maude and wondered about the nature of her "engagement," but she was already drifting toward the door, pausing only briefly to exchange words with John Rickenbacker and partake of his hospitality with the cocaine spoon. As she slipped out, alone, unescorted, moving quickly, Dale reflected on the rumor that Maude Logan was said to be a woman not in the best of health.

Hell. He fixed himself another drink.

He mingled with the party, distressed by the increasing feeling that he was a member of a wake. When he reached his wife, Emma, he remembered that Maude, just like Emma, was one of the very few patients of the reclusive Andrew Conturas.

The kid parked his VW in a side street, noticing how grubby it looked beneath a streetlamp. Then he made his way along the brown cobblestones (cobblestones, yet) toward the apartment building. He paused in front of the glass door and a feeling of hesitation went through him, a doubt of some kind taking shape in his mind.

Okay, you could get back into the Beetle and just drive the hell away from Las Cosimas, you could hit that old open road and pretend you hadn't come here at all. Sighing, he pushed the glass door open and looked at the flight of stairs stretching ahead of him.

No, you'd come this far. You'd entered the world of button-down shirts and designer jeans and you might as well stay put for a while. He climbed the steps, reached the landing, stopped again.

He gazed at the door in front of him.

And for a moment he felt puzzled, disoriented, almost as if he weren't sure that this was the right door, the right apartment building, his surroundings just slipping away from him.

His head cleared.

He reached out and turned the handle and stepped inside the apartment, where the air smelled stale.

Like the kind of useless air you imagine inside a locked crypt.

He went into the empty living room and sat down, putting his feet up on the sofa, taking off his glasses and pinching the bridge of his nose. He stared at the dead TV, the groups of framed photographs, the pile of old newspapers on the coffee table.

It's something you have to confront.

It's something you just can't run away from.

His analyst's words. What a laugh.

He used the remote device and turned on the TV and, as he studied Johnny Carson's face, he wondered what kind of salary Ed McMahon took home for the strenuous task of laughing at everything Johnny said.

The kid closed his eyes.

Drifting.

Drifting away from the pain of things. From that iniquitous candleflame that drew him back time and again to the source of all his sorrows.

Opening his eyes, he rose and walked through the apartment.

Inside the bedroom he paused, studying the haphazardly made bed.

There were more framed photographs on the round table by the window. Quite a little gallery. (Jesus Christ, why did his father keep them? Why did he surround himself with all those aspic relics of the defunct past? Why didn't the man make one mighty bonfire of all his antique longings?)

Those damned pictures—why did they accuse him like this? Why did those sunlit faces stare back at him like members of a jury that had found him guilty of a terrible crime?

A crime, he thought.

My only crime is being alive. That's all.

That's my only sin.

When she left her drunken husband at the Hamlett party, Maude Logan drove quickly home, let herself in, listened to her heels click-clack on the fine ceramic tiles of the entranceway. She went into the spotless kitchen (a room whose appearance suggested something other than the preparation of food—neurosurgery, say) and she helped herself to a fistful of sunflower seeds. She chewed these slowly for a time and then climbed the stairs to the enormous master bedroom with the stained-glass ceiling. Inside the bathroom, she swallowed a pill, then studied her face in the mirror. A slight palpitation crossed her chest, but it wasn't painful. She stepped out of her clothes, unclipped her bra, kicked her panties aside, and found a short black negligee which she put on. Abe, she thought, would not be home for hours.

She descended the stairs, shivered a little in the slight breeze that blew through an open window, and felt a second palpitation. She was accustomed to these tiny tremors, but nevertheless there were times when they scared her. Times when she imagined herself dead and lying pale and romantic and embalmed inside a velvet coffin.

She thought a moment before she picked up the telephone in the living room and dialed a number. It was ten o'clock and not a convenient hour to be calling her physician, but fear hovered around the edges of her awareness and fear answered to no clocks.

She heard Andrew Conturas's voice.

She said, "Dr. Conturas? This is Maude Logan."

"Yes," was all the physician said. He had one of those dry, expressionless voices that would recite the Gettysburg Address as though it were a weather report.

"I don't mean to trouble you at this hour. I've been having a couple of palpitations and—"

Conturas was heard to sigh. "My dear woman. Let me see if I can guess. You've been pushing yourself too hard at those wretched exercise classes of yours, for one thing. For another, I can deduce from the way you speak your words that you've been drinking alcohol. In short, Mrs. Logan, you have been courting needless stress."

Maude Logan thought how much she hated Conturas at times. He sat up in that dreary, dusty little house of his and issued edicts and commandments like he was God and made deductions like Sherlock Holmes.

"Well," she said, fingering the strap of her negligee and looking out across the darkened garden at the phallic significance of the gazebo, which, spotlighted by a fine moon, had the appearance of a Buddhist shrine.

"Moderation, Mrs. Logan," said the doctor. "In exercise. In stimulating beverages. Moderation in all things. My suggestion to you at this late hour is to go lie down and relax."

Maude thought she saw a shadow pass in front of the gazebo and there was a tight feeling in her throat. Small drops of perspiration stood out on her brow. The shadow passed even as her own heartbeat fluttered. He's out there already, she thought. He's out there, waiting.

"Thank you, doctor," she said and hung up.

She went to the sliding glass doors that led outside and felt the grass press upward against the soles of her bare feet.

The night breeze, billowing through the canyons from the ocean, blew between her legs.

Palp, palp, palpitations.

She took a couple of deep breaths.

And then she paused in front of the gazebo.

Moonlight made mazes in the latticed wood.

Maude Logan thought: He's nearby. He's close now.

She could feel the excitement rising in her stomach, rushing through her bloodstream. Nothing strenuous, my dear woman. Go lie down and relax.

I intend to lie down, she told herself.

She stepped into the gazebo and stood in the center of the floor.

Wood creaked nearby.

She shut her eyes.

She held her breath. Palp, palp, palp.

He made hardly a sound. She felt his cool hands against her shoulders, his body pressed to her spine, and still she didn't open her eyes. His warm breath played upon the back of her neck and then his hands were lowering the negligee down and down until it lay, like a wrinkled cocoon, around her ankles.

It was the silent way he always took her that blew her mind.

Unexpectedly expected.

She could hardly breathe on account of her anticipation. The world was not turning. She heard the sighing noise the zipper of his pants made as he undid it, and she reached behind herself, stretching her palm, holding him.

She turned now, facing him, barely seeing that beautiful expression in the dimness of the gazebo. She slid to her knees and looked upward at him and as he started to bend toward her she shut her eyes and her brain was filled with cheerleading noises and she was a young girl again, bouncing up and down on the sideline and yelling at the sky.

# 8

No pun intended, but Tobias found his night patrol through Las Cosimas a beat idea. His walk took him on a round trip of some eleven miles. His feet invariably hurt, his chest ached from too many cigarettes, and he dreaded the occasional eruptions of the walkie-talkie attached to his hip. Rezabek was given to checking his exact whereabouts without warning, like the guy was making a series of little surprise assaults on enemy positions.

As he made his way down Esmeralda Canyon Drive, he stopped to roll a cigarette, sniffed the night air, checked his watch. He continued to walk, glancing at the houses as he went past. It was close to 0300 hours and almost time for him to head back down to the Quarter before calling it a night.

A car, he thought.

What I want is a goddamn car.

Dark houses and sore feet.

Tonight the tension in the air that came in the wake of the murder seemed to make the houses diminish, as if they were huddling in toward themselves, hunched against all the possible ravages of the night.

He passed the dark house of Andrew Conturas and he paused a moment, gazing up through the jungle of weeds at the black windows of the place. It was rumored in Las Cosimas (where rumor had more validity than scientific fact and more market value than U.S. currency) that Conturas, who had once held a position of some prominence at a teaching hospital in Boston, was now involved in lonely research of such an esoteric nature that even the eggheads around here couldn't understand it. Now and again, he took a few patients privately, but for the most part he stayed in that grim little house doing his thing, whatever it was.

Tobias had taken Edith there a couple of times, toward the end. . . . A flicker of pain coursed through him right then, not his own sensation but that of his late wife, as if he carried around inside himself a set of experiences that had belonged to the dead woman he had loved so much—and his heart turned quickly to ashes.

He wasn't sure what he'd expected to find in the mysterious home (although he had entertained lurid notions of slices of cadavers in pickle jars or brains floating in formaldehyde), but everything had been ordinary. Your average furniture, an old grandfather clock, stacks of medical tomes. Of course, he hadn't been in the upstairs part of the house, and so there was still the possibility of something mysterious going on in an upper room—ah, Jesus, Tobias, the worst part of these patrols is the way you let your imagination go to the circus. The guy's a retired doctor, takes on a few heart patients; he isn't constructing his own Frankenstein monster out of spare parts, for God's sake.

Downhill now, and he could see the welcoming lights of the Quarter. He walked a little faster; suddenly he was thirsty and looking forward to his Dos Equis. The warmth of Enrico's, the cold beer, the end of another day and a step nearer to heaven. The flecks of tide that fell on the beach sparkled in moonlight and suddenly he was thinking of the dead woman again. Rezabek, he knew, had taken it on himself to go back to Henry Sharp's house. The Great Sleuth. What was it exactly that Rezabek had to prove to himself? His problem was his own sense of personality. He had indecisive thoughts about how decisive he was.

Tobias gulped the sea air into his lungs.

Nicholson had fingerprinted Isadora's room. Nothing strange there except for prints that matched those of the maid, a Puerto Rican girl called Elizabeth, a couple belonging to Henry—and all the rest were Isadora's. Fingerprints, unanswered questions, a stab wound.

Then he was thinking something else, something that hadn't occurred to him before but should have, something that hadn't entered his brain because he had become rusty here in Las Cosimas—what if it had been a motiveless crime?

What if it had been one of those random slayings without purpose, without meaning, a killing that had nothing personal about it?

Tobias was filled with dread all at once.

You hardly ever caught the perpetrator of a motiveless slaying.

And—

What was worse—

Much worse—

That kind of killer often struck again.

Out of the labyrinthine depths of his madness, out of the wild senseless maze of his own demented brain, that kind of guy reared up in the dark like a monster and took another life, and all the lives he took were for reasons of sheer whimsy. (Or, if not that, then the guy heard Voices from the ether telling him to kill, or maybe swore it was a command he heard when he'd listened to a Black Sabbath record backwards.)

The wrong place at the wrong time.

Had Isadora been at the wrong place?

Tobias reached the Quarter and suddenly he wasn't

thirsty anymore. He was tired, he'd go home, stretch out, just as soon as he'd gone to the station and signed himself off-duty and done the right thing by Karl's Holy Book of Rules.

Then he was crossing Hermosillo Square, passing the snooty boutiques and the canvas awnings and the pomegranate trees in their concrete tubs, seeing the artfully lit windows and the glistening espresso machine in the coffee shop where all the chairs had been inverted on the tables. Tobias had an impression of lifelessness, of all forms of vitality sucked away into a vacuum.

Hermosillo Square.

Caroline's apartment—

He glanced up at the unlit windows of her place, imagining her lying in there asleep, yellow hair stretched on the pillow, bare feet maybe peeping out from the bottom of the sheets.

He paused.

There were two cars parked on the other side of the square. One was Caroline Cassidy's Datsun, the other the sleek Lincoln with the Wisconsin plates, and something in this conjunction of vehicles made him uneasy, even if he wasn't sure why for a moment.

And then the shadows made it clear.

The movements in the shadows.

The girl was leaning against the man, her arms around his shoulders. Her face was pressed into the side of his neck. The guy's hand was flattened upon her lower spine, the material of her white skirt crumpled, rising up her thighs. A soft sound of laughter floated across the square to Tobias and he stepped beneath one of the spindly trees, hoping he hadn't been seen, caught like a Peeping Tom.

Caroline Cassidy and the guy who owned the Lincoln.

Lovers. Only a blind man could fail to see they were lovers.

Tobias felt a weird nerve move in his throat as he watched the guy's hand rise up under the girl's dress, and then there was more soft laughter and the two shadows melted together, fusing into one entity that Tobias could no longer bear to look at.

He stared upward at the moon, but, like a moth to its own doomed flame, he had to turn back to look at Caroline and the man, who had moved his face directly into the soft glow of a streetlamp.

And something about that face rang a tiny chime in the deeper recesses of Tobias's brain.

Not quite as strong as familiarity. Not quite as definite as that. Not a recognition exactly—but rather the insubstantial echo of a face you might have seen in an old dream.

A shimmering picture.

Tobias could feel himself flex and unflex his fingers.

That face—

But then the man had turned away from the flood of the overhead lamp and he was no longer visible.

Tobias moved quietly across the square.

Sickened. A lump of lead in his heart.

When he had turned into Mascota Street he felt like a total fool.

What's the bottom line here, Tobe?

Sweet Jesus, what's the bottom line?

You run into a pretty girl a few times, chat, pass the time of day in mundane fashion, and somehow in your mind you create a world of unlikely possibilities, you hack chimerical opportunities out of the cold quarry of your solitude. You imagine, maybe, that you and Caroline might . . .

Might what?

And abruptly he needed to laugh at his own downright foolishness. To even dream that something might come to pass between them! Yeah, Tobe, in the windmills of your mind, that's where.

But why then did he feel the curare-tip of jealousy pierce him so sharply? And why had he written down the registration of the Wisconsin Lincoln?

Why the untimely pain?

Moving down the darkened street, he whistled, as if he were a character in a Walt Disney movie afraid of all the silent places of night. Caroline Cassidy and a stranger holding her—and this conjunction suddenly passed out of the realm of his own misshapen personal jealousy into a sense of protectiveness, as if there were a possibility that Caroline could be in danger. As if the man who'd stuck his hand up beneath her white skirt could be the killer responsible for that pathetic corpse on the sands—

Boy, Tobias, you're hallucinating. You're seeing things.

Do you want that lovely girl to be in danger so you can arrive on your white charger at the last possible moment and rescue her? You ridiculous middle-aged fool—your horse would be some broken-down nag and your armor would creak and you'd be hacking for breath.

Then he saw the grubby VW Bug parked along the block and everything changed for him. Caroline in the arms of her lover. The dead woman on the sands. The need to sign off-duty. Everything fell away like the feathers of a sad molting bird.

He ran in the direction of his apartment, filled with an unusual sense of joy.

He didn't mean to snoop, she was certain about that much, but as she unlocked the door of her apartment and stepped wearily into the living room, Caroline Cassidy reflected on the way she'd just seen Tobias Manning lurk in the shadows of Hermosillo Square. She flopped down on the sofa and let her arms dangle toward the floor. It had been unexpectedly charming of Daniel Romero to make sure she got home safely (yet another side of his character, she thought—how many facets did he have, for heaven's sake?), but the idea of Tobias eyeballing them like that took the bloom off Romero's act of courtesy.

She lit the end of an old joint she found in an ashtray and then it occurred to her that she was being too hard on the cop. For one thing, it was his job to walk the streets. For another, in the present climate of Las Cosimas he would be acting even more conscientiously than usual. Maybe, if you put the best possible light on things, Tobias was like a Big Brother, looking out for her interests. Seeing her intimately wrapped around a man, he was bound to take more than a mere passing look. After all, cops were suspicious by nature, and it might just have crossed Tobias's mind that Daniel Romero, a stranger, was a candidate for dark deeds—possibly Isadora Sharp among them.

Tobias, she thought.

He was always pleasant to her when they met on the street.

He was always charming, interested.

And something else. A little bonus of sorts.

She thought she detected the nimbus of sexual interest around him. A little halo encircling his head. The way his eyes, as they said in romantic novels, "drank" her in. The casual straying of his look to her tits. She was mischievous enough to play on this, albeit harmlessly. He was an attractive man in a kind of street-rough way and he had the quality of sandpaper at times. But there was always this tragic look lurking behind his expression. And she knew it was because of the dead wife, Edith. The same wife Tobias had wheeled through the streets of Las Cosimas with the proud look of a father on his face. That look of intense love. She might be wasting, she might be dying, but I love what's inside this woman and I don't give a damn and I won't waste whatever minutes I have left of her on this earth. You had to admire Tobias's love for the dying woman. And you also had to admire the woman's constant cheerfulness, despite whatever excesses of pain racked her body.

There was a dead son too, she remembered.

And another, Paul, whom she'd met only once, briefly, at Edith's funeral. He was about twenty and cute in an awkward, tousled way, as if he was still growing out of adolescence. You'd want to mother Paul.

Caroline shut her eyes a moment.

She was high on both dope and Danny Romero.

In her mind, she'd gone through a list of possible occupations for the Great Lover.

A Mafia hit man.

A professional gigolo.

An international diamond smuggler.

Or a guinea pig wearing the prototype of a computerized cock.

Whatever.

Exhausted, she realized the joint was burning her fingers. She sat upright quickly, blew smoldering ashes away, rose and went inside the bedroom.

The glaring red eye of her answering machine was lit, which indicated a message. For a second, she wanted to dismiss listening to it until she was wide-awake—whenever that might be—but she popped the button and the tape wound back and when she pressed PLAYBACK she heard . . .

"You know you're sick, Caroline."

She caught her breath and a muscle in her head stiffened and suddenly she wasn't stoned anymore.

"You know how sick you are, don't you?"

A pause, and somehow that was more horrible than the message itself because then her mind became a flood of images—a guy hunched over a receiver, his eyes shut and a half-smile on his lips and something in the palm of one hand, something bright and deadly that she knew was a knife. Maybe it was the same knife that had pierced Isadora's heart, and just maybe somebody out there was planning the same demise for herself.

Then: "You can't get better, Caroline. Unless . . ."

She heard the click as the message ended inconclusively. Just like that.

Unless.

Unless what, you insane asshole? Unless what?

She walked to the window and twisted a slat of the blind and looked down into the square, because she knew whoever had left that message was standing down there right now, right at this very moment looking up at her window and smirking secretively in the dark.

The square was empty. Nothing. Lamplight and plants and nothing else.

She pressed the palm of one hand to her forehead. At any other time she might have attributed her sense of a presence in the square to the paranoia that accompanied marijuana, to that discomforting instinct of being obliquely observed (eyes peering from a closet or somebody in a shower stall), but there was that god-awful creepy message and even as she stood at the window she heard it run again and again through the tape in her own mind.

That voice. She didn't recognize it. She ransacked her

memory banks and came up with nothing like it. The caller most likely had disguised it anyhow.

She walked through the apartment, checked the locks, and then she picked up the telephone and dialed Daniel Romero's number at the country club. When she heard his voice it was sleepy, drawling.

"It's you, Danny, isn't it? I mean, it's you that's leaving these messages, isn't it?" She heard the whisper of hysteria in her own voice, which had the sound of a razor blade quietly sliding over the surface of skin. "Tell me it's you. Then I can write it off to your demented sense of humor and I can get some sleep. Confess."

"I was dreaming about a blue lagoon," he answered. "I was on the edge of discovering what lay beneath Esther Williams's swimsuit. You just interrupted an important discovery."

"Please, Danny, I'm not talking about Esther Williams and her goddamn swimsuits, I'm talking about these phone calls—"

"Tell you what I really think," he said. "I think you've got a very shy secret admirer out there. Although I can't say I blame him, I don't exactly admire his lack of guts, lady."

"It's you, you creep," she said.

He was quiet a moment.

Then, simply: "Good night, Caroline."

Leaving her with all the silences and all the whispers of her locked apartment.

Tobias didn't move. Years slipped away like the skins of old reptiles. He let his hands hang at his sides although he knew he wanted nothing more than to reach forward and touch the sleeping boy's face, but this lack of motion, this watching, was enough in itself. And what crept through him was a sense of warmth, almost as if the blood in his veins had quickened its circuits of his body. Paul, he thought. Dear Paul. He studied the thin face a time, then saw how the kid's glasses lay folded in his limp hands and how the crumpled shirt had risen out of his pants, leaving a space of pale flesh. The quiet, perfect moment in a lifetime of loss and imperfection. A history of geometric angles that didn't add up the way they were supposed to. The hypotenuse of love—it was Paul, only Paul, he was left with. All the rest was dross.

Still he didn't move.

He listened to the regularity of the kid's breathing and he thought how closely Paul resembled David. Facially, at least. Otherwise, they'd had nothing in common except the bonds of brotherhood and a love that, while it existed between them, seemed to exclude anyone else. The closed circle.

David had been the gregarious one, outgoing, always switching girls, a party animal. David had been more charming and socially better equipped than his brother to deal with the intricacies and cruelties of the world and its relationships. Paul built things—he stuffed ships in bottles, drew elaborate blueprints for science-fiction cities of the future, wrote poems in a big notebook in a handwriting too cramped for almost anybody to read. But they had loved each other fiercely, their differences only helping to harden the adhesive that bonded them.

There was a kicker, though.

A hard one.

Both boys, the one living, the other dead, resembled Edith. It was almost as if Tobias had had nothing to do with their births, made no contribution, had given nothing of himself.

He shut his eyes tight, trying not to cry.

Because what this apartment needed now was the smell of Edie's lemon meringue pie from the kitchen and David's infectious laughter and then things would have been complete again.

The closed circle.

Dear God, Tobias thought. Death is a stalker, a sneaker, it comes up behind you like a dark Halloween figure and touches you on the shoulder even when you don't expect it and don't want to confront it. He rubbed his eyes with his knuckles and he was suddenly standing beside an open grave and staring at a hideously beautiful wooden casket while a minister, one of God's strangers, intoned words that brought no comfort because there was none to be found anywhere on the planet, a cold orb without joy, a chilly globe with no security. Twice in his lifetime he had buried the people he had loved most, and all that was left to him now was this kid asleep on the sofa.

And he moved toward his sleeping son, filled with a love too strong for him to embrace, a wordless love, feelings that soared beyond dictionaries and theories of linguistic structure and all the other bullshit people needed to apply to their raw, gut sensations.

He stood over the kid.

Without moving his lips, he said: I love you.

Then he could hear Edith in the kitchen saying that supper was ready and David was regaling them with some tale of a party he'd just been to and Paul, his head tilted and his eyes bright behind his glasses, was laughing. And Tobias just stood there, hands in his pockets, a feeling of the most enormous happiness working through him.

But it was a silent apartment with a TV playing soundlessly and a folded-up wheelchair in a closet, and the illusion, like a mirror smashed by a mallet, fell apart around him in cutting shards.

I bleed, he thought. My blood runs out of me.

He cleared his throat and the kid opened his eyes, grinning, gazing up at his father.

"Surprise surprise," the boy said.

Tobias choked something back. "You never called—"

"And spoil the surprise, Pops?"

Tobias bent down, hugging the kid, holding the thin body against him as if his world depended on the embrace. Pops, he thought. It was always Pops with Paul. David hadn't ever called him anything but Dad. Tobias, a little awkward suddenly, ran a hand across the kid's head.

"I could've baked a cake," he said.

"You could've burned something, sure," Paul said.

"I would have tried—"

Paul said nothing. He blinked, put his glasses on, smiled. Between the two men there was a quick silence in which you might hear the roar of pulses and the hammering of hearts. Tobias, still awkward, punched the kid lightly in the chest.

"You're skin and bone, sonny. Skin and bone. What's the matter? Don't they have food in L.A.? The UCLA grub unnourishing or what?"

Paul yawned, stretching his thin arms. "I burn the midnight oil too much, I guess." A pause. "God, you know, it's good to see you, Pops. I mean that."

"Likewise," Tobias said, his voice husky. What pressed upon him again was the awful emptiness of the apartment, accentuated by the hissing of the dead TV. Likewise, he thought. What kind of conversational oddity was that anyway? What happened between fathers and their grown sons that they just couldn't plunge right into each other's arms and avoid such stupid words as "likewise"? Some essential emotional arsenal had been robbed. A vocabulary stripped down by the turpentine of uneasiness.

Tobias shut the television off and the test card shivered away into some electronic purgatory. "Come here," he said, and as the boy moved toward him he caught him again and held him as hard as he possibly could and this time there was no awkwardness, no gap between father and son, just this single unashamed physical connection between them, almost as if grief had never entered their lives, as if the other members of the circle had never lived and therefore never died. Joy, astonishment, the surprises of love. Tobias never wanted to let the kid go because if he did then something bad could happen to the boy, that same vile fist of death that had crushed both Edith and David could crush Paul too, and he wasn't sure he could stand that kind of loneliness, he wasn't sure his sanity would be strong enough to take another loss. And so he clutched the boy because he was more precious than anything else could be and the love he felt caught the air like a bird set suddenly free.

Tobias felt his eyes water, his own thin tears streak his son's cheeks. Then he stepped back and sniffed and raised the cuff of his shirt to his eyes.

"I work too hard," said Paul, and his eyeglasses caught the light in such a way that his expression was hidden, but Tobias knew there was moisture in the boy's eyes too.

"How hard is hard?" Tobias asked. "Too hard for girls, or have you got one stashed away somewhere?"

"I don't have much time," Paul said. "For girls."

David, Tobias thought—always there were girls calling on the phone to speak to David, hopeful young voices with a slight squeak of expectation in how they sounded. Is David home? Can I speak to him?

There had never been such calls for Paul.

Those that had come for him were from the Manhattan Chess Club or the Museum of Modern Art (where he was a part-time guide) or from bizarre little magazines with names like *Sonnet* and *Son et Lumière* and *Grub Street*, wondering about his latest poem and when they could expect his work.

My boy, the poet, Tobias thought.

"They work your butt off, do they?" he asked.

"Pre-med isn't exactly a day at the beach," and Paul got up from the sofa, yawning again. He wandered into the kitchen, poured himself a glass of milk from a cardboard carton that was probably out-of-date. "I've seen empty refrigerators," the kid said. "This one wins the blue ribbon, though."

Tobias shrugged. "I eat out mostly."

A sudden silence.

The squeak of the wheelchair. Edith's voice. A whisper. Tobias ran cold water over his hands. "How long are you staying, kid?"

"I'm not sure. Summer school's pretty demanding."

Tobias turned and gazed at the boy. Long, skinny, eyeglasses perched on the bridge of the fine nose, a good generous mouth—but you always had the feeling with Paul that he showed you only his surfaces, none of the hidden places of his personality, none of the secret abysses. A private person, someone who didn't give easily of himself unless he was one hundred percent sure you could be trusted. David—Paul had always trusted David best of all.

"How's your social life?"

Tobias made an empty gesture with his hand. "I find myself busy with garden fetes. Fund-raising drives. Too many parties . . ."

Paul was smiling. "I think I was hinting at other possibilities."

"Like what?"

"You know."

"No, I don't know—"

Paul sighed. "Are you seeing anybody, I mean."

I see a lot of ghosts, Tobias thought. He shook his head, smiled at his son, and there it was again, Caroline caught in the stranger's embrace. He pushed the picture aside.

"I don't get the opportunities to meet women often," he said.

"Come on. An old fox like you? You trying to tell me you don't get your good threads on every now and again and try your luck at the country club? Pull the other leg, Pops."

Banter, Tobias thought. There was something heavy-handed about it, a fake gaiety, a mirth that wasn't felt. "I'm not a member. I can't afford the fees."

Paul finished his milk, wiped his lips, looked around the kitchen. The expression on his face suggested that he was searching for something, something he'd mislaid. Suddenly Tobias wondered how deep the lode of grief ran inside his son, how far down it went, how he coped with the loss of family.

"What kind of doctor are you going to be anyhow?"

"A faith healer," Paul said. "I figured I'd get my own TV show and cure people who aren't suffering from anything anyhow."

"Seriously," Tobias said.

"I'm not sure yet," the kid answered.

Tobias went back into the living room and sat down. Paul lay once more across the sofa, closing his eyes. He thought: I shouldn't have come. I should have stayed in L.A. He rubbed his hands together nervously and remembered his analyst, a small European with one eye that wandered indiscriminately, as if he were searching walls and ceilings for clues to his clients' identities.

You need to confront, Paul.

You don't need to run away right now.

The kid rubbed his eyes, blinked at his father. That handsome, tired face made him feel a slight flinch of pain. Where did he live these days? Where did the old man really live? The past, most likely. Wasn't that the place where they were both doomed to live anyhow? Wasn't that more of a bond between them than anything blood might mean?

"Did I mention our murder?" Tobias asked.

"Murder?"

"Right here in lovely Las Cosimas. A dead woman on the beach. Stabbed once."

"Violence in paradise," Paul said.

Tobias nodded. He was filled with the need to pace the room, so he got up and walked in aimless circles. "Violence in paradise is right," he remarked, and he paused beside the silent TV, resting one hand on the cabinet.

"You've probably got a whole gang of suspects right now," Paul said.

"Don't I wish." Tobias yawned.

"You'll get your man. You're like the Mounted Police, Pops."

Tobias moved toward the bedroom door. The fatigue he felt ran through him like rivers of lead. "You'll be comfortable on the couch?" he asked.

Paul smiled. "Go get some sleep. You look like you need it."

But suddenly Tobias didn't want to sleep, suddenly his adrenaline was pumping through him, and he turned away from the bedroom door to sit down in the armchair that faced the sofa. What he wanted was to talk with the boy, to run through old memories, catalogs of old times, almost as if he needed reassurance that there had been a past and that past had been filled with laughter.

He rolled himself a cigarette, gazed at his son, then he heard himself drift off into a memory of the time when they'd all gone on a car trip to Montreal and a sudden blizzard had robbed them of any sense of direction and they'd quite forgotten the name of the hotel where they'd had reservations. And before Montreal there had been the Summer of the Garden, when they'd all decided to grow their own organic vegetables behind the house in Queens and how the starlings had eaten the goddamn seeds and the only produce that ever made it to the kitchen table was a handful of limp peas. Old times, old times. Even as he talked, and Paul nodded his head in response to these memories, Tobias could hear the sound of Edie's wheelchair coming across the floor toward him, and he almost wanted to turn his face to look, knowing he'd see nothing save perhaps a dim specter risen from a recent grave, something that wouldn't be Edie at all. A thing of bone and old hair and horror.

Now Paul was mentioning a camping expedition to a place in the back of the beyond of the Adirondacks. They had trudged into this godforsaken wilderness, pitched their tent, primed their old Coleman stove, unloaded their canned food—only to find that the can opener had been forgotten, each then accusing the other of poor planning. A memory of trying to puncture the lids of Campbell's cream-of-chicken soup with sharp stones, making gashes and dents.

Old stories, old fables, family myths. And both men worked them over like a couple of miners digging for precious metals. The stories trailed off finally into weary silences, private moments when father and son lapsed into recollections too fragmented to utter, and then Tobias raised one hand wearily and stepped toward the bedroom.

He covered a yawn, then smiled. "I better get some sleep."

He went inside the bedroom and sat on the edge of the bed. Memories and ghosts. He lay back and gazed at the ceiling and he thought of the fractured skeleton of his life, as if it were an exhibit behind a glass case he was destined to look at day after day after day.

Edith, he thought.

Alone, Paul picked up the old newspapers and flicked absently through them. This apartment, he thought. This place he so dreaded. He shut his eyes. He'd plunged for a time into the world of nostalgia only because his father had seemed to find it necessary to rummage through old experiences. But now it left a bitter taste inside him and a sick sensation in his stomach. He felt helpless: it was as if the past were a vast army massed against him and he could do nothing to control the advance of the hordes. Sickness and death. . . .

Grief is perfectly natural, Paul.

It's only unnatural when it doesn't begin to mend.

Tell me, Dr. Streicher. Tell me that grief is just nature's way of doing a repair job on the rubber raft of your feelings. A way of stretching adhesive over a split in the old seams.

Tell me, Dr. Streicher.

Then write me another script for Seconals so I can sleep nights.

He stared at the telephone for a time, thinking that he might call Streicher right this minute, that he might just inconvenience the guy, as if to do so could prove some kind of point—but when his hand touched the receiver, he froze, overwhelmed by the sheer futility.

# 9

Andrew Conturas had decided when he was forty that he had chosen the wrong profession. Human beings, taken as a whole, did not interest him in the least, and their illnesses, for the most part, could be cured by aspirin and diet and exercise. When he had been teaching in Boston he had received a stunning revelation in the midst of a lecture concerning systemic circulation that if he could have stepped back in time he would have become a marine biologist and spent his days dissecting eels or exploring the brains of sharks or examining the nesting habits of the three-spined stickleback. At least, in this watery world, one was not at the beck and call of the hypochondriac, since fish were not known to have severe mental problems. However, it had been too late to make such a radical change in his profession, so he did the next best thing. He quit his teaching post, moved to Las Cosimas before Las Cosimas had become an executive enclave, and he filled the upper part of his house with aquariums of various kinds. Saltwater mainly, since Conturas's principal interest was in the sexual dimorphism of the hideously beautiful anglerfish, which he purchased at considerable expense from houses that supplied exotic marine specimens.

In pursuit of this hobby, naturally he needed funds. So he was obliged to take the occasional patient, none of whom he liked (since misanthropism was his main philosophical tenet), but all of whom came to him with various forms of heart disorders. For some reason, it had gotten around Las Cosimas that Conturas was a specialist in diseases of the heart. He was no specialist, for sure, but he knew more about the malfunctions of the human heart than any of those highly paid whores who strutted the fluorescent corridors of Las Cosimas General Hospital.

Conturas, who enjoyed the company of his anglerfish, was a man in love with solitude. Consequently, he was more than a little irritated by the man who sat at this very moment in his living room, a buffoon who was doing a damn good job passing himself off as the local sheriff. Rebook, Rubadeck, a name like that. Andrew Conturas, who had saturnine features and lips that were full and purple, pretended to be listening to what the sheriff had to say.

"She was a patient of yours, I believe," Karl Rezabek remarked.

Conturas nodded. The faces of his patients tended to blur one into another. "I treated Mrs. Sharp, yes."

"What for?" Rezabek asked.

"There is a principle of confidentiality involved," the doctor answered. He pondered matters a moment. A dead woman dumped on the sand. A well-aimed knife (or scalpel) through the heart, puncturing the pulmonary arteries.

"I thought that under the circumstances, doctor, you might give me some background on the late Mrs. Sharp."

Conturas picked at his lower lip. He became conscious of a fragment of lint clinging to the vest of his black three-piece suit. Under the circumstances, he thought. A matter of ethics. This man who represented law and order could go in search of a warrant and the principle of confidentiality would go straight down the toilet. Conturas felt uncomfortable.

"She had a disorder of the heart, Sheriff." What was the damned man's name? Rubadubdub. No, there was a Z in it somewhere. Sheriff Berzerk, the physician thought.

"Can you be more specific?"

"Would it be of assistance to you if I were?" Conturas airily waved a hand. The dimorphism of deep-sea anglerfish—why was he being bothered by this trivial inquiry? "Would it help if I were technical?"

Karl Rezabek found himself listening to the sonorous tick of the big grandfather clock in the corner. Through a half-open door he observed a massive number of books in great untidy stacks. There was dust everywhere, and fine cobwebs hung in high corners. Physicians were supposed to be obsessed with hygiene, were they not?

"When did you last see Mrs. Sharp?"

"Three weeks ago," Conturas answered. "I don't encourage my patients to make regular visits. A waste of time usually."

"Was her disease terminal?"

"She suffered from a malfunction of the tricuspid valve," Conturas said.

This is one cold fish, Rezabek thought. He talks about a patient as if he's discussing a machine. He studied the physician's features a moment. You couldn't read that face, those black eyes, you couldn't get a damn thing out of just looking at the guy.

"And that's serious?"

"Yes, Sheriff. The valve in question controls the flow of blood into the right ventricle."

Ah, I see, Rezabek thought. The right ventricle. He leaned forward in his chair and said, "Have you any idea who might have killed her?"

"An odd question," Conturas said. "How could I have such knowledge?"

"Well, sometimes patients confide in doctors, don't they? Tell them things. You know."

"I don't encourage intimacy like that, Sheriff."

"She never told you anything about her private life? Friends? Enemies?"

"Had she done so, I wouldn't have listened," Conturas said flatly. "People come to see me. I examine them. I provide medication. They go home. The rest is of no concern to me." The physician looked at his watch and started to rise. "You'll have to excuse me, Sheriff. I have some work to do."

Rezabek stood up. "Thanks for your time anyhow, doctor."

Conturas was already moving out of the room and heading toward the stairs, as if Rezabek were nothing more than a distant, unpleasant memory. When he reached the landing at the top, he listened with some satisfaction to the gurgling sounds made by the aquarium pumps. Downstairs, the front door closed.

Conturas paused before going inside to study the anglerfish.

Isadora Sharp, he thought.

He had never liked the woman at all.

The blue fish gaped at him through the sizzling bubbles as he entered the room.

No, he had never liked Isadora Sharp in the least.

He sat down before his fish tanks and picked up a knife from a small table to his right. With the tip of this implement he poked the index finger of his left hand and drew to the surface of his skin a small bubble of blood, at which he stared with some distaste. Then he placed the knife aside and, hunched forward a little on his chair, studied the motions of fish through glass.

He wondered why he had jabbed his own flesh the way he had done. Testing the sharpness of the blade? Checking its usefulness for dissecting purposes? A small shapeless cloud drifted through his mind, and as it loomed larger in his consciousness he felt an uneasiness, as if shards of broken glass were being applied, like some sadist's poultice, to the side of his head. He shut his eyes very tightly, squeezing the lids so hard that he could see colored flashes in his blinded visual field.

A knife through flesh, he thought.

And he saw what he wished he hadn't seen—he saw the woman's face and the way her mouth contorted in pain and the stiffening of her fingers as if she were trying to catch things that slid awkwardly through the air around her, he saw all this in a sequence of speeded-up pictures almost as if he had stumbled inside a darkened movie theater operated by an insane projectionist.

He pressed his eyelids even harder than before.

Then he stood up, rubbing his hands together briskly, determined to get back to work, determined to still the discomfort the idiot policeman had left in his passing.

Tobias woke, discovered that Paul had gone—maybe to pick up a morning paper—and prepared some strips of bacon and two fried eggs for himself in the kitchen. When he laid the food out on a plate, he realized he had no appetite whatsoever. Dipping an oblong of bread into the heart of the undercooked yolk, seeing a slinky length of mucus cling to the crust, he thrust the plate aside. He strolled toward the window and looked down into the street.

He dressed and shaved and walked down to the station. Charlie Nicholson was standing at the water cooler, turning the conical waxen cup around in the palm of his hand. Charlie's face was streaked with sweat. An abrupt bubble rose inside the cooler and exploded near the surface.

"Morning, Tobe. What brings you in here this time of day?"

Tobias sat down. He was dressed in pale blue slacks and a navy cotton shirt, a relaxed contrast to Nicholson's uniform. He rolled himself a cigarette and lit it.

"Restless, I guess," he said.

"Can't keep away, that it?" Nicholson crumpled his cup in his big beefy hand. He shook his head and stared up at the whirring ceiling fan. "I hate to disappoint you, my man, but we haven't turned up the killer as yet."

"Where's Rezabek?"

Nicholson shrugged his wide shoulders. "He's out there like Dick Tracy, I guess."

"Figures." Tobias watched the smoke curl away from his cigarette. "Christ knows what he expects to find."

Nicholson leaned against the wall, hitching up his pistol. "He took old Dunbar's tirade to heart, so I guess it's his neck on the chopping block, Tobe, which is why he's out there now doing his solo act."

"With the emphasis on 'act'," Tobias said.

"Right," and Nicholson drew more water from the cooler. Tobias looked at the wall calendar. July 2. Two days until the annual Fourth Fireworks Display. The usual elaborate outburst in the night sky over the country club and the usual burn cases with kids who got too close to their firecrackers. He put his hand to his shirt pocket and took out his notebook, flipping the pages.

"Charlie, you ever see a big Lincoln parked around here with Wisconsin plates? A black mother with tinted windows."

"Can't say as I have. Why?"

"I was just curious," Tobias said. He looked at the number he'd written down, then he shut the notebook. So what? Caroline had a lover with Wisconsin plates on his car? Big deal. And it isn't just idle curiosity you're suffering from, is it, Tobe? You want to know the name of her partner, don't you? He stuck the little book in his breast pocket. Forget it, he told himself. Don't hang albatrosses on yourself.

The door of the office opened and Karl Rezabek stepped in, cap in hand, shirt collar slightly undone, necktie slackened. He had the look of a man put through a wringer. He said nothing, just moved to his desk and sat down, tilting his chair back at the wall. He didn't have to ask anything—he knew from the expressions of the two officers that nothing had broken in the Sharp case. Karl sighed and let his hands go slack in his lap. Something of the sheen, Tobias thought, has been rubbed off the old soldier. And for a moment Tobias felt a slight sense of pity. This wasn't a case of food pilfered from the canteen or some jerk turning up on parade without his socks on or the U.S. flag flying upside down.

This was murder.

The office was silent save for the bursting of another bubble in the cooler, which had the sound of a quiet, liquid fart.

Tobias stood up. He'd take a stroll down to the Quarter, maybe run into Paul in the street, have a beer with him. It didn't matter, he just needed to get out of the morgue the office had become—and away from the corpselike pall on Karl Rezabek's weary face.

"Something's going to break," Rezabek said.

Charlie Nicholson nodded. "Sure. Sure it will."

Tobias concurred with a slight movement of the head.

Anything to bolster Rezabek's spirits, anything to give the poor guy a boost.

"Something always breaks when you least expect it," he said as he moved toward the door.

He hoped he sounded optimistic.

* * *

On her second espresso, which she needed to get her circulation flowing, Caroline Cassidy became conscious of the fact that somebody was watching her as she sat at the coffee-shop counter. It was not the kind of realization filled with menace, it was just mildly disturbing, the sort of nuisance you might feel when a fly keeps buzzing around your face. She lit a cigarette and listened to the hiss of the chromium espresso maker. Trouble was, the coffee shop was crowded and noisy and you couldn't just look around in the hope of catching somebody's eye.

Antonio, who owned the shop, leaned toward her and smiled. "Getting ready, huh? Getting ready for the big day, huh?"

"The big day?"

"Whoom! Zoom!" And he threw his hands upward, rolling his eyes.

Whoom, zoom, what? It took several seconds for her to filter Antonio's meaning through the murky corridors of her brain.

"The works of fire!" he shouted.

"The fireworks," she said.

"Right, right. The Big Day. Patriotic!" Antonio, who had recently become an American citizen, had his certificate of citizenship framed and hung on the coffee-shop wall.

The goddamn fireworks, she thought.

It was a task that J M Dunbar charged her with annually, the preparation for the display. Although he did not appear in person, he liked to sit down in San Diego and think that the Las Cosimas display was the greatest thing this side of Coney Island.

"I've been too busy with my own fireworks lately, Tony."

"Huh?"

"It's okay. It doesn't mean anything." She drained her espresso and Antonio filled her cup again. She fidgeted with it nervously. I am being observed, she thought. And now it occurred to her that perhaps it was the Caller who had crept out from beneath his sleazy stones of darkness to observe her openly in the sunlight of the day. She twisted her head from side to side, noticed nothing unusual, sipped her drink. The fireworks display.

She shut her eyes. A slight pain was beating against her inner eyelids. Each year in the past she'd used a company from Carmel to put on the display, a pair of charming faggots whose artistic notions of fireworks displays involved elaborate rockets that burst into avant-garde shapes which, though they lit the sky, somehow always left the crowd a little disappointed because they'd come to see red-white-and-blue flags burst into life over Las Cosimas, not some queer roses and violets and odd spirals that suggested stairways to the stars. Maybe this year she could ask them to forget the poodles and the flowers and archangels and go with something more, well, traditional.

She made a mental note to call the people in Carmel. Then she stubbed her cigarette and turned her face to the side and she saw the young man with the glasses on the other side of the room. The faint feeling of familiarity became one of firm recognition. The young man rose and crossed the room toward her.

"I know," he said. "I was staring."

She smiled. "It's Paul, isn't it? Paul Manning?"

The kid nodded and shifted his weight around uncertainly.

"It's been quite some time," Caroline said. "You here to see your dad?"

"Yeah." He looked past her, his attention drawn by the hissing of the coffee machine.

"So, how have you been?" she asked.

"Pre-med. UCLA. The usual stuff."

"Right, I remember that now." She didn't, of course, but the kid looked so ill-at-ease, she wanted to make him feel comfortable. There were times when she had this kind of effect on young men; she made them nervous and they tended to behave around her as if they were smitten by the virus of infatuation. "How long are you staying?"

"A day or two, I guess."

She studied his face a moment. It wasn't a bad face, maybe a little on the gaunt side, but the eyes burned and you could see an intelligence behind them.

"Maybe . . ." He started to say something, then stopped.

She tilted her head, waiting. "Maybe what?"

"I thought we could have a drink together while I'm in town."

Ah, she thought. How deep down did he have to dig for that question? She looked at his eyes, insecure behind the glasses now, as if he lived in stark terror of a refusal. Very lightly she let the tips of her fingers brush across the sleeve of his jacket. Christ, he'd have to show ID in any bar around here, a prospect she found both funny and embarrassing.

She pushed her coffee cup aside. The look on the kid's face was so damned appealing that she didn't want to let him down with a bump.

"You promise not to molest me or anything?"

He smiled. "I swear."

She slid down from the stool. Really, when you thought about it, there was something flattering in his invitation. He'd gathered his nerves together, he'd summoned his courage to cross the room, he'd popped the question. Besides, he was a pleasant kid.

"I'll tell you what, Paul. Why don't you call me later and we'll see how things shape up?"

"Tonight? Tomorrow? When?"

The eager squeak in the voice. She felt suddenly and quite unexpectedly maternal. "Make it tonight. Sevenish. Maybe we can set something up," and she let her hand trail across his sleeve again.

She smiled at him and stepped out into Hermosillo Square.

What the hell am I doing? she asked herself.

Sunlight struck her face and she thought: All bets are off if Daniel Romero calls me before seven o'clock.

A quiet drink with a nice kid was one thing.

Dynamite Danny was something else.

Paul finished his coffee and noticed that his hand was trembling as he set the cup down. He turned to look at Caroline Cassidy cross the square, then she was lost to him in the morning light that fell in dappled sequences over the movements of shoppers. But even after she had disappeared from sight he could still see something of her, a shadowy imprint on his retina, a ghost. He placed a fingertip against his lower lip, remembering the way she'd touched him, how her hand had lingered against his arm—and he was convinced he saw something in those eyes of hers, a smart little light of invitation maybe. (Or was he deceiving himself? Was he running himself through the gauntlet of his own expectations?)

She was beautiful, she was desirable, but even as he considered these qualities he was filled with a deep sadness and he blinked his eyes and his perceptions shimmered in front of him.

He went out into Hermosillo Square, fighting the sorrow that had abruptly welled up inside and wondering—as he always did, as he always wondered whether he was alone or whether he was arguing with Streicher—if life ever held out anything more than the promise of grief and pain.

He could hear the insidious whisper of Streicher's voice inside his mind, the kind of voice that answered inquiries at the information desks of public libraries, soft and in its very softness, its sweet quality, curiously imprecise, as if there were no hard meanings attached to the words.

Your mother is dead, Paul. David is dead too.

You are alive. Your life goes on.

I'm paying you money for greeting-card messages, doc?

No, Paul, you don't stop loving the dead because they're no longer alive, but you must confront the grief and you must set aside your bad memories of their pain, you must unload the baggage—

Memories as luggage.

Things to be checked in and out of airports of the emotions.

He stared up at the sun, blinked. His eyes hurt. But that was nothing, that was a minor inconvenience, a smarting sensation compared to what his mother and his brother had gone through in the last stages of their lives. Dragged down into the humiliation of pain, bedpans, nurses sticking rectal thermometers into you like your ass was a pincushion . . . and those bad days, those really bad days, when you were beyond pain, afloat on the morphine clouds and communing with cherubims and talking in long dreamy sentences that stripped you of your logic, your basic human dignity, those awful days when your continued existence made no sense at all.

David. His mother.

Suddenly the sun was chill against his face.

He took off his glasses, wiped his eyes with the sleeve of his shirt.

Streicher said: You want to be a doctor so you can help people like your mother, people like David, am I right?

Yeah, Streicher, real perceptive.

Real bright.

I'm awed.

I can hardly breathe on account of my admiration for you.

Paul walked to the corner of the street. The sadness was a palpable thing in his blood.

Sometimes, in these moods, the inside of his own mind seemed to him like a graveyard and all his thoughts nothing but epitaphs.

A hangover suggested something more than death, something less pleasant than a lingering, incurable cancer. A part of your brain had been amputated and messages of even the most mundane kind—such as "Get out of bed" or "Go to the john"—became tangled in the frazzled wires of your own short circuits.

Dale Hamlett, or the hulk that was performing a passable likeness of him, a counterfeit man, an impostor, rolled out of bed and squatted on the floor and blinked like a pit pony at the white sunlight that, screaming through the bedroom window, pierced his brain with the accuracy of a laser.

He put a hand to his mouth. The teeth were in place.

He studied his toes. There were ten in all.

His hands were still attached to his body, although, in the way they shuddered, they seemed to have an existence independent of himself.

A folk remedy occurred to him.

A raw egg dropped inside a stiff Bloody Mary.

He let his eyes roam around the room. No Emma. Presumably she had risen earlier and was downstairs even now doing horrible things with food. Dale Hamlett prodded the inside of his mouth with an index finger, for God knows what reason other than at the command of some broken-down synapse. Then, with a gargantuan effort, he rose, stumbled toward the bathroom, and plunged his head into cold water. It sang in his ears and filled his nostrils and coursed wonderfully across his scalp.

There had been a party, that much he remembered.

He wandered downstairs, dripping, and he surveyed the ruins of what had been a social gathering.

Empty wine bottles lay across carpets or were stuffed between cushions of sofas, and broken glasses had been scattered around the fireplace. The conversation pit, that sunken feature in which Dale and his wife mainly practiced the art of marital silence, was strewn with crushed canapés and hardened streaks of fondue and skewered olives. On a table lay an oval mirror, a razor blade, half of a drinking straw, and a small empty brown bottle encrusted with a white substance.

It was the day after Pompeii, Dale Hamlett reflected.

A minor Vesuvius had erupted, leaving artifacts behind, but no bodies.

So far, he thought.

He stepped over the debris, dogged by the skunk of his own hangover.

He called his wife's name in a voice that shattered the delicate crystal connections of his own brain.

Emma! Emma!

Outside the living room, he looked over the edge of the balcony that hovered above the large kitchen. More wreckage assailed him.

He started down the steps, his bare feet slapping on the unvarnished wood. The twin porcelain sinks were piled high with glasses, dishes, more empty bottles. The white tiles had been sprayed with what might have been an exploding bottle of Pepsi-Cola, ragged brown streaks crusted to the Mexican ceramic.

Bloody Mary, raw egg. Raw egg, Bloody Mary. Screw the celery stalk.

Dale's was a one-track mind now and his throat felt like gritty sand. He stumbled toward the refrigerator, took out an egg, found a bottle of Stolichnaya and a can of Bloody Mary mix and threw the lot together after cracking the egg.

He swallowed his drink rapidly and his brain cleared and he looked around the kitchen.

Where the hell was Emma?

He padded about for a while, mixed himself a second drink, and started to feel like a whole person again. At least he knew his own name and he understood the fact that he somehow fitted his own body again.

Emma, dear . . .

Perhaps she had fallen asleep in the sitting room, sprawled out on the sofa. He'd go check.

He passed more of the same Pepsi-like stains on the walls as he made his way across the hallway to the door of the sitting room, which was halfway open.

Something made him pause.

It was almost as if a piano chord had sounded at the back of his brain. An E-flat minor, something with a melancholic echo. Holding his glass precariously, he nudged the door open a little way further and he stepped inside the room.

The expensive wood-slatted blinds were half-closed and the sunlight that sneaked through the spaces created an impression of bars.

Dale Hamlett called his wife's name again and wondered why, all of a sudden, he was whispering.

Emma . . .

Emma, darling . . .

He moved across the room, skirted the octagonal coffee table that Emma had bought in Rome, and he paused by the sneaky light at the window.

Emma. Where are you?

He was struck by a weird sense of finality, as if he had heard the pages of a heavy book being slammed shut. Struck by silence, by the odd quality of this quietness, this void of sound.

And he was touched by a fear as light as the wing of a moth fluttering past your face.

Emma . . .

Em Ma . . .

Something dark and sticky adhered to the soles of his bare feet and his first thought was that Pepsi had been spilled in this room as well.

But when he spun suddenly around, as if directed by instinct, and saw the twisted way Emma lay across the couch, he realized that his first thought had been a mistake, that it wasn't Pepsi or any other kind of syrupy drink that stuck to him, and he opened his mouth to moan or shout or scream but no sound came out of him.

# 10

There was a warm breeze blowing up Libertad Street as Tobias strolled past the windows of the small shops. He went as far as the edge of the beach. White and yellow sails, catching wind, puffed up like the wings of strange birds. He stared at the ancient pier, at the far end of which a couple of fishermen sat hunched in the manner of crumbled statues. Then he walked back the way he had come, pausing only once to glance in the direction of the place where Isadora Sharp had been found.

He was moving toward Enrico's when he saw Caroline Cassidy on the sidewalk ahead of him. She had just stepped out of the cigar store and she was clutching a tiny box against her side and Tobias felt a quick arrow of awkwardness go through him. Cigars. Presents. For the guy with the Lincoln.

Her loveliness was a stunning thing. The breeze scattered her hair back across her shoulders and her pale blue miniskirt (a garment that went in and out of fashion more frequently than a cuckoo in a Swiss clock) was blown slightly backward, the front flattened against her trim stomach. Tobias had the mental image of himself inside a confessional, peering at the face of the priest through the grille.

I have lust in my heart, Father.

Give me penances. Thousands of them. Heap them upon me.

Caroline had seen him and was smiling as she walked

toward him. The breeze flapped through her thin blouse. No bra, Tobias observed.

"It seems like I can't get away from Mannings today," she said.

"Oh?"

"I just ran into your son, Paul, not an hour ago." In the coffee shop," she said. "He's a sweet kid."

A lowrider went honking past, stuffed with more passengers than any car could logically hold. Tobias, taking his eyes from Caroline's face, watched it go.

Caroline moved the box of cigars from one hand to the other.

"Taken up smoking?" Tobias asked.

"They're a gift."

"He's a lucky fellow."

Caroline pushed a strand of hair out of her eyes. "You could say that."

Tobias jingled loose change in the pockets of his pants. He watched as the girl gazed past him in the direction of the oceanfront. A moment of silence here. Something Tobias didn't know how to fill.

"Maybe I shouldn't tell you this, but your son asked me for a date," she said.

"A date? Paul did that?"

"Date is too heavy. I mean, he invited me to have a drink."

"Paul?" Tobias asked again.

"Why not? He's old enough, Tobias."

Paul, Tobias thought. Was there a hidden fire deep down in the kid's gut? Some horny little flame? Tobias wasn't sure whether to feel proud or envious. He just couldn't imagine Paul coming up to this girl and asking her to go out with him.

"Did you accept?" he asked.

"I left it at maybe," she answered. "I hope I didn't do anything wrong . . . I mean, you wouldn't object if we had one drink together, would you?"

"Object?" Tobias managed to laugh. He noticed, with a rush of warmth, that the girl was laughing too. She had the most splendid mouth. Perfect lips. And he wondered how it would feel to press his own mouth against hers, but suddenly he was back to Hermosillo Square and Caroline was all locked up in the embrace of her lover and the prospect of kissing her dissolved in his mind with all the sadness of a wilted birthday candle. Now Paul—Christ, I didn't think the kid had it in him.

Caroline was staring at the cigar box in her hand. Quietly, almost mischievously, she said, "I saw you this morning in the square, Tobias. You didn't manage to conceal yourself very well—"

A hot flush went up the back of Tobias's neck. He heard himself stammer, "I was finishing my patrol, I just happened—"

Caroline laid one hand on his wrist. "It's okay. I'm just giving you a hard time—"

"I wasn't spying, Caroline, I mean, you shouldn't think that, but with this murder just happening, I . . ." And his voice became a flute with a flawed reed. Embarrassment all around. He wondered if he was blushing.

"I know you weren't spying, Tobias. Just doing your job, right?"

"The job, yeah—"

"And wondering about my companion, right again?"

"Right again, I have to keep my eyes open—"

Caroline seemed to be enjoying herself enormously. "If you haven't already found this out, he's called Daniel

Romero, he lives at the Resort, and he's from Wisconsin."

"You don't need to tell me—" Tobias suddenly saw himself as a snoop. The class creep. The Chief Nerd in the High Order of Nerddom.

"I'm a big girl, Tobias," Caroline said. "You might have noticed."

Tobias numbly nodded. The palms of his hands perspired. He saw Romero's face in lamplight and there was a dry thickness at the back of his throat. "I wasn't spying," he said again.

"I know that." Caroline clutched her cigar box to her side and now she laughed. "It's a comforting feeling to know that there's a cop nearby. Especially now." She was silent a moment before she asked, "I don't suppose there's anything new happening?"

Tobias shook his head. The girl stared down at her feet a moment, as if she were remembering Isadora Sharp. A flag at half-mast, a moment of silence.

Then she said, "I've been receiving strange phone calls. I guess I ought to report them."

"What kind of calls?" Tobias asked.

Caroline shrugged. "You'd loosely describe them as the work of somebody with his shoes on the wrong feet, I guess. Crazy." She tapped the side of her head.

"You recognize the voice?"

Caroline shook her head.

"Well, does the caller make threats, anything like that?"

"You couldn't say they were threats. He doesn't make any sense." She paused. Something in the way she blinked made Tobias's heart teeter at the edge of a high-dive board. "Still, it's kind of unpleasant, Tobias. What do you suggest?"

I have all kinds of suggestions in this black heart of

mine, Tobias thought. "First, you change your number. Then if you get any more calls, we could put a tap on the line."

Caroline seemed to consider these possibilities for a moment. She rattled the cigar box in her hand and Tobias thought sickeningly of the recipient of the smokes. She said, "I'll contact the telephone company."

"And make sure you get an unlisted number," Tobias said. But give it to me, don't forget to let me have it, just in case, you never know, it might come in handy, because a night might come when I can't take any more loneliness and images of you will drive me crazy with lust. He thought suddenly of Edith and his whole married life of complete fidelity and he was touched by an illogical sense of betrayal.

Caroline smiled at him.

"I'll see you around," and then she was gone, high-stepping it along Libertad Street, collecting a couple of wolf whistles from the sidewalk lizards who lounged around shop doorways. Tobias watched her go and then he went inside Enrico's. Instead of his usual Dos Equis, he ordered a tequila, which he threw back in one shot and gasped.

Caroline and Paul.

Hell. Good luck to the kid. Maybe the company of Caroline Cassidy was just what he needed. Somebody to bring him out of himself.

He ordered a second shot and couldn't concentrate on what old Enrico was telling him as he turned the name Daniel Romero over in his mind.

The face of the guy. And now the name.

Tiny bells ringing in the far distance.

Ships' horns on a foggy horizon.

He leaned against the bar and watched the pool players

and then he was conscious of the incongruous sight of Karl Rezabek stepping inside the bar and approaching him slowly.

"Slumming, Sheriff?" Tobias asked.

Rezabek shook his head slowly.

Something is wrong, Tobias thought. All at once the air around him had changed. Some wicked current of electricity flowed through the barroom. He was conscious of several things at once. The kid Carlos with a pool cue in one hand. Enrico running a towel over the damp counter. And Rezabek's pale face.

One of those frozen moments.

"Tobias," Rezabek said.

Tobias put his glass down. He needed to be stone sober for this, whatever it was.

"Tobias . . . there's been another one."

Tobias shut his eyes a second. His head was suddenly clear. Another one.

"A woman called Emma Hamlett," the sheriff said, his voice cracked.

Tobias pushed himself off the counter and said, "Let's go," and Rezabek followed him out onto Libertad, like a soul wandering through the unpaved, unsigned streets of purgatory.

"Look, man, I don't know, you know what I'm saying, I don't know." The little guy called Sammy shrugged. He had a boxer's mannerisms, shifting his shoulders from side to side as if he expected to be punched. He shuffled his feet, bounced from side to side, then he glowered fiercely at himself in the men's-room mirror, across the surface of which a jagged crack ran. Sammy had oiled black hair and he wore a sharp powder-blue suit and two-tone shoes and he had a reputation in the Quarter for having one hand, if not both, in any kind of action that might be going on. He sold photographs imported from Tijuana and Juárez that were reputed to depict enormous ladies undergoing various forms of sexual intercourse with beasts such as donkeys and bears. He pimped for a couple of women who lived above the Farm Workers' Union on Javelina Street. Some who knew Samuel Suarez spoke of a safe in his apartment which contained hundreds of counterfeit green cards, blank MasterCards, and birth certificates that only required a name to make them legal.

If he had a weakness—at least one that could be isolated from so many—it was the fact that he was quite unable to pass up a bargain. A watch, a bracelet, a ring, it didn't matter to Sammy: when he saw something that glinted, when he realized that the item was reduced to the kind of price that you wouldn't even find at a fire sale, a certain yearning filled him and a complex series of chemical reactions set up business in his head. If a man had something to sell at a loss, then it stood to reason that Sammy would be the only victor from such a transaction.

He ran a comb through his hair and said, "Hey, look, I don't know, kid. I don't know you and I don't know where the merchandise is coming from and I don't like sitting out on a goddamn limb listening to the sound of a buzz saw just below me, *comprende*?" Sammy made an expansive gesture with his arms and looked at his young companion. "Hey, maybe you're okay. Maybe you're on the level. I only know your name, kid. And I got a reputation I don't like anything . . . *sucio*, you know?"

The kid nodded. Sammy stared at the delicate gold chain the young man held between his hands, stretching it like the web of some gorgeous *Araña*. the bait, Sammy thought. The kid dangles the bait in front of me and I'm a *payaso*, brainless, knuckleheaded. He tore his eyes away from the gold chain as some old hombre came inside the lavatory, peed quickly, belched, then left. The old guy knew a transaction when he saw one.

Sammy Suarez put his hand on the kid's shoulder. "Listen, kid, I like your goods. Okay? I like what you're showing me."

"I got more," the kid said.

A cash register went off in Sammy's head. "Like what?"

"Other stuff, good stuff," and the kid looked at himself in the mirror, pulling his upper lip back and studying his gums.

A kid comes along, Sammy thought. Pretty soon he's taking over your territory and stealing your customers and you're just another onetime enchilada in the Quarter. "Listen, *compadre*, I don't know you. So, I take a chance. Fifty for the chain."

"Fifty?"

Sammy nodded.

The kid laughed. He had wonderful white teeth. Sammy didn't like the feeling of being laughed at, especially not by some handsome kid for whom half the gringo wives in Las Cosimas had the hots. I used to kick them out of bed, Sammy thought. Time was when those cocksuckers begged me.

"Two hundred."

"You are crazy," Sammy said.

The kid shrugged and rolled the chain into a little ball, then shoved his fist beneath Sammy's chin, a gesture of contempt.

"Kid, okay," Sammy said. "One hundred. On this condition."

"Condition?"

"You tell me where you got it, okay?"

"The honor of a certain lady is at stake," the kid said.

"Honor, my ass." Sammy whistled through his teeth. "You're screwing some bitch up there, I don't care. All I got to know is she isn't the woman who turned up unfortunately dead on the beach. You understand my position, kid?"

The kid nodded. "A gift, okay? For services."

Sammy winked, shuffled his feet. "And this woman is alive, right?"

"My word," the kid said.

"Okay. Since I like you, seventy-five."

"One-twenty."

"Ninety."

"One-ten."

"An even hundred."

The gold chain, unrolling from the kid's hand, slinked into Sammy's palm in exchange for five crisp twenties. Transaction completed.

The kid smiled, an arrogant look. "You should see my other stuff sometime, Sammy."

*Sammy*. Too familiar. Suarez ignored his discomfort. He smiled back at the kid. "Get in touch with me when you're ready, Carlos. Okay?"

Saying nothing, Carlos Ayala stepped out of the lavatory and returned to the bar, leaving Sammy to gaze at the exquisite gold chain which he pressed quickly to his lips, in the manner of a man kissing a rosary, then stuffed inside his wallet before old Enrico got suspicious about what might be going on in the toilet of his tavern. Enrico was scrupulous about anything that went on inside his cantina.

A house of death always had a certain quality to it, as if you might hear the fading echo of the recently deceased. Half a phrase, an unfinished sentence, a whisper. This was especially true of places in which violence had been committed, because there the echoes were louder, clamoring for your attention. Dale Hamlett, who sat in the kitchen in an atrophied position, hands dangling between his legs, a Bloody Mary stain on his canary-colored Jockey shorts, stared at the window as if there, inscribed in the hieroglyphic of sunlight, he might find the name of his wife's assassin.

Tobias, who had examined the corpse in the sitting room, who had seen a single stab wound through the heart, felt that his worst fears were being confirmed. Las Cosimas had a lunatic killer running through the streets.

A madman.

The same crazy MO.

Tobias picked his way through the debris of the Hamlett house and noticed, in passing, a cocaine spoon attached to a bottle that lay on the kitchen table. In bygone days, the sight of such a thing would have been enough to fetch out the entire narcotics squad—but the world had changed and the recreational habits of people had changed with it and if the highly paid executives of Las Cosimas wanted to stuff portions of their bank accounts up their noses, if they wanted to drive Lamborghinis into their mucus membranes, then there wasn't a narcotics squad anywhere that could prevent such things. Even marijuana had the profound impact these days of Tylenol.

Tobias sat down at the table and looked at Hamlett, conscious of Rezabek stumbling around in another room. A physician had been called and a needle was on its way to assist Dale Hamlett over the first frontiers of grief and bewilderment, though God alone knew how Hamlett would be when the soporific wore off. Men carry grief in different ways, Tobias thought. Henry Sharp had shouldered his like a bricklayer climbing a ladder (at first anyhow) and Dale Hamlett looked as if he'd been given enough Thorazine to mellow out the entire city of Santa Barbara . . . and he,

Tobias, had yielded to days of the most utter emptiness imaginable. Just emptiness. The shallows of a life. Not even tears, grief, the tearing of hair, the insomnia filled with toxic tobacco smoke.

Just nothing.

The recognition of nothing.

He touched the back of Hamlett's hand a moment and the big man stirred, as if he'd been disturbed in his sleep.

It's tough.

It's lousy.

I'm sorry.

Sure, Tobe, you could say these things.

But words were as useful as pebbles at the bottom of a quick-moving stream sometimes, just as glassy, just as glossed, just as treacherous.

Nothing changed the fact that Emma Hamlett had been stabbed to death somewhere in the dark.

Tobias gazed at Hamlett's vacant moon shaped face a second, then he got up from the table. I know your emptiness, he wanted to say. He wandered through the house, thinking that some kind of Social Bomb must have struck this place last night. Taittingers dropped from three thousand feet. Chablis hoisted through doorways like Molotov cocktails.

Prowl, Tobias told himself.

Look for something . . . awry.

Call Art Frye, ask him.

Why does somebody stab a matronly lady called Emma Hamlett anyhow?

It's close to home, Art would say. Always look close to home. Never go out searching for strangers, Tobe, my man.

As he was staring around the debris, he heard Rezabek's voice coming up from below and then there were sounds of footsteps on the stairs and Andrew Conturas, black bag in his hand, entered the kitchen. Why did the guy's appearance so surprise Tobias all at once? Maybe it was the three-piece black suit and that undertaker's look and the pallid flesh that seemed never to have been kissed by sunlight.

Maybe something else.

Memories of Edith. Recollections of the times he'd taken Edith to see this physician, as if Conturas were the last hope left to her. Tobias looked across the cluttered kitchen at the doctor and Conturas smiled in a thin way, a look of faint recognition. Then the secret black bag was being opened and out came the paraphernalia of oblivion, the needle that would go in Dale's bloodstream and render life, at least temporarily, tolerable. The poor guy sat motionless, like an extra in the midst of a movie he didn't remotely comprehend. Tobias watched the sharp needle glint, saw a tiny slick of blood on Dale's arm, then looked away.

Needles.

Edie had had all the needles the world had to offer.

Suddenly, he was upset by the memory of his wife, angry that she'd been taken from him, angry at the heart disease that had wasted her away, angry even at the cheerfulness with which she'd faced her own death, as if it was a party to which she'd been invited. Tobias shook his head and looked back at the physician, who was leading Dale Hamlett out of the room. Dale, the Zombie. Tobias could hear Hamlett settle down on a sofa in another room, then Conturas came back.

"It's Manning, isn't it?"

Tobias nodded. "We met a few times."

"Edith. Of course." Conturas snapped his black bag shut

firmly. He looked around the kitchen. "This is an unpleasant business."

Master of the understatement, Tobias thought. "You saw the body."

Conturas ran a hand across the kitchen table, a gesture of disapproval at the litter there. "A single stab wound."

"Like Isadora Sharp," Tobias said.

"As you say."

Tobias could hear a broken sob issuing from the room where Dale Hamlett lay. The drug hadn't kicked in yet. The guy hadn't been awarded his ribbon of oblivion. The sound tore at Tobias and, although he tried, he couldn't ignore it.

"Emma Hamlett did not have very long to live in any case," Conturas said.

Run it past me again, Tobias thought. "You knew the woman?"

"I treated her now and again."

"What was her problem?"

Conturas shrugged. "There were a number, Officer."

"Like what?" Tobias watched the guy. There was a glacial quality to the man: you could imagine touching him and finding your flesh covered in ice. Maybe for a heart he had frozen tundra. For a soul, layers of permafrost. Tobias had never been happy on those occasions when he'd taken Edie to see Conturas, because he treated her as if she were nothing more, nothing less, than a machine with which he was impatient.

"There was a deterioration of the mitral valve and a related set of circulatory problems. . . ."

Conturas might have been talking about the engine of a car.

Tobias went to the window. From another room he could hear Rezabek move around and he wondered what the sheriff was up to other than maybe destroying evidence in his hapless manner.

He turned to look back at Conturas. This guy loses patients like they're going out of style, he thought. A bad batting average. Some he lost because they were beyond the feeble assistance of medical science, but now two of his patients had met violent deaths. Coincidence, Tobias thought.

Art Frye had always said there was no such beast as coincidence. Always look for patterns, Tobe. Skip the random bullshit.

Patterns of what? Tobias wondered.

A physician who kills off his patients?

He wandered around the kitchen, suddenly restless. It was as if the existence of a killer in Las Cosimas was a personal affront to him, somebody out there in the shadows taunting him. He turned to Conturas, who was moving toward the door.

"Can I ask you a question?"

Conturas looked impatient. "Do."

"Can you think of anyone who would dislike you enough to start killing off your patients?"

"My dear Manning," Conturas said. "The kind of enemies I might have tend to exercise their animosities in the pages of medical journals. And the only time they use a knife, so far as I know, is in the course of surgery."

Tobias watched the doctor leave. Then Rezabek came into the room.

"You know anything about Conturas?" Tobias asked.

"I know he doesn't give much away," Rezabek said.

"Maybe we should find out a little more about him."

"Why?"

"He's pretty careless with his patients, it seems. They have this tendency to come to unfortunate ends."

Rezabek nodded, looking thoughtful. Tobias was aware of a slight role reversal going on here, as if by some form of transmutation he had become the sheriff and Rezabek was just along for the ride. He found this notion a little satisfying.

He pressed his forehead against the warm pane of glass and he could hear, scouring through the canyons, the terrible sound of an ambulance.

He stepped toward the sitting room and gazed at Emma Hamlett and the darkening stain that had spoiled what must have been an expensive dress.

"This killer . . ." Rezabek said.

"What about him?"

"You think he's likely . . ." The sheriff, unhappy with his own train of thought, stared at Emma Hamlett as though hypnotized.

"Yeah," Tobias said. "I think he's likely. If I were a gambling man, I'd put good money on it too."

Out there in Las Cosimas, he thought.

Walking the sunlit streets even now.

A killer.

And what coursed through him then was a sense of determination he hadn't felt in a long time, like a pilot light going on in his mind and flaring up suddenly, a large blue flame that wouldn't be extinguished until this madman was incarcerated.

Conturas paused on the sidewalk, sniffing the clear afternoon air into his lungs. He considered the corpse of Emma Hamlett, but only for a moment; he reviewed the single stab wound in the heart, the precision of the cut. It had taken a sharp knife and a steady hand, he thought. And he pondered the image of the blade going through the pulmonary arteries—a picture that was so hard and clear in his mind that for a second the force of it surprised him. Then he was remembering again, memories churning inside him, cluttering those spaces in his brain that he liked to keep otherwise occupied—red memories, scarlet, flaps of flesh peeled back by scalpel and blood spurting from thin tributaries that widened and opened out into gullies through which blood rushed more quickly than he could ever control.

He yielded there on the sidewalk to a temporary panic.

Then he straightened his back and carrying his black bag close to his side, moved in the direction of his car.

Anyone observing him might have noticed a temporary look of anguish cross his face and the motion of a nerve in the hollow of his neck.

But there was nobody.

Nobody to see the good doctor drive away from the house of violent death.

# 11

The guys in Carmel tried to be charming in a rather flustered way. They made it perfectly clear that their fireworks displays were not specifically created to pander to the mazes because they were, sweetie, respectable artists working in a highly technical, if not altogether academically respectable, medium and that this year they intended to unveil something rather original—to wit, nothing less than the Evolution of Mankind. Holding the telephone in her damp hand, Caroline tried to imagine the sky over Las Cosimas bursting with Neanderthal shapes and doubtless terrifying the children. She couldn't make an image.

"Gus," she said. "I'll go with the mankind bit, if you'll just throw in Old Glory at the end. Can you do that?"

"It's all a question of balance, sweetie," said Morton, who was Gus's partner and was talking on another line. "It's a delicate question of arrangement and taste, don't you see?"

Gus said, "I daresay we could drum up Stars and Stripes, although God knows it does turn my stomach, Morton."

Caroline sighed. This pair in Carmel were about to squabble with each other.

Morton said, "Over my dead body, Gus."

"It would please the kids," Caroline put in.

"I am not in this business to please infants and fill their little heads with patriotic nonsense, sweetie," Morton said.

"A flag is all I'm asking, for Christ's sake," Caroline said.

Gus said, "Humph. I suppose we could do a teensy-weensy flag right at the end, Morton."

"It's all bull," Morton answered.

Caroline hung up even as they were bitching at each other. Morton & Gus, Fireworks Artistes. You'd think they were fighting about the Sistine Chapel or something. She rubbed her eyes. She had it in mind to postpone the Fourth of July entirely this year (and perhaps forever), although not on account of the squabbling faggots in Carmel but rather because there was something distasteful in the idea of celebrating anything in Las Cosimas these days. She wandered around her office, paused by Cindi's vacant desk, studied the necklace of paper clips that lay beside the IBM typewriter.

Isadora Sharp.

And now this, Emma Hamlett.

She paused by the window and looked out at Hermosillo Square. It was early evening, the day softening to twilight. There was a certain hazy quality in the air, perhaps a faint mist blowing in from the ocean. But two murders hadn't stopped the Saturday shoppers in the square, even if she did seem to detect a certain quick, furtive manner in how they darted from store to store, as if leisurely browsing might be construed as an invitation to the killer in their midst.

She saw Paul Manning shuffle along the sidewalk. Although he was a tall kid, he tended to stoop somewhat, almost as if he were afraid of facing the world ahead of him. She wondered why a slight flush of pity went through her all at once. Turning from the window, she moved back toward Cindi's desk. Paul Manning, Christ, had she really half-accepted a date with him? Maybe she could make up an excuse of some kind when he called.

Which would be a rotten thing to do.

She picked up the telephone and dialed Daniel Romero's room at the country club but it didn't answer. She looked at her watch: it was six-thirty. Maybe Paul Manning was just walking around killing time until seven. Getting his nerve up all over again.

She placed the palms of her hands against her face and she thought about Emma Hamlett. A decent kind of woman, a little different from the average wives of Las Cosimas. Caroline remembered that she wrote poems she published in obscure magazines and at one time she'd been a writer with Hallmark Cards. It was funny how one suddenly remembered things like that. She's always liked Emma, although they hadn't met quite as often as Caroline would have liked. But that was because Emma didn't get around much on account of her heart condition. In fact, the last time they'd spoken together was maybe three, four months ago when they'd met at the country club and the talk had turned to health and the subject of Emma's physician, Andrew Conturas.

At that time, Caroline had been concerned with the birth-control device she'd been using—an IUD she thought interfered with her menstrual cycle—and Emma had recommended a visit to Conturas. And so Caroline had made an appointment with the doctor, who admitted, in an offhandedly candid way, that he disliked what he called "female plumbing complaints" and had he known in advance the nature of her problem he'd never have made the appointment. End of discussion. Interview over. Caroline had thought: Misogynist sonofabitch. And all the charm of a goddamn embalmer. Now she wondered what it was that poor Emma had seen in the man in the first place. Maybe he was good with heart problems—at least that was what people said about him. But female plumbing—forget it, brother.

Her telephone rang. She hesitated a moment before picking it up because right then she was in no mood to hear the Breather tell her how sick she was, how incurably sick.

"I couldn't wait until seven," Paul Manning said.

Ah, the impatience of youth. The eagerness in his voice was something she couldn't bring herself to puncture.

"You old enough to drink?" she asked.

"I'll bring my birth certificate."

She was silent a moment. Then: "Where do you want to meet?"

"It's your town. You suggest a place."

"You know Oaxaca on Juárez Street?"

"I'll find it," Paul said.

"There's a nice bar. Give me an hour, okay?"

"An hour," the kid said.

Caroline hung up. What the hell was she doing? She massaged her eyes, sighed, and remembered that at least Oaxaca had a well-lit parking lot and Juárez Street wasn't exactly a shady lane either. Given the awful conditions of the time, she had a real longing for bright electricity and an absence of shadows.

She left her office and went upstairs to her apartment. As she stepped into the shower stall she wondered if she'd remembered to lock her door.

This was no time for Janet Leigh flashbacks.

This was no time to let all her fears crystallize and congeal in her brain.

"Fucking fingerprints," Charlie Nicholson was saying. "I got more prints than there are people in the whole of goddamn Las Cosimas. It must have been one hell of a party out there."

Tobias drew water from the cooler and drank thirstily. "A hell of a party that ended badly," he said. Dipping his fingers into the waxen cup, he splashed a few drops of water across his face.

"Come to Las Cosimas," Charlie said. "See people drop like flies."

Tobias crunched the cup in his hand and looked around the sterile office. Karl Rezabek had gone home. Exhausted, he had looked like a man in search of a few hours' sleep, which Tobias seriously doubted he'd get. For one thing, old J M Dunbar was sure to be on the telephone to Karl as soon as this new item of information reached him.

Charlie Nicholson wandered over to the computer, his hand dangling lightly on the printer. This computer, which had been donated to the department by Schwartz Electronics, was linked to other computers all across the republic. In the flash of an eye, you could find out almost anything about anybody, especially if the subject of your inquiry had broken the law at one time. Charlie felt uncertain around these gadgets, as he did in the vicinity of most machines. He had a tendency to press wrong buttons and cause malfunctions—cars, stereos, it didn't matter what. He was, in a word, ham-fisted. Now he backed away from the device and looked at Tobias.

"We ought to be getting something on the old snoopbox any moment now," Charlie said.

Tobias sat up on the edge of Karl's desk. He gazed at the blank console a moment and waited for the information he had requested some minutes before. He imagined complex grids of wires humming all the way across the country, machines talking to other machines, data being sucked out of banks. The Microchip Connection. Computers knew it all, didn't they? Stored deep in their mazes of silicon, they had their electronic fingers on every pulse going. Soon as you were born, they fed you into a computer, like some kind of sacrifice of infants. The computer had created whole new sets of rituals.

The console flashed a message.

INFORMATION BEING PROCESSED
YOUR DATA INQUIRY 2 JULY 1933 HRS
CODE 8Z5PPR

"It's all bullshit," Charlie said as he stared at the numbers. "What the hell does it all mean?" And he stepped back, a little afraid that his presence would stall the whole thing.

Tobias stared at the screen.

CONTURAS, ANDREW JOHN
DOB 8/8/35
POB CHICKASHA, OKLA

"Chickasha," Charlie Nicholson said. "The guy's a goddamn Okie."

The screen was blank a moment.

Then more words appeared

GRADUATED MD UNIVERSITY OF BOSTON
1960.

Now there was a series of computerized squiggles, signifying nothing.

*And the screen blanked out again.*
*Then back to life.*

CRIMINAL RECORD

Pause.

"Criminal record," Charlie said.

"I hear skeletons rattling in a closet, Charlie," and Tobias leaned closer to the screen, the palms of his hands damp.

CRIMINAL RECORD

"It's taking its own sweet time," Charlie said.

Impatiently Tobias rolled himself a cigarette rather badly, and tobacco stuck to his lips.

ARRESTED BOSTON, MASS 7/5/64

Arrested for what? Tobias wondered.

Then the console began to spew forth, in its stilted fashion, a tale that might have been taken by a cheap novelist and turned into something lurid for the checkout stands in supermarkets.

ARREST SHEET # 78/B/7334
ANDREW CONTURAS.
ARRESTING OFFICERS CASHMAN, MACDONALD
ON OR ABOUT 26TH MAY 1964. THE SUBJECT, CONTURAS,
PERFORMED AN ILLEGAL ABORTION ON MARYANNE
DEVINE. SUBSEQUENT INTERNAL COMPLICATIONS
RESULTED IN DEVINE'S DEATH.
MURDER CHARGE WAS BROUGHT BY STATE
ATTORNEY'S OFFICE ON THE BASIS OF EVIDENCE
PROVIDED BY DECEASED'S MOTHER, ESTHER DEVINE.

Another computer pause.

DEATH BY MISADVENTURE WAS RECORDED, ANDREW CONTURAS ACQUITTED, LATER STRUCK OFF MEDICAL REGISTER, REINSTATED DECEMBER 1970.

The screen went blank and stayed that way.

"That's all she wrote, I guess," Charlie said.

Tobias pressed two buttons on the keyboard and the printer began to bang out the information that had come over the console.

"Well, well," he said. The trouble with computer information was the way it was condensed: it told you nothing about nuances, about the shadings of circumstances, all the stuff that might be hidden beneath electronic surfaces.

Charlie Nicholson sat down. "What do you make of it, Tobe? You think maybe the guy was unhinged? Bad publicity. Disgraced. Suddenly decided he'd take out his revenge on women, something along those lines."

Tobias said nothing a moment. "Yeah, except it isn't anything sudden, is it? We're looking back twenty years here. You think Conturas has been sitting planning these deaths for twenty goddamn years, Charlie? I doubt it."

Charlie Nicholson looked thoughtful, running a hand across his red face. "Okay. Try this one. Conturas hides out in Las Cosimas. The mother of this dead girl, this Devine woman, hunts for him. Revenge motive, right? It takes her a while to locate the killer of her daughter, but let's say she's got a devilish turn of mind, and instead of offing the doc, she does away with his patients—"

Too complicated, Tobias thought.

Too untidy.

"Makes Conturas look bad," Nicholson added. "Pretty damn cunning, you ask me."

Tobias shook his head. Theories—you could play with the goddamn things until the cows came home, but meantime there was some lunatic in Las Cosimas with a sharp blade. He drank more water. He looked at Charlie, whom he liked, but Charlie wasn't on the ball the way Art Frye had always been. He remembered hours when they'd toss theories and ideas back and forth like a couple of demented philosophers.

"Blackmail," Nicholson said. "Maybe these two victims were blackmailing Conturas about his squalid past and so he had no alternative except to put them permanently to sleep." Charlie wiped his brow with a handkerchief the size of the U.S. flag. "No? You don't think so?"

"I don't think so, Charlie. Not really."

He leaned back against the wall, folding his arms. The rattle of old bones. Old skeletons.

It was an encouraging sound even though he wasn't sure what the noises meant or where, if anywhere, they might lead him.

But locked closets were always interesting to open.

And old dust deserved to be stirred.

In the bar of the Oaxaca restaurant, which had been built from expensive materials to resemble a cheap Mexican cantina, Paul ordered two margaritas and watched as Caroline Cassidy licked salt from the rim of her glass. It wasn't quite that she did this lasciviously, but he had the feeling that many of her gestures were sexual because she wasn't altogether conscious of them. Rather, they came to her naturally. She was wearing a gray shirt and tan slacks and a simple pendant hung from her neck. He was aware that he was staring at her and so he turned his face to the side and looked across the half-crowded bar.

"Nice place," he said.

Caroline nodded. The kid was not at ease, she thought.

What could she do to help him relax? Offer to screw him? "I don't come here often . . ." Swinging chitchat, zipping right along. She glanced at the TV over the bar and saw a baseball game.

Paul watched her light a cigarette and realized, too late, that he should have struck the match for her. She blew a stream of smoke upward.

"Why are you in pre-med?" she asked.

He shrugged lightly. "I don't know. It just seemed the right choice. A few years back, I was going to go in for sociology, then all of a sudden that seemed just academic bullshit. And a couple of things happened that made me change my mind. . . ."

A couple of deaths, Caroline thought. She smiled at the kid and, reaching forward, slipped off his glasses. A vague defensive expression flitted over his face, then he appeared to relax.

"I can't see a damn thing without them," he said.

She stuck them on her own face and said, "Jesus Christ, they make me dizzy," and she handed them back. She crushed her cigarette and watched the young man a moment. Inexperienced, awkward, uneasy in a social situation—and yet he was not without a vague charm.

"You got a girl in L.A.?" she asked.

He shook his head. "I don't have the time."

Caroline leaned back against the booth. "What does a young man like you do with all your healthy appetites then?" Paul said nothing. He stared at the tabletop, sipped his drink, then casually rubbed the corner of one eye. The world he saw without his glasses was a blurry place, a universe without hard edges. Healthy appetites, he thought. And there was Streicher's voice whispering in his ear: You need to get out more, Paul. You need to meet more people. Become involved. Involved in what, doc? Suppose you tell me what exactly. A relationship that would be doomed anyhow—whether by its own erosions, its inherent flaws, or finally by death itself?

He stroked his jaw, conscious of his leg touching Caroline's, aware of a warmth that was spreading through him. A nerve began to work in the pit of his stomach and he experienced a vague nausea—and then he was thinking of the girl who called herself Brandy and how he'd picked her up three successive Wednesday afternoons on Hollywood Boulevard, the tiny box of a motel room and her underwear stark and white against the chocolate color of her thighs and her large breasts pressed against his face, he was thinking of the way she'd touched him and how, with his eyes wide open, he'd been conscious of three ten-dollar bills lying on the chipped bedside table—and the girl had told him, Honey, hey, you gotta relax, you gotta let yourself go just a little, you're an ulcer case, kiddo, if I ever saw one. And he hadn't been able to tell her that something was making him afraid, something that stalked him always like a spectral avenger, something whose name was Death.

He glanced now at Caroline and for a moment he was struck by the extraordinary transience of her beauty and what he perceived was her face as it would become eventually, networks of wrinkles, bloodless, the veins empty and stilled and the pulses dead as old radio signals. He shook his head and he thought: No. He wanted to reach out and touch her hand and be reassured that she was young and real and lovely. Then he was imagining that it was Caroline and not the pseudonymous Brandy who accompanied him to the Bolero Motel on Wednesday afternoons.

Caroline turned her face away from the kid's expression. What did she see there? Sorrow of an intense variety? Whatever, it made her uncomfortable.

"You okay?" she asked.

He smiled and said, "Sure. Oh, sure."

"You don't mind me saying it, but you don't exactly look like you're having a terrific time, Paul."

"I wouldn't want you to get that impression, Caroline."

Pardon me, she thought. You just happened to look like a guy who came straight from a funeral. She picked up her drink. And a curious sensation went through her, one she tried to turn aside: it was the feeling she had suddenly of wanting to mother this kid, to hold his face against her breasts and rock his body gently back and forth—Oh, for Christ's sake, she thought. You're not the type, Caroline. You are definitely not the type for these bizarre maternal instincts. Nevertheless, she did put her hand on his fingers and left it there. He needs something, she knew that. He needs human contact. Affection. Call it what you like. And she wasn't bothered by the pressure of his leg against her own. This kid carried too many old pains, old sores.

She stroked the back of his hand. Abruptly, he did something that surprised her: he pulled his hand away, as if her touch had been that of a hot coal.

"What's wrong?" she asked, and in her question was the tone of a woman vaguely offended. After all, she didn't have to be here. She needn't have accepted this ridiculous date. And she didn't have any obligation to be kind.

Paul looked at his own hand in the manner of someone watching for signs of blisters. Why? he asked himself. Why the hell did I do that? Fear rose inside him, indefinable, all the more awful in that it lacked definition. "I'm sorry," he said weakly. "I don't know why I . . ." His voice faded away. He cupped his hands around his drink and he said, "I saw you at my mother's funeral. I remember that. You were very kind that day. You've probably forgotten it now."

Caroline smiled. "I remember that day well," she said. "You looked genuinely sad. That's what I remember. Sincere."

Paul opened a book of matches and lit one, then applied the flame to the remainder and set the sudden bonfire down in the ashtray, where it sizzled and died. Fire, Caroline thought. The crematorium. Was that what the kid was thinking now? Morbid embroideries in the brain. She closed her eyes, sighing inwardly, entertaining a strange picture of herself and Paul Manning tangled together in her bed, and the image was less sexual than it was comforting, almost as if she might provide a certain therapy for the young man, a release from all his obvious tensions. Jesus, what exactly was she doing with her mind? She couldn't possibly go to bed with Paul. How could she? There would be inevitable complications—he'd probably turn out to be the kind of guy who sent roses and wrote poems and stared up at her window from the street like some lost romantic soul. I won't be a sexual Florence Nightingale for him, no way.

Paul rose and she watched him go in the direction of the men's room. There was a quality in his movement, maybe in the way he seemed to drag his feet as he slouched, that depressed her slightly.

"Cradle-snatching, are we?"

It was Maude Logan who stood over the table, smiling. She was dressed in a flimsy black cocktail thing through which you could see her black underwear. And she looked utterly radiant.

"An old friend, dear," Caroline said.

"Old? He looks twelve if he's a day."

"He's at least half your age, Maude. Say, twenty-one?"

Maude Logan smiled stiffly. "Does he have a name?"

"Paul," Caroline said.

"Paul," Maude echoed, as if she were searching the letters of the name for something obscene. Failing to find anything, she changed the subject. Emma Hamlett. She'd heard it on KOCO news and wasn't it dreadful?

Caroline agreed.

"I hope our police are doing something to catch this lunatic," Maude said, angling for some inside information, a line on the latest gossip.

"I'm sure they are," Caroline said, and watched as Maude, with a grin and a flighty little wave of the hand, skipped away.

Inside the white-tiled men's room Paul locked himself in a cubicle and stood with his back against the wall, his hands clenched in front of him. Unaware of the men who came and went outside the locked door, who flushed the urinals and dried their hands beneath blasts of hot air, he raised his face up to the yellow ceiling and tried to forget where he was and why he'd come here, but he kept seeing pictures as if through veils of swirling mist, and the picture he mainly saw was that of Caroline Cassidy on the day of his mother's funeral, the way she'd carried herself with a grace that seemed to defeat death, to transcend the inevitability of endings—grace and loveliness at the heart of darkness. He took his glasses off and pressed his fingertips to his eyelids. Caroline, Caroline. Why had he even asked her to meet him for a drink anyhow? She only reminded him of that terrible day when he'd last looked on his mother's face and seen it devoid of life, absent of meaning, in the casket, when he'd leaned over and pressed his lips against the cold forehead and felt, as surely as if a finger had touched him, the black stretches of death that lay beyond the sunlight of the day, beyond the grass and the trees and the colored flowers, black fissures waiting to open up, to swallow, as if death were a hungry mouth—

Caroline Cassidy and death. He had to separate these two entities, but he couldn't. His eyes were moist and his throat dry all at once. He said to himself: Go back out there. Go back out among the living. Where people smile and pretend there's no pain. Go, go. And the voice inside his own head was that of Streicher, almost as if the man had come to possess him. He slid the bolt on the door and made his way back into the bar, crossing the crowded room and feeling light-headed, as if he were floating an inch or so above the thick rug.

"You want another drink, Caroline?"

Caroline shook her head. "I don't think so." She looked at her watch. She didn't want to sit here any longer. Feeling she'd fulfilled some imaginary obligation, she wanted to leave. "In fact, I guess I should be on my way."

"So soon?"

Caroline smiled, a little expression of disappointment. "I'm sorry."

"I'll walk out with you," Paul said.

Caroline slid down from her stool and Paul followed her to the door. Outside, the night was balmy, the air tranquil in such a way that suggested nothing dark, nothing terrible, had ever happened in Las Cosimas. Caroline rattled her car keys in the palm of her hand. And the feeling swept across her again that maybe she could invite this young man back to her apartment, maybe she could alleviate the sadness that so obviously inhabited him—she pushed the thought, fragile as it was in any case, aside. She raised her face and, as if she were doing him a kindness, kissed him quickly on the lips. It was a cold kiss and its spontaneity seemed to startle him. He stepped back a foot or so.

"When are you leaving Las Cosimas?" she asked.

"In a day or so. I'm not sure," and he shrugged.

"Call me before you go," she said and she moved toward her Datsun, still rattling the keys in her hand.

As she drove away, she saw the thin young man in her rearview mirror, watching motionlessly.

* * *

When she stepped inside her apartment, Caroline entered the bedroom and took off her shirt and slacks. Not nine o'clock yet on a Saturday night and she could think of nothing better to do than go to bed. Alone, too. She sat on the edge of the bed and wondered what had come over her back there with Paul Manning, because she'd never found the qualities of sadness and sorrow, with their concomitant little-boy-lost expression, intriguing in any sexual way. But something else, something she couldn't quite define, disturbed her about the kid. What was it?

More than the mourning look in his eyes, more than the downward turn of his mouth when he wasn't smiling, more than the nervousness he displayed when she'd been faintly affectionate.

It was—if she were to put a phrase to it—a sense of smoldering beneath surfaces, of inchoate emotional reactions, as if, were you to pick him up and shake him, you would hear what you heard when you rattled a kaleidoscope.

She got up from the bed.

She checked her answering machine.

No messages.

Nothing from the Caller.

She went inside the bathroom, considered the prospect of getting dressed again and hitting the country club for a few drinks—but the notion depressed her. All the conversation out there would be about Emma Hamlett and she didn't need that right now. Instead, she picked up the telephone and dialed Daniel Romero's room number, but there was still no answer. Maybe he'd checked out. Gone his own merry way.

She took off her bra and panties and stared at her reflection in the mirror. A sensation of vulnerability went through her, as if her nakedness were a target focused through the sights of some sniper's rifle—

Which was when she realized that she wasn't alone in the apartment—

Cold terror. A chilly instinct—

Somebody was here—

She listened, holding her breath, then moved toward the bathroom door, thinking that if she locked it she'd be safe.

As she reached for the handle, the plastic shower-curtain shivered and crackled and the small curtain hooks rattled together and a shadow moved at her side and a strong hand was clamped over her mouth.

Then laughter, unexpected laughter.

The hand fell away, releasing her.

"You bastard," she said. "You scared the shit out of me!"

And then Daniel Romero was drawing her down to the tiled floor, his hands exploring her body with a hard urgency.

An outrage of fear that almost made her heart explode.

It didn't last long.

She closed her eyes and spread her legs for him and she moaned as he entered her, and her fear turned to the kind of pleasure at whose heart there is the shadow of a nameless danger.

# 12

Andrew Conturas stared into the big tank, tapping his fingers against the glass. The anglerfish—the smaller male attached to the female—paid him no attention. A curious species, this fish. The male spent his life with no independent existence from the female; instead, he attached himself to the female's body, taking his nourishment from her. Astonishing dimorphism. In return for sustenance, the male provided sperm. Conturas was in the middle of writing an academic paper on the behavior of anglerfish, and the desk in the big room was strewn with notes and folders and photographs he'd taken himself.

He moved toward the desk, turned on the lamp, examined some papers. When he sat down, studying the photographs, he picked up a pencil and began to write captions on the backs of the pictures. He had always been a systematic person, methodical in his working habits. He paused, laid the pencil down, rubbed his eyes in a tired fashion. There was a small card-index box at the back of his desk. This contained notes on his human patients, details he'd written in his crabbed handwriting. Absently he reached toward the box and moved it slightly, so that it lay flush with the back of the desk. Since he hardly ever used this card-index system, he had no idea why it might have been moved, even so slightly.

When he'd written up the Hamlett woman's death, perhaps then he hadn't put the box back in its exact position. On the other hand, it crossed his mind that there might be something more sinister involved here: had someone been in this room in his absence? Was such a thing possible? Had someone come here—possibly that inquisitive policeman—and gone through his card-index system?

A policeman, he thought, hating the notion of somebody trespassing in his private dominion. Policemen were inclined to be like dogs attached to old bones, forever gnawing on them even when there was no meat left. He gazed at the little box for a time and dismissed the idea of an interloper, even though a shadow lingered at the edge of his mind.

There had been other policemen in his life once, and when that recollection drifted up through the silt of his unconsciousness he became nervous.

He rose and paced up and down his room, rubbing his hands together. Isadora Sharp. Emma Hamlett. The names of the two dead women echoed inside his head as if they were distant bells, wind chimes heard from a long way off. At the small window he paused. Two dead women, he thought. Both cut through the heart.

Clean cuts, administered with economy and precision.

He stared out of the window across the canyons of Las Cosimas. He thought of the whole spread-out community not as a collection of families living beneath rooftops but as beating hearts, as disembodied organs pulsing in rooms, and the sound made by blood being pumped through veins filled his mind for a time. He turned away from the window.

He scrubbed his hands at the sink, in the fashion of a surgeon, and then he opened a small refrigerator in the corner of the room. Carefully he took out the corpse of a female anglerfish and, with a sharp knife, dissected the creature accurately. He studied the ventral aorta and the branchial arteries, marveling as he always did at the fact the fish had evolved with such complex economy, a creature perfectly adapted to its invironment. Which was something he could not claim for mankind.

Cheerfully he severed the head from the female and held it in the palms of his hands as if it were a cherished object, a keepsake of some kind, and the cold dead eyes stared up at him as though, even in a state of death, the fish had conscious perceptions.

Sammy Suarez said, "It's pure gold, Enrico. You think how nice that's gonna look on your wife's neck, eh?" And he watched Enrico's wizened fingers touch the chain. Enrico, although he considered the chain pretty, and probably a bargain at one and a half, knew that if Sammy Suarez was selling it, then the item was as hot as a jalapeño. Besides, he'd seen Sammy and Carlos go back into the john some time ago and he suspected that the necklace came from the kid in the first place. The cocksman's rewards, Enrico thought.

"I can't afford it, Sammy—"

"Hey, I'll take payments. An arrangement of some kind," Sammy said.

Enrico shrugged. "I'll pass, man."

"Okay okay," and Samuel Suarez stuffed the chain back in his pocket. "You just missed the bargain of the month." He turned and studied the pool players, listening to the click of balls on the green baize. He turned back to Enrico.

"Listen, I'll make you a deal. One-twenty-five, huh?"

"If you offered me the chain for fifty, I still couldn't do it." Enrico served a drunken customer and thought that maybe it was really a bargain and how pleased Carmelita would be with the thing, but he didn't need to get involved in anything to do with Sammy Suarez. A man could buy a bunch of trouble that way. He looked across the bar at Carlos now, picking his teeth and looking like a cheap gangster in his tight white pants and matching jacket.

Enrico felt suddenly old. He wiped the countertop and then he thought of Carmelita, to whom he'd been married for years, and whom he loved deeply. He'd never given her much. She'd never really asked for material things anyhow over the years—so maybe, what the hell, this chain would be a way of showing his gratitude for love.

He called to little Sammy. "That chain, how do I know it ain't hot?"

"Hey, Enrico, I got it on good authority."

"And how do I know it's genuine gold?"

"Because I say it is. What I don't know about precious metals, compadre, isn't worth knowing." Sammy could sense the fish rising to the golden bait. He flashed the chain again.

Enrico shrugged. "You'll take fifty down. Fifty next week. Then twenty-five at the end of the month?"

Samuel Suarez rubbed his jaw, shuffled around. "Wait. We got ourselves a different proposition now. Fifty at the end of the month. I'm carrying your note, Enrico. That means a little interest, no?"

Enrico sighed, imagining the chain shining on his wife's neck.

He took fifty from the cash register and, with great reluctance, handed it to Sammy Suarez.

"You will not regret this," Suarez said, with a flashing smile.

The quality of the smile did not illuminate Enrico's soul—rather, he felt a strange heaviness in his heart, as if he'd done something very wrong. Even the image of Carmelita's smile did nothing to dispel the sudden gloom.

When Tobias stepped into the apartment, the place was in darkness. He turned on the living-room light, blinked against the sudden burst of white electricity, then popped a can of beer inside the kitchen. No Paul, he thought. Maybe the kid was getting lucky with his date. Tobias kicked off his shoes and lay down on the sofa, turning things around in his mind—running the mice of his thoughts and speculations through mazes, but they kept coming back to Andrew Conturas, they kept leading him in that same old direction.

Could the good doctor be killing off his patients?

Naw. This didn't sit well at all with Tobias. But there was the troublesome matter of the abortion the computer had spewed out and he felt he wanted to know a little more about that. The Boston cops involved in that business had been called Cashman and MacDonald—maybe they'd remember something, something that hadn't been fed into the electronic data banks, the kinds of details only cops would know.

He rubbed his weary feet, massaging the toes.

If Conturas wasn't doing away with his patients, then who was?

The sound of the telephone startled him.

"Tobias Manning," he said.

And for a moment dread filled him. Was there another out there now? A fresh corpse?

The man's voice said, "I'm trying to contact Paul Manning."

"He isn't here right now."

A silence.

"Do you expect him soon?"

"Hard to say," Tobias answered. "I'll take a message for him."

Another silence, then the soft voice said, "Tell him to call me. Streicher. Dr. Streicher. He knows the number."

"I'll pass it along." Tobias put the receiver down. Dr. Streicher. Presumably one of Paul's professors, somebody he worked with at UCLA. Tobias crumpled his beer can, tossing it toward the wastebasket and missing.

Then he rose and wandered the room restlessly.

He stopped at the window, looking down into the street. Darkness, pale nimbi created by streetlamps. Above, the night was starry and the moon looked inscrutable in its fullness. A perfect sky, vast and mysterious.

A lovers' moon, he thought.

And his mind turned to the idea of Paul and Caroline, a conjunction he couldn't quite see.

Why did nights such as these make you so damned restless?

No, the nights themselves didn't do it, it was just the way the great dust of the stars underscored your own sense of loneliness. The way they reminded you of the things that had been once.

He put on his shoes and left the apartment, thinking he'd perhaps take his old Chevy and drive through the canyons and maybe, just maybe, stop out and see Conturas and discuss the little matter of the criminal charge that lay concealed in the man's history. In the street, he changed his mind and began to walk, reaching Hermosillo Square, where he saw Caroline's Datsun but no sign of Paul's little Beetle.

Maybe they'd gone for a drive together. The canyons in moonlight. The great dense shadows and the breeze stirring the trees. Or the beach, perhaps. A walk across the sands. Getting acquainted. Moonlight on calm water—was there a better aphrodisiac? He and Edie, in the early days of their marriage, back before the kids were born, used to drive the old Studebaker up to Lake Pleasant and sit there holding hands, enjoying the kind of exquisite silence that only lovers really knew how to share. Not that washed-out quietness that afflicted most marriages, not the awkward absences of speech across restaurant tables, but a true stillness, a welding together of selves in a place beyond the reaches of language.

He passed beneath the pomegranate trees and then he stopped quite suddenly.

The black Lincoln was parked in a side street.

Tobias touched its gleaming surface.

Something wasn't adding up here.

If Caroline had gone out with Paul, what was this big black car doing parked so close to her apartment?

Mysterious night, mysterious moon.

He hardly heard the approach of the man until the guy was practically alongside him.

"You want to buy it?" the man asked.

"Beyond my means, I guess," Tobias said. He looked at the other guy, the steely hair, the grayness of the eyes. He guessed he was maybe in his middle forties but clearly he kept himself in shape. The body beneath the dark suit was hard, well-muscled. Caroline's lover, he thought. Daniel Romero.

And there was that goddamn tinny little bell going off in his head again. Romero, Romero, Romero—what was so familiar about the man?

"The upkeep runs high," Romero said.

"I guess it would," Tobias answered, looking back at the slick lines of the car. "I always liked big babies like this," he went on. Maybe if he kept the guy talking it would come back to him. Where? When? "You from Wisconsin?"

Romero nodded.

"Passing through? Staying?"

"I was looking at houses."

"Find anything?"

Romero shook his head. "I've seen a few," and shrugged.

Tobias wondered how long he could keep the questions rolling. "You in the industry?"

"Industry?"

"Everybody in Las Cosimas is in computers."

"I wouldn't know a computer from an abacus," the guy remarked. "I'm retired."

"Lucky man," Tobias said. It isn't coming back, he thought. It's not taking shape in the old memory banks, is it? Unreal, the number of cells that popped forever inside your head when you were relying on them for information. Tiny little explosions of gray matter.

"You in computers?" the guy asked.

Momentarily Tobias looked across the square at the windows of Caroline's apartment. They were in darkness. "I'm a cop," he said.

"You must be a busy guy these days," Romero said.

Tobias nodded. "Yeah, yeah. We got some problems, all right."

Romero unlocked the door of his car and smiled, showing bright teeth. "Good luck," he said and, slamming the door, he started the motor and the car slid inaudibly down the street.

Tobias watched the red taillights disappear and then turned once more to stare at Caroline's windows. He walked to a phone booth and, without entirely understanding the vague sense of alarm he suddenly felt, he stuck a quarter in the slot and dialed the girl's number. With each ring he could feel a tense nerve work in his brain.

Answer.

Pick up the goddamn phone, Caroline.

He heard a click and the the sound of her voice, at which point Tobias hung up. He strolled across the square.

Something got to you just then.

Something touched you inside.

The idea that something had happened to Caroline Cassidy—

That Romero had—

Had what?

Killed her?

He smiled at himself.

Jumpy tonight, Tobe.

Very jumpy.

And as he continued across Hermosillo Square he kept asking himself where he'd seen Daniel Romero before, but there were still no answers.

When he started to drink, Abe Logan went through various stages of aberrant behavior, beginning with a tendency to sing "When Irish Eyes Are Smiling" and working, downhill quickly, toward garbled recitations of Robert Burns. The last stage of all, which Maude relished, was when he started to dig through his collection of country-western records and constantly play and replay Charlie and Ira Louvin singing "Don't Let Your Sweet Love Die," but usually when he'd stumbled to the stereo a few times his eyes began to turn glassy and his movements became ever more precarious. Finally, when he'd listened to the Louvin brothers for the fifth time, he slipped between the sofa and the footstool and lay there in the awkward, openmouthed pose of the sleeping drunk.

She took the album from the stereo, deliberately scratching the goddamn thing, and stood over the fallen body of her husband, looking down at him as if he were a large sluggish insect she would enjoy squashing underfoot. He turned once, raised his head, said, "Silicon Valley" aloud and then went back to sleep.

Maude went inside the bathroom and let her hair down over her shoulders. Dabbing a little eye shadow on her lids, she admired her own reflection for a while, and then she checked on Abe again. After, she slipped open the glass doors to the back garden and looked out toward the gazebo.

Nothing stirred out there, save the breeze that worked secretively through the shrubbery. Perhaps he wasn't going to come tonight. Perhaps he'd found something else to do.

More like SomeBody else, she thought.

She peered through the night just as the moon passed under a luminescent cloud and the sky, as if crayoned by a kid angry with a coloring book, went quite black.

Maude shivered. She was filled with a great desire tonight. She needed her young lover. She wanted to step inside the gazebo and let him come up behind her . . . she wanted to be taken from behind.

She wanted his brute force.

She moved barefoot across the grass and entered the gazebo and she whispered the young man's name, but there was only silence all around her and somehow this very quietness quickened the flow of her blood as if the night were a fragile thing made to be broken by the sheer animal brutality of being fucked by him. And fucked hard and swift, feeling him swell inside her.

Her heartbeat fluttered.

For a second, a sensation of panic went through her and she wondered if she'd need to go back indoors for her medication, but then the sense of having a bird beat inside her chest passed away and she stood very still in the gazebo.

As the moon reappeared.

As it touched shrubbery, lit trees, shone against the flimsy blackness of her dress.

As it fell through the slats of the gazebo and sparkled in her eyes.

Yes, she thought.

The sound of a footstep now.

He's coming.

Yes, indeed, he's coming.

She stood very still as she heard him come up behind, felt him press his body against hers, and she shut her eyes, sighing—even as she realized there was something wrong—

Something different tonight—

He didn't feel the same—

Didn't smell the same—

Was different in some way—

She turned to face him as the moon was sucked behind cloud again and the sound of a solitary woodpecker began to rap rap rap on a nearby tree.

Rap.

Rap.

Then, in a furious brushing of wings, there was silence.

# 13

It was 0547 when Karl Rezabek reached his office and found Tobias leaning against the desk, smoking one of his foul-smelling hand-rolled cancer sticks.

"Logan," was all Tobias said. "Maude Logan. You know her?"

Rezabek shook his head.

"According to the husband, she was struck in the chest."

Rezabek drew a hand across his face. He lacked the constitution for murder.

"When?" he asked.

"A very hysterical, extremely drunken husband called about thirty minutes ago. Found his wife in the gazebo. You want to run over there with me, Sheriff?"

Rezabek nodded. "Yeah, yeah," although his voice was without enthusiasm, without life. As they left the office and walked toward the Honda, Rezabek sighed and looked at Tobias. "Back in New York, you must have seen hundreds of murders."

"I saw plenty, sure," Tobias answered.

"You ever get used to them?"

Tobias looked curiously at the sheriff. "You don't get used to them. You develop a kind of shellac around you. That make sense to you?"

"I'm not sure," Rezabek said.

Rezabek took the wheel and then they were driving though the canyons of Las Cosimas as dawn filled up all the hollows with pools of beautiful light. Neither man spoke for a long time. Tobias looked at the road twisting ahead; Rezabek held the wheel as if, were he to let go, he would plunge into an abyss.

"We need 1300 Sierra Madre Boulevard," Tobias said,

"Thirteen hundred," Rezabek repeated in an empty way. Then, out of nowhere, he suddenly said, "I used to be a damn good soldier, Tobias. Damn effective. I always had the respect of my men." A pause. "I don't have yours, do I?"

"I'm just an old street cop," Tobias said, embarrassed.

"Doesn't answer my question," Rezabek said.

Tobias yawned, one hand to his mouth. "Some men are suited to some jobs. Others aren't."

"Meaning?"

"Meaning I'm too tired to know what I mean, Sheriff."

"Karl. You can call me Karl."

Tobias looked out of the window as the Honda hit Sierra Madre, where the road rose up into thickets of trees and houses you could barely see from the pavement. All this lovely privacy plundered by murder. All this rich peacefulness soiled by a madman with a knife. What was the point of all this wealth if it couldn't protect people from dying by violent means? He put on his shades and stared at the rising sun. Shades, he thought, a real California hardass cop.

1300 was a large redwood affair with the statutory levels of sundecks and a pool in the shape of a geranium leaf. A man, presumably Abe Logan, was standing in the manicured grass alongside the gazebo. He was smoking a cigarette fitfully. When Tobias and Rezabek approached him he stubbed the cigarette underfoot and gestured toward the gazebo, as if he didn't want to acknowledge its existence. Tobias wanted to say, I know, I know, you think this is a dream, something you'll wake from, I understand the feeling. . . .

He stepped inside the gazebo.

The woman, her black dress up around her stomach, her arms thrown to her sides, her hair spread as if the appearance of death were akin to the look of sex, lay in the center of the small room. Tobias stepped over her, seeing his shadow fall on the body. She comes out here in the dead of night, presumably, maybe to meet a lover, maybe for some clandestine tryst (otherwise why the flimsy dress and the sexy underwear), only she meets the madman with the knife. Like Isadora Sharp. Like Emma Hamlett. The same spreading gash in the center of the chest.

Tobias moved back into the sunshine. Abe Logan, red-eyed, turned his face away.

Rezabek looked at Tobias. He could read it in Manning's eyes. The same method as the other two. The same means of death. He could hear, like trees falling in a forest, the sounds of his world come crashing down around him.

"You hear anything, Mr. Logan?" Tobias asked.

"I'd been drinking. I fell asleep. I woke up and I looked for her and . . ." Logan shut his eyes very tightly.

"You any idea what she was doing out here?"

"None," Logan said.

Tobias leaned against the gazebo wall. Fond of midnight strolls, maybe? A lover of the dark places? Or a lover *in* the dark places?

"Did she wander around at night? Some kind of habit? Insomnia maybe?"

"Usually she took sleeping pills," Logan said. He was a short man with a head a trifle too large for his body, and his eyes, especially red as they now were, seemed like stalks attached to his skull.

"Sleeping pills," Tobias said. Scripts, prescriptions. This

is too close to the impossible edge of unlikely coincidence. Scripts. Physicians. He could feel the question form in his mind even before he asked it. And even then he didn't want to ask it anyhow. "Who wrote her scripts?"

"Conturas," Logan said.

Karl Rezabek made a low, moaning sound and Tobias squinted at him through the dark safety of his sunshades.

And Maude makes three.

Tobias looked past Abe Logan toward the house, which had that scrubbed California look of untainted wood—all natural and yet, in this dawn sunlight, synthetic somehow, as if it were built from laminated plastics. A bird was singing nearby. A thrush, Tobias thought. A birdsong of death.

It sprang upward, a branch bouncing, a motion of feathers.

"Why was she seeing Conturas? Was it just insomnia?"

Logan blew his nose into a blue silk handkerchief. Jesus, he looked rough, as if he'd lain all night long in a trough of Jack Daniel's. "No," he answered. "Her heart."

I could have laid odds on that one, Tobias thought.

I could have cleaned up.

In the distance there was the sound of an ambulance and Tobias thought how accustomed he'd become to its screeching whine lately. The noise seemed to remind Abe Logan, through the mistiness of his wretched hangover, that the corpse in the gazebo was that of his wife, that this was no terrible dream, this was the Real Thing.

Tobias strolled toward Rezabek and spoke to him very quietly.

"I'm going to pay a call on our friend the doc."

"Maybe you can get something out of him," Rezabek answered. "I couldn't."

"I'll take the car, if that's okay."

Rezabek turned, watching the ambulance come up the driveway. "I'll hitch a ride with the corpse, was all he said."

And then Tobias was gone, striding through the sunlight toward the Honda.

Carlos Ayala's apartment was located above a bakery on Cinco de Mayo Street, a narrow thoroughfare that lay behind the main drag of the Quarter. Its only window overlooked a couple of misshapen shanties. You could see washing flap on clotheslines and a skinny dog sniff among garbage. Carlos, however, wasn't exactly looking at the view as he stood at the window. When he turned, absently surveying the walls of his small room on which he'd taped a variety of centerfolds and some of the more curious sexual conjunctions from *Hustler,* he could feel a tightness in his chest and his throat was dry as an old bone. He opened the icebox and removed a bottle of cheap tequila, from which he drank for several seconds.

Then he sat down on the edge of the narrow bed, the bottle dangling from his hands, and he waited.

This shit apartment, he thought.

He deserved better than this dump. Cockroach palace. The crawlers came and went like a stream of commercial travelers to a sales convention. He saw one right then and popped it with the sole of his foot.

Loco.

Everything was crazy.

Inlcuding the need to get the hell out of Las Cosimas.

He gazed into the clear liquid of the tequila, took another swallow, gasped.

This comes from fooling around with the gringo wives of this dump, it comes from being the big macho man—hell, it hadn't been altogether his fault. They begged him for it. Crazy bitches.

He rose, opened a closet, took out a battered suitcase, which he opened and looked into. A couple of good shirts, a few pairs of pants, his two suits.

And the little cardboard box, which rattled as he lifted it out.

He stood very still when he heard the sound of footsteps on the stairs. Then the door of his room was knocked three times lightly. Carlos opened it a little way and looked out at the sleepy face of Sammy Suarez.

"Seven A.M.," Suarez said as he slipped into the room. "I never heard of such an hour. What's the big rush, kid?"

Carlos thrust the cardboard box at the little man, who opened it and looked inside. There were several silver bracelets, an expensive wristwatch, a gold pendant.

"How much for the whole works?" Carlos asked.

Sammy rattled the goods around, touching them deftly with the tips of his fingers. Then he looked at the kid's face and what he saw there was trouble, Big Trouble.

"Seven A.M.," Sammy said. "A man don't want to sell stuff at seven A.M. unless he's in one sonofabitch hurry, Carlos."

Carlos gestured impatiently. "Five hundred for everything."

Sammy Suarez laughed. "Who did you kill, kid?"

"Kill?" Carlos gripped the little man by the lapels of his jacket and shook him a second. "What do you mean kill?"

"A manner of speaking, kid. Take it easy." Sammy, a little ruffled, stepped away. Big Trouble. Danger. He could smell it from the kid's skin.

"My mother's dying," Carlos said. "I got to get home fast. Five hundred for everything."

Sammy shoved the box back into the kid's hands. "I'm not interested. Naturally, I'm sad about your mother, Carlos, but I'm not interested in the goods. Okay?"

"Three hundred."

"Not at a goddamn dollar."

Carlos sat down, staring at the box. He had the look of a person who had just imploded. "Sammy, please, I got to get out of here fast and I need the bucks."

Samuel Suarez turned and walked to the door. He wasn't feeling so good suddenly, remembering the chain he'd sold to Enrico and now seeing these other items in the kid's possession—a man had to wonder about sources. A man had to stay out of trouble, especially one like himself whose business enterprises took him around the outer limits of the law.

He stopped at the door and turned to look at Carlos, noticing that the tough kid had damp eyes and his lower lip was trembling like that of a baby with a grazed knee. Where was the tough guy from the night before? And why this sudden hurry to get out of town anyhow?

He believed the story of the dying mother as much as he believed the moon was made of Jack cheese.

That little box of goodies. That *joyería*. It was tempting, but no thank you.

"Fifty and it's yours," Carlos said.

Sammy Suarez shurgged. "Suddenly I don't like the thoughts I'm having, Carlos. Suddenly I just don't want to know about your collection there and how you might have come to own those things." Sammy opened the door, looking out across a dimly lit landing. Women were dying in Las Cosimas and Carlos had a bunch of jewels, and he himself, Samuel Suarez, entrepreneur, had been greedy enough to already purchase one of those hot objects and sell it to somebody else.

Mother of God. A hot item was one thing.

But if it came from a cold body, that was quite another.

* * *

Tobias parked the Honda in the driveway of Andrew Conturas's house, behind the dilapidated Chevy Impala that belonged to the physician. He noticed cobwebs strung between the tires of the car, which meant that Conturas wasn't a man who went out a great deal in his old blue car. Tobias looked around the car for a moment, searching for nothing in particular and yet knowing he was seeking something. The old trained eye, he thought. A bloodstain on the seat, maybe. Or a sharp instrument lying carelessly on the dash.

Oh, sure.

Sure thing, Tobe.

Then he stared up toward the house, which was strangled by its own tangled shrubbery. The windows, as they had done before, gave him the impression of dark rooms beyond. Or maybe Conturas had had them painted black and the windows themselves were no more than cunning illusions. He wandered up the pathway to the front door, expecting to have to ring the bell, knock myabe—but the door was already open and Conturas was standing in the hallway, a coffee mug in one hand, his body draped in a wine-colored robe.

"Officer Manning," Conturas said. "An early-morning visit, eh? I have a sense of foreboding and I'm not sure why," and the guy was smiling in a thin way.

Tobias stepped inside the hallway. "I need to talk," he said.

"Someone else has died," Conturas said, and it wasn't a question. The physician turned and went inside his living room and Tobias followed, glancing up the darkened stairway as he passed.

The living room was cluttered with old furniture. Conturas sat, sipped his coffee, and Tobias remained on his feet.

"Maude Logan," Tobias said. "Killed in exactly the same way as the other two. And also a patient of yours, doctor."

"Maude Logan," Conturas said, looking thoughtful. "Yes, she was a patient. I always thought she lived too energetic a life for somebody in her condition. It surprises me she didn't die from natural causes."

Natural causes? I tell him about a murder and he mutters about natural causes? What kind of creep do I have here? Tobias rolled a cigarette, noting the faint look of disapproval on Conturas's face.

"What was her condition?" Tobias asked.

"Angina pectoris, Officer. You know that term, of course."

"I know it," Tobias said. He was angry suddenly. He could feel his fists clench and he knew that a small nerve was working in his jaw, which he hoped wasn't visible to the doctor. This guy is without feelings, he thought. This guy has no heart. His patients are dying and he doesn't even look surprised! What did he have in his gut? A bag of crushed ice? Some kind of silicon device?

Tobias sat down. There was no ashtray and Conturas made no move to provide one either, so Tobias was obliged to catch his own ash in the palm of one hand, which made him feel awkward.

"Three patients, Conturas," he said. "You've lost three goddamn patients."

"I hardly lost them, did I?" Conturas said. "It isn't as if they died on my operating table, is it—"

"You know what I mean, dammit—"

Conturas sipped his coffee. "I do not take kindly to being visited by a police officer at this time of day. Nor do I like your tone of voice—"

Tobias flicked his cigarette butt toward the open fireplace and, with a sense of satisfaction, watched it smolder amid the carefully arranged logs. He'd never liked Conturas when he'd brought Edith here and he liked the guy even less now. But you couldn't let your personal feelings get involved when you were staring at somebody and wondering if that person were capable of gross murders. Your professionalism flaked away when that happened. You lost the edge and, Jesus, that edge was something you needed.

"Why are your patients being killed?" he asked.

"Coincidence, I assume," Conturas said.

"Twice, maybe. Three times, I doubt it."

"Coincidence still, no matter how you try to interpret it, Manning." Conturas drained his coffee and Tobias noticed that the mug had his initials on it. AC and a couple of little flowery emblems. A gift from somebody? Yeah, who'd give Conturas a gift? A grateful patient?

My ass.

"Maybe somebody is sytematically going through your list of patients, Conturas. Hacking his way through them, so to speak—"

"For what reason?"

Tobias shrugged. The physician's composure appalled him. The icy front filled him with disgust. He wanted to seize and fracture it, he wanted to see the mask slip away and reveal what, if anything, lay beneath the veneer.

For a second, Tobias was quiet.

Then: "Tell me about the Devine girl."

Nothing.

Nada.

Conturas did not flinch, his expression didn't change, and he spoke as flatly as a man measuring the meters of his own words in time to a mental metronome. "It was a long time ago. The laws of the land were different. Abortion was not the legality it can be today, Manning."

"Why did she die?"

"Uterine bleeding," Conturas answered. "She had already attempted to abort the fetus with a twisted coat hanger before she came to see me. I did what I could. I aborted the fetus. I tried to save her life. For my reward, I was prohibited from practicing my profession for a number of years. But you obviously know all that already." No bitterness, no anger, just the flat voice. Conturas stood up. "I assume it passed through your limited imagination, Manning, that I might have harbored a paranoid resentment against all women. That I began to kill them regularly." The physician smiled. He shook his head.

Tobias was quiet a moment. He could let the insult go over the top of his head because he'd heard them all his working life. He'd been called pig, had stones thrown at him, he'd been spat at during crowd-control duty, and at least three times somebody had taken a potshot at him. No, the insults were nothing, but what galled him was how he couldn't shake the structure of this guy in front of him now.

"I may dislike the human race with irrational intensity, Manning, but I have better things to do with my time than go around stabbing women."

Tobias gazed through the open doorway of the living room, looked at the hallway, saw the flight of stairs that led upward into shadows. What was up there anyhow?

A freak's laboratory?

Pieces of slivered lung afloat in vinegar or something?

The occasional human heart.

Maybe it was the physician's version of a wrecking yard where prospective customers could browse through spare parts.

"The fact remains, your patients have this extraordinary tendency to die, doctor," he said, trying now to take the reasonable tack. Go with the fair-weather version. The old wind of fake affability in his sails. "And it would help me if you could provide me with a list of your other patients . . ." Provided any remained, he thought, biting his tongue. "For their own protection, you understand?"

Conturas studied the cop a moment.

"It's out of the question, Manning. There is such a thing, as I told your so-called superior officer before, as professional confidentiality. I would not willingly make a list available to you. Now, you can go in search of a warrant, if you like. That's your prerogative. But I have my ethics to protect—"

"Did you have ethics when it came to the Devine girl?" Tobias snapped. Shit, he'd gone way off track, he'd alienated the guy all over again.

"I'll have to ask you leave, Manning."

Tobias turned toward the door. "We'll talk again, I'm sure."

Moving along the hallway, he thought: Or I'll come back here when you're gone and I'll have the place all to myself. . . .

He heard the front door slam behind him, disturbing a flock of quail that squawked and rose clumsily into the trees.

Mad doctors, Tobias thought, had gone out of fashion somewhat these days. There had been a time in the 1930's and 40's when the deranged man of science had been something of a staple in low-budget horror movies—they were always guys with a strident grudge against humanity because a woman had spurned them or people laughed at their inventions and they underwent the kind of humiliation that transformed them into maniacs with hypodermic needles. Had Conturas been spurned? Maybe it was different nowadays, maybe all that had to happen to drive a scientist mad was a rejection slip from the Ford Foundation concerning the request for a grant. Tobias drew water from the cooler in the office and gazed out of the window.

He sipped his water, listened to the noise of Karl Rezabek in the john—coughing and flushing, accompanied by an occasional escape of air—and he turned his mind back to Conturas again. It was a bit like listening to a symphony played by an orchestra with one instrument slightly out of tune. Enough to notice, but not enough to quite put your finger on. Was it the oboe? the violin in the second row? Tobias rattled his fingertips against the windowpane for a time. He tried to imagine a girl called Devine dying as a consequence of Conturas's attempt at abortion, and what he perceived was a pale young face with dark hair plastered to a damp forehead, legs upraised on a stark table, a slippery gloved hand holding a steely instrument.

He moved toward the desk and looked at the telephone. A girl called Devine. He picked up the hard copy the computer had printed out and he ran his eyes over the words, wondering at the way the data banks reduced emotions to a language so stilted, so stripped of nuances, as to be almost useless. A girl dies, her mother brings a complaint, two cops investigate, the doc is struck off and then reinstated—what the hell else was there to all this? What lurked behind this functional language?

He reached for the phone and, thinking how much time had passed since Conturas had been arrested, asked for the number of the Boston police. There was always a chance that the officers—Cashman, MacDonald—would still be associated with the cops in Boston, and another chance, perhaps slimmer, that they might remember something. Tobias was shunted from department to department, from one unhelpful voice to another, until he found himself talking to a woman with a hard Boston accent who seemed to have something to do with personnel records. He was informed that Officer Cashman was dead (1974) and that Officer MacDonald was now with the Phoenix police. Tobias thanked her, put the phone down a moment, then decided he'd try Phoenix.

He was shuffled around again until he was put through to a detective called Patrick MacDonald, who spoke with a Scottish accent that had been modified for American purposes. Tobias introduced himself and the old cop fraternity sprang into action—MacDonald might have been a long-lost cousin or an old partner Tobias hadn't seen in twenty years or so. MacDonald, when he heard the name Andrew Conturas, was quiet for some time and Tobias could almost hear the shuffling of kalamazoo cards in the guy's memory.

"There was a young girl called Devine," MacDonald said. His pronunciation threw Tobias momentarily. Girl came out as "girrel."

"Devine, right. An attempted abortion," and Tobias was forcing the cards of the other man's memory.

MacDonald was heard to sigh. "Conturas performed an abortion on the girl and she died soon afterwards. . . . Aye, I remember, I remember. I was with Jimmy Cashman then." MacDonald was quiet once more. "It was a weird business, as I remember. Weird and bloody."

Tobias watched Karl Rezabek emerge from the john, buckling his belt. The sheriff's face was ash-gray.

MacDonald said, "Weird and bloody."

"Like how?"

"Well, first, there was always the suspicion that the child was Conturas's, although nobody ever actually proved that one beyond any doubt."

Tobias held the receiver closer to his ear: there was interference along the line. The doc's own kid, he thought. Well, well. "What else?" he asked.

"The mess, man. The goddamn mess of it all."

Mess? Tobias wondered. What was MacDonald driving at?

"An awful lot of blood," MacDonald said.

Silence. Karl Rezabek lowered himself slowly into his chair, like a man whose muscles are causing him to suffer. Tobias waited, tense all at once.

"I never thought a doctor would risk his professional life the way Conturas did," MacDonald said. "Which is why I always thought it had to be his own kid he was aborting. Getting rid of a nuisance, know what I mean? Didn't want the kid, didn't want the girl to have any claims on him, that kind of thing."

"Why was it a risk?" Tobias asked. "I always thought abortions were pretty straightforward."

"If you catch them in time," MacDonald answered. "But not when the fetus is six months old."

Six months old? "Run that past me again," Tobias said.

"Conturas had to perform a cesarean section, Manning. That's what I'm telling you. He had to make a big cut and he fucked up. He didn't get it right. In fact, he fucked it up like a butcher and when he couldn't stop the blood maybe he panicked. Maybe the sight of that baby kicking and breathing scared the shit out of him and he went to pieces. Who knows for sure? Anyhow, the girl died. She died."

Tobias thanked the man for his information and then hung up. He stood with his back to the wall, motionless, trying to sort out the various pictures that flooded his mind as if he were a man attempting to catalog old postcards. Six months old, he thought. Six months pregnant and Conturas had to go in with the knife and he blew it so badly that the girl didn't survive—and he saw blood everywhere now, spurting from the girl's open body, slithering over the physician's gloves, dripping to the floor. He saw the formed infant dying blindly, ripped out of the warmth of it's mother's body, and he felt the panic—the panic of the unborn child, the panic of the mother, and the desperation that must have seized Conturas's mind as he saw what was happening. It sure as hell wouldn't have taken place in an operating theater and there sure as hell wouldn't have been nurses around to help—just a physician, a young girl, and an unborn child.

And Conturas had lied to him.

Bullshit about a coat hanger. Bullshit about trying to mend the results of some amateur abortion. Unadulterated crap, nothing more.

And what Tobias wondered now was whether that tragedy had truly left Dr. Andrew Conturas unhinged enough for him to start killing his own sad patients. If some madness had lain dormant inside him for twenty years, awaiting the right moment to awake and begin destroying anew.

Enrico's wife, Carmelita, threw the gold chain across the room. It struck the wall and fell to the floor, curling like some skinny metallic snake.

Hurt, Enrico picked it up. He'd just given her the thing, thinking she'd wear it to church, show it off a bit, impress the *vecindad,* but instead she'd examined it a moment and then hurled it violently across the room.

"Your intentions are good. I do not quarrel with your intentions, Enrico. But there are ways of insulting a woman that perhaps you are not aware of," and she gazed at him from the bed, where she sat with her feet in a bowl of tepid water containing Arm & Hammer, which she considered good for her muscles.

"It's a beautiful thing," Enrico said.

"I will not quarrel with that either," his wife replied.

"Pardon me, then, if I don't understand the problem."

"Examine the chain. Look carefully at the clasp."

Enrico did so. He saw nothing, even though he squinted. It was just a large gold clasp.

"Don't you see?" Carmelita asked.

"It's just some writing, is all."

"There are initials on the clasp—"

"Maybe the manufacturer—"

"ML, it says—"

"ML," and Enrico noticed it for the first time. Holy Christ, who but a woman would perceive such a tiny detail?

"It belonged to somebody else, Enrico—"

"Perhaps . . ."

"So where did you get it?" Carmelita rose and walked awkwardly on her toes across the room. There was the sound of little bones cracking. She ran her hands through her black-silver hair and Enrico, as he observed this gesture, was filled with an old lust.

She said, "The smile you can remove from your face, Enrico. I am talking about the clasp of the chain." She stared at him with that look which had been seeing straight through him all the years of their marriage. "That little *zorrillo* Suarez talked you into this, didn't he? Every time he tries to sell you something, you buy it like an *idiota*, Enrico. Where are your brains? Huh? In your *nalgas*?"

Enrico looked down at the floor, like an ashamed kid.

"It's stolen, Enrico. Samuel Suarez doesn't possess anything that wasn't stolen. What was it last time, Enrico, eh? You bring me home a watch which leaves a green stain on my wrist first time I wear it and you believed it had come all the way from Switzerland, didn't you? Either stolen or cheap. That's Sammy Suarez, Enrico."

She softened suddenly, a change of mood, and she put her arms around his neck, pressing her face against his cheek.

"You're a good man, Enrico. And I love you. But you're sometimes one big *payaso*."

She kissed him and he felt better.

"You take the chain, Enrico. And you show it to your friend. What is his name? The cop, I mean."

"Tobias?" Enrico asked. Running to a cop, even a friend like Tobias, was maybe a little more sneaky than he wanted to be. "Listen," he said. "Maybe it's not stolen. Maybe somebody sold it to him."

Carmelita laughed. "Then you can bet your last peso, my dear, that whoever sold it to Sammy Suarez stole it in the first place."

Enrico pressed his face against his wife's ample breasts.

Carlos, he thought.

Carlos Ayala.

From the adjoining bedroom he could hear the stirring of his son-in-law Manuel. A lazy bum who lived off his wife, Enrico's daughter, Rosa. Enrico had been against the match in the first place, but who listened to an old guy like him?

The door opened and Manuel came in, wearing striped pajamas, scratching his fat head, yawning, looking no doubt for some sign of breakfast being cooked.

"Hey, you hear the radio?" he asked.

Enrico said nothing. The fewer verbal exchanges he had with Manuel, the better he liked it.

"Another body," the young man said.

Carmelita moaned. "No . . ."

"Some woman called Maude Logan up in one of the big

houses. It just came on the news. One of those flashes when the announcer breaks in with something big to tell you!" Radio was one of Manuel's great enthusiasms. He had come, not so long ago, from an obscure Mexican village where only the priest owned one, and that had been a portable whose batteries were forever running down.

Maude Logan.

Carmelita exchanged a dark look with Enrico.

"Mother of God," Carmelita said.

Tobias went inside the apartment and found Paul curled up on the sofa, asleep. He gazed at the kid for a while and then, when he reached out to touch the boy's tousled hair lightly, Paul opened his eyes.

Tobias sat down in an armchair and watched the kid come to wakefulness.

"What time is it, Pops?"

"I make it nine."

Paul stretched his arms and swung himself into a sitting position. He rubbed the sides of his face lazily, in the manner of someone checking the stubble on his jaw. Tobias rolled a cigarette and, for some reason, tried to conceal the small leather pouch from Paul, as if by so doing he could hide the memory of a death.

But Paul said, "Still using the old thing?"

"I figure I always will," Tobias said. He was about to mention the most recent slaying but he changed his mind. What he desired right now was emptiness, the silence of a good cigarette, making his mind a blank. Shove the big matters aside a moment and concentrate on the trivial because sometimes when you do that the big things take care of themselves. So he pushed Conturas out of his mind and with him all the bloody images he'd received from MacDonald. He thrust that agony away.

"Say, some guy called Streicher called you, Paul."

"Streicher?"

"Yeah. Said it was important you get in touch with him. A doctor, I guess he said. Friend of yours?"

Paul nodded, ran his fingers through his hair, looked across the room in the evasive way he'd always had as a small kid. It was as if he'd concentrate on some mundane object with a slight shift of his eyes so that whatever else was on his mind would dissolve. Tobias had always been able to see through this ruse. He puffed on his cigarette, studying the kid.

"So who is this guy Streicher?"

"Like he told you, Pops," Paul said. "He's a doctor."

"Somebody you work with? A professor maybe?"

"Streicher's a guy I see sometimes at UCLA."

"A physician?"

"A therapist . . ."

"I'm not quite sure what you mean by therapist," Tobias said.

"A psychiatrist, Pops, that's all."

Tobias was silent, watching his son.

A shrink.

Paul was seeing a shrink.

Tobias stubbed his cigarette and stood up. "I never knew."

"It's no big deal. You know how many people see therapists these days?" Paul smiled, and there was something just a little patronizing in the expression.

Tobias said sure, he understood, but he knew from Paul's expression that the subject was closed. The shuttered rooms of grief. All those little locked corridors of the mind. And the kid needed a shrink to help him open these doors. Suddenly, Paul seemed a stranger to him, someone whose depths he couldn't plumb.

He shrugged and for a time there was an awkward silence between father and son and Tobias could see grief in the boy's eyes.

Change the subject. Quit walking on thin ice.

"You have a nice time with Caroline?" he asked quietly.

Paul said nothing, looked sullen.

"First date," Tobias said. Romero. Daniel Romero. In a distant phone booth a telephone was ringing in a muted fashion. Daniel Romero. It kept coming back, wave after wave. Without any enthusiasm, he went on: "Call her again. Fireworks display tomorrow. Could be nice. You got to give these things time," and he wondered if Paul knew that he had one rival for the girl's affections.

Paul smiled. "She said I should call her before I leave."

His smile was feeble. Maybe he knew about Romero.

Maybe he'd seen Caroline with the guy, something like that.

With Daniel Romero.

Danny—

Now, why the hell did he suddenly abbreviate the guy's name like that?

Why would he do that with somebody he barely knew?

Danny

Romero

dannyromero—and why did he suddenly have this faded image of Romero in a mug shot?

He flicked on the TV. Sunday-morning preacher pleading for funds. A toll-free number was written across the screen. These polyester beggars for the Lord, he thought. These blow-dry creeps for Christ.

He was about to change the channel when it hit him, it

came at him like a baseball bat smashing the top of his skull.

Danny Romero.

Of course. Of course.

Suddenly the years rolled away like the parting of his own personal Red Sea and he could see the opposite bank as clear as hell.

He moved quickly to the telephone and picked it up and dialed a number in New York City that he'd never forgotten and never would forget and then he was connected with Art Frye who, with a mouth stuffed no doubt with a hot dog and sauerkraut and dollops of French's mustard, was saying, "Tobe? No kidding? I thought I saw your obituary last week. Quarter-inch *New York Times*. Had to use a magnifying glass." Pause, chew. "If you're calling from beyond the Great Divide, Tobe, you better speak the hell up."

# 14

The guys from Carmel unloaded their equipment with all the wariness of two nuclear specialists in the depths of a silo regarding their doomsday keys. Caroline watched them go in and out of their van, which was painted with the slogan LIGHT UP YOUR SKY INC, a purple Dodge which shone meticulously in the early sunlight. Sunday, July 3. She adjusted her sunshades, folded her arms, watched as Gus and Morton emerged with vast rolls of wire fencing. She could never get them straight in her mind (not that anyone could have managed that feat, given their sexual proclivities); was Gus the red-haired skinny one or was he the squat little man with the beard and red silk shirt? They squabbled constantly as they unrolled their wire and began to hammer posts into the soil. Caroline turned and glanced in the direction of the country club a moment. The idea of fireworks left a bad taste in her mouth.

She put her hands in the pockets of her corduroy jeans, feeling the sun warm against her maroon silk shirt.

Maude Logan, she thought.

She hadn't liked Maude, but nobody deserved to die like that.

The concept of a fireworks display suddenly seemed like a tasteless funeral pyre for the poor woman.

Gus and Morton were coming toward her, still bitching back and forth at each other. The red-haired one was munching on a whole-wheat sandwich from which protruded bean sprouts and little cubes of tofu. Now she remembered. This one was Morton, the smaller guy was Gus.

Morton said, "You'll be delighted to know, Caroline, that we're going to include our beloved Stars and Stripes as a finale—"

Gus had bright, birdlike eyes. He said, "In a manner of speaking anyhow—"

"A compromise, darling, an artistic compromise," Morton said.

Caroline nodded. Her attention had strayed toward the country club, where she noticed a police Honda turn into the driveway and saw Tobias Manning get out. The Honda, she observed, was parked right alongside Daniel Romero's Lincoln.

"We've altered the colors," Morton said.

"Taken liberties, so to speak," said Gus.

"Instead of red white and boring old blue—God, it makes me cringe to think of that particular combo—we're going with pastels. Pastels, Caro, sweetie. Think about that. Red has been replaced with pink—"

Caroline smiled politely and wandered away, leaving the two men to their pastel descriptions. She reached a knoll that overlooked the entrance to the country club and she paused there for a moment. Maude Logan, for God's sake.

Who was going to be next?

The next victim?

Despite the sunlight, she felt cold. She walked down the knoll toward the club and went in. Although it was early, she needed a stiff drink. She entered the Piano Bar, deserted and quiet at this hour, and she ordered a gin and tonic. She realized she was expecting to see Tobias Manning and find out what had brought him out here at this time of day and whether it had had anything to do with the murder of Maude Logan—a weariness went through her. She stared at her wrists. There were reddish-blue marks against her skin and as she self-consciously tried to tug her cuffs down over them, she felt a moment of annoyance with herself.

When Daniel Romero had broken into her apartment, by means of a MasterCard inserted into the door, she'd let herself go again.

God. It had never been like that in the past, not with any other man. She had always enjoyed the gentle lovers best of all, the ones who were considerate and attentive—

Daniel Romero was something else.

Somebody who created a darkness inside her.

A spell, she told herself. He's a fucking sorcerer, that's what he is. Svengoddamngali.

Her hand trembled as she tasted her drink. Now she was wondering about her own safety, which seemed a fragile concept right then, because if Danny Romero could enter her apartment that easily, then anyone could. The Caller, even. Shit, maybe she should have taken Tobias Manning's advice and had her number changed—

She shut her eyes. There was the start of a horrible headache.

She swung around on her stool, looked across the empty bar, the silent piano, the shadow of a corridor that led toward the rest rooms.

Suddenly she heard herself being paged from the foyer and she was momentarily surprised. Then she remembered she'd left a message on her answering machine that she could be reached at the club. She slid down from her stool, walked across the bar, stepped into the foyer—which seemed needlessly bright to her—and she paused a moment before picking up the telephone on the reception desk.

This fear of telephones, she thought.

This is something you have to overcome.

She raised the receiver slowly and said her name in a voice that came out quite unintentionally as a whisper.

She hoped she wouldn't hear somebody remind her about how sick she was.

The goddamn Malibu had a lousy starter, a bad solenoid, a faulty water pump, and a body that had mainly been consumed by rust over the years of countless owners, most of whom had had little respect for either cars or papers of ownership. It ran out of energy a mile before the freeway ramp, and steam was belching from under its loose hood. Cursing, the kid got out and kicked the tires, as if violence might work some kind of mechanical magic, but the steam kept storming out and there was a weird hissing now as well, like the whole crazy thing was going to explode in his face. He wiped sweat from his eyes and looked helplessly up and down the road that led from Las Cosimas to the highway. He could hear the drone of cars from the freeway and they seemed an impossible distance away, but then again, he didn't exactly have too many options left to him except to take a hike. He whipped his suitcase out from the tattered back seat and started off in the direction of the freeway, where, he hoped, he could travel by means of *el pulgar*—which could be big trouble, because the highway patrol didn't look kindly on guys hitching rides on freeways.

A little fucking money, he thought, and I'd be on a bus, a plane, I'd be a hundred miles away from this dump. That cheap bastard Suarez—Jesus, why hadn't he tried to help out?

He searched the road once again with a hopeless expression on his face. Maybe he could go back and hide in the Quarter, an idea that took shape in his mind like a sudden little flower. Hey, who'd think of looking for him there?

He didn't move.

Suitcase in hand, steam hanging around him like vapors emerging from the fissures of hell, he just didn't move. All he could think about was the dead woman in the gazebo and the blood spread across her black dress.

Paul said, "I was wondering if you'd like some company for the fireworks display. . . ." He heard his own voice echo on the line and he had the odd feeling that there were two versions of himself, the one seated in his father's apartment, the other a ghostly double trapped in the electronic intricacies of the telephone system. (What would Streicher say about that phenomenon?)

Caroline said, "That's very sweet of you, Paul. But I believe I have another date."

"Oh," and Paul was silent a second.

Caroline said, "If you're coming to the display, though, we'll probably run into each other."

He detected it just then. A slight impatience in her voice. She wanted this whole conversation to end. He said, "Yeah, maybe."

Maybe maybe maybe. There was no future with Caroline, no future for that matter with anyone else.

When he'd said good-bye and hung up he wandered idly around the apartment. Inside the kitchen he opened closets absently, finding his mother's old wheelchair folded away in one. He touched it lightly, then pulled his hand away as if scalded. Why did his father keep that thing? Why did he keep a reminder like that around the place? Then he was thinking about the expression that had gone across his father's face when they'd talked about Streicher: it had been one of disappointment, almost as if Tobias had been saddened by the fact that his own son felt it necessary to take his emotional problems to a stranger and hadn't brought them to his father. Paul was filled right then with an intense longing for wholeness, for things to be complete, for a fractured world to be put right. A yearning for family . . . for all those times when grief hadn't shattered the stained-glass loveliness of shared lives.

He stepped into the bathroom. He looked at himself in the mirror, then ran a hand across his face. What did he see there? The face of someone who could be a physician? Who had ambitions and dreams of restoring sick people to health? He thought of Caroline Cassidy again and as he did so he could feel a pulse beat in his throat, beat beat beat, his blood sounding like a muffled drum. He imagined her lying spread out in front of him, the buttons of her shirt undone and her nipples visible, and he could almost feel it, feel the way her smooth skin would yield to the gentle pressure of his hands, he could see her open mouth and the way her lips would glisten and that faraway expression in her eyes—

Leaning forward, he splashed cold water all over his face and head.

Then he looked at himself once again in the mirror.

A physician, he thought. A physician in reflection.

He could make the sick well.

Tobias stepped inside the room when Daniel Romero, half of his face covered with shaving cream, opened the door. Romero smiled, waving an old-fashioned open razor in the air, then turned and moved into the bathroom. Tobias could hear the sound of running water and Romero mumble something from behind the folds of a towel.

Tobias looked around the room. He realized it was the first time he'd ever been inside any of the rooms at the resort and he was a little disappointed to discover that Romero's room, at least, was nothing more than a kind of upgraded Holiday Inn lodging. The bed was unmade. Romero's clothes lay across a chair. An open suitcase sat on a small oval table alongside an ice bucket.

Romero came out of the bathroom, the towel in his hand. He was still smiling, but there was a certain perplexity behind the expression, as if he were wondering why a cop had come to visit him.

Tobias moved toward the window and looked out across the green hollows and sandy bunkers of the golf course, noticing a couple of guys following the flight of a small white ball as it flew, like some emaciated gull, over a stand of sunlit trees.

"We met, didn't we . . . ?" Romero said. "You're the cop that wanted to buy the Lincoln, right?"

"I'm the cop that couldn't afford it," Tobias answered.

He looked at Romero. There was a slight razor nick on the man's jaw, and a hairlike line of blood slid across the skin. But it wasn't the shaving wound that interested Tobias, it was the face itself, and he found himself remembering, trying to remember . . .

"Right," Romero said. "If it's any consolation, the car isn't all it's supposed to be. It's got terrific computerized gadgets, if you're into digital readouts . . ."

Tobias glanced once more at the golfers, then back at Romero. "I think we met long before that, though, Romero."

"Did we?"

"New York City. Fifteen years ago."

Romero threw his towel down on the bed, a casual gesture. "It's a small world, like they say, but you'll have to forgive me if I can't recall exactly. What did you say your name was?"

"Manning, Tobias Manning."

Remembering, remembering...

Tobias was silent a moment. The telephone on the bedside table started to ring but Romero made no move to pick it up. Tobias sat down at the oval table and drummed his fingertips on the laminated surface. "Fifteen years ago," he said. "Georgina Sullivan," and he felt the name slip out of his mouth as if it was the pit of some sour fruit.

"Who?" Romero asked.

"Georgina Sullivan. A nice kid. Used to do grocery shopping for old people in her neighborhood. Worked a lot as a baby-sitter. People had nice things to say about her. Always a smile on her face, she was that kind of kid. She was sixteen years old when she died."

Romero sat on the edge of the bed and studied Tobias a second. "Should I understand what you're talking about, Manning? I mean, should I sit here and nod my head and understand you?"

Carefully, Tobias began to roll a cigarette. He was nervous, and the act of making a smoke calmed him a little. Fifteen years ago, he thought. And Art Frye, whose memory was vast and complicated, who could recall batting averages from the 1940's as well as the most mundane details about every person he'd ever interviewed or interrogated, had confirmed the name. Yeah, Romero, Daniel. A punk kid. Smartassed. Sullen. Knew it all. Couldn't pin it on him and he took a walk. That one really bugged me, Tobe. I was so goddman sure...

Romero said, "Well? Are you going to explain to me why you're talking about a girl who's been dead for fifteen years or am I meant to guess, Manning?"

Tobias watched Romero while holding a match under his cigarette. Fifteen years—hell, a face could change a lot in that amount of time. Lines, creases, a change of hairstyle, differences in the way a person moved, the whole stance, the poise, everything could be altered. And what he was trying to see, as he observed the other man, was the punk kid he and Art Frye had hauled in off the streets on a summer night in 1969 when the city had been frying and hydrants had been opened and kids were screaming under the waterfalls. A punk kid called Danny Romero. Hair greased back, leather vest, blue jeans, sneakers.

This is it, Tobias thought.

This is the place where you work.

The nebulous point where you try to make connections.

"Georgina was going home one night after a baby-sitting gig. She stopped at a grocery store. She bought something, a candy bar, something, talked with the clerk for a few seconds. Then she left." Tobias paused. His cigarette was falling apart in his hands. And he noticed that Romero seemed amused by the sight of tobacco shards spilling over his fingers and onto the table. "Next day, some kids found her body on a vacant lot. She'd been stabbed repeatedly. Stuffed inside a trashcan, Romero."

Stabbed, stuffed.

Tobias crushed his dilapidated cigarette in the ashtray, annoyed with himself for his architectural incompetance.

Romero stood up. "I'm sorry about the girl, Manning. I'm sorry somebody killed her. But I got better things to do than sit around and listen to your reminiscences—"

Cool, Very nice. Tobias had to admire the guy's style. Already he was standing in front of the dressing table and brushing his hair, gazing at his own image in the mirror.

"We pulled in a kid called Danny Romero for the killing," Tobias said.

God damn.

Why was this bastard so expressionless?

I am talking to myself.

"Did you hear me?" he asked.

"Sure."

"That kid was you, Romero."

Romero smiled and for an instant Tobias saw him in bed with Caroline Cassidy, saw her sprawled beneath him, her legs wide—and the image unraveled him more than a little because it made him wonder if he'd come here for all the wrong reasons. If he was making faulty connections because he was jealous as hell about Romero and Caroline.

"Run that past me again," Romero said.

"You, was what I said. You were the kid, the killer—"

"The alleged killer," and Romero turned, still smiling. He put his hand out and clapped Tobias on the shoulder, somewhat patronizingly. "Let me see if I can follow your thinking, Manning. Women are being killed around your town at the rate of one every seven minutes. Stabbed, according to what I hear on the radio or see on TV. Okay. Fifteen years ago, a kid who happened to have my name, was a suspect—a suspect only, remember—in a similar kind of slaying in New York City. And now you come to my room with your head filled with the idea that maybe this particular Daniel Romero is back on the streets with a knife. Have I got it right?"

Tobias said nothing. He listened to Romero's words echo through his head and he understood that the other man was trying, in his own cool way, to reduce Tobias's thinking to the absurd. Even the touch of the man's hand on his shoulder was a kind of physical punctuation, an underscoring of Romero's strategy.

I might be the same Daniel Romero.

Or I might not.

Either way, in the present or in the past, my sheet is snow-white.

Prove it otherwise, if you can. Link me to a fifteen-year-old slaying first, then see if you can tie the knot the whole way.

Tobias felt a surge of powerlessness.

"You're going to have to do a whole lot better, Manning."

From the window, Tobias watched the two golfers disappear in a stand of trees. You've lost your touch, he thought. You came running here to Romero's room without even thinking the goddamn thing through, for Christ's sake. It's this place, it's taken your edge away, left you blunt and unprepared and as useful as a rusted razor.

Las Cosimas.

He faced Romero, who was busy with a silver necktie. "I could have your prints here in a matter of minutes from New York, Romero. I could take you down, establish positive ID, keep you for questioning—"

"Notice how I'm shitting on the rug, Manning." Romero smiled at his own reflection in the mirror, knotted his tie, turned away from the glass.

"When are you leaving Las Cosimas?"

"Did I say anything about leaving?" Romero asked.

"You intend to stay here?"

"Hell, why not, there's another thousand women I lie awake thinking about killing."

"Like Caroline Cassidy?" It slipped out, Tobias thought. It just slipped from his mouth and there wasn't any way in the world of retrieving it.

"You've been snooping already, huh?" Unflappably, Romero fastened his cufflinks, and there were quick little flashes of silvery light, like fish seen darting in water. Tobias clenched his fists because suddenly he wanted nothing more than to smack this character in the face and see where that imperturbable look would go then, see how his sarcasm might dramatically dissolve. Instead, he moved toward the door of the room.

Romero called to him. "Keep an eye on Caroline, do you?"

Tobias paused in the doorway.

"Worth looking at, Manning," Romero went on. "She tastes even better than she looks and she fucks even better than that—"

And Tobias slammed the door as he stepped out into the corridor, cold with rage, bitter about his own clumsiness, annoyed with the way he'd let Romero get under his skin with all the subtlety of a surgical blade.

Inside the elevator, he started to sweat.

You've forgotten how the game is played, Tobias.

You've forgotten how to get to the heart of the maze.

And it was a maze filled with people who had blood on their hands. Andrew Conturas. And maybe Danny Romero too.

With all that blood dripping, Tobias, there ought to have been some kind of trail.

The trouble was the way these people kept babbling in Spanish mixed with English. It made for very poor comprehension and Karl Rezabek had already had it up to here with confusion. He turned on the air-conditioning unit of the office and wished Manning were here to deal with these Mexicans because he had an affinity with them for some reason—but he hadn't heard from Manning in hours.

Weary, weary me, he thought.

He ran a hand across the bullet of his head and looked at the faces of the elderly couple in front of him and then at the other guy, whose name he knew was Sammy Suarez, some kind of small-time crook in the Quarter.

"Maybe if we quit getting so goddamn excited we can reach an understanding here," Rezabek said.

The woman, a stout mamacita with pendulous breasts, was shouting at Suarez, and her husband, who kept a tavern in the Quarter, was trying to mediate, but he was about as useful as a guy trying to umpire a tennis match between overpaid jocks with operatic mannerisms.

Rezabek stepped into the throng, gripping Suarez by the shoulders and pulling him aside. The little guy, bobbing like a pugilist, twisted his body away, his small fists upraised—a gesture that was so obviously automatic that he appeared not to comprehend the seriousness of threatening a police officer.

"Cool, cool," Rezabek said.

There was silence for a moment.

Then the stout woman said, "*Ladrón!*" And this set everyone off again until Rezabek regained control by slamming his fist hard on the counter.

Suarez said, "Look, I come down here to protect my good reputation—"

"I gathered that already," Rezabek said.

The woman, whose name was Carmelita, made a slightly obscene gesture. "He has a pig's reputation," and here she dangled a gold chain in the air a moment, before letting it fall on Rezabek's desk.

Suarez, nonplussed, went on: "This woman accuses me of selling her stolen property."

"Worse," the woman said. "Worse than stolen!"

Karl Rezabek picked up the gold chain and ran it across the palm of his hand.

The old guy, Enrico, said, "I bought it as a present for my wife, Officer. From Samuel Suarez."

Suarez: "I do not deny it—"

Carmelita: "You're worse than a thief—"

Suarez: "I have a lawyer, a good lawyer, and I'll make sure he files papers against you because of the way you're making me out to be such a bad guy—"

Rezabek tuned out these voices as he examined the chain. Sturdy links of gold and a large, somewhat unusual clasp on which the initials ML had been inscribed. He sighed and wondered why these Hispanics had to be so damned excitable all the time. Why couldn't they be reasonable and Caucasian? Logical and cool?

"You don't deny you sold the chain to Enrico?" he asked Suarez.

"I don't deny it, sure, but I didn't steal the goddamn thing."

"Look at the initials, look at them," the stout woman was shouting.

"I am looking! I see them!" Rezabek studied the clasp again. What was so important about—

The chain slid from his fingers to the desktop.

Suarez said, "Hey, don't look at me like that, Sheriff, I didn't have nothing to do with stealing the chain—"

Rezabek could feel his office go suddenly dark around him and he was filled with a sensation he'd never known before—a dizzying elation, a dryness of mouth, a tingling coursing through his veins. It was either the onset of a coronary or the realization that the killer was only a step away.

"I bought the chain in good faith from Carlos Ayala," Suarez said.

"You didn't ask him how he'd acquired it, did you?"

"I forgot to—"

"Yeah, sure you did—"

Suarez looked ashamed. "I can take you to him. I can show you where he lives," said Sammy, still ashamed, but more conscious of a desire to save his own neck than to observe the meaningless dictate of honor among thieves. "He also tried to sell me other things, other jewels, only this morning, he had like this big box filled with good stuff, but I backed off because I knew he was in trouble—" And Sammy was babbling now, running off at the mouth because there was something more serious here than mere stolen property. A vision of a gas chamber went briefly through his head.

Rezabek was already moving toward the door. Suarez followed him out into the sunshine, shuffling to keep up with the sheriff.

There was a department Honda parked across the street and for a moment Rezabek was dismayed to see that it wasn't the one with the word SHERIFF on the panel, but this feeling lasted only a moment.

His nostrils were filled with the perfume of a sweet triumph.

While Manning was off shooting wild geese, the sheriff of Las Cosimas was about to catch himself a killer.

# 15

Night over Las Cosimas, a picture postcard of hillside residences, shaded canyons, tall firs—and beyond, beyond the saunas and sundecks and hot tubs and whirlpools, the Pacific, silvered by shards of broken moonlight, slithering up beneath the struts of a dying pier. Caroline closed her eyes and leaned against a support beam. She liked to think she was romantic enough still to enjoy sea-dampened wood and scents of brine and the feel of watery moonlight against her face. The breeze, stirring sand, blew against her lips. When she opened her eyes, she saw Daniel Romero looking at her with a smile that was more than a little infuriating—as if he understood some big secret about her, something the rest of the world didn't.

And so he did, she supposed.

She shivered as the breeze blew harder.

Romero put his hands against her shoulders. She remembered now that he had suggested this walk along the sands because, in the morning, he was leaving. The sailor's farewell, she thought. Shore and sand and this rotten pier and maybe the breeze should be piping a lament.

"It's not my kind of town," he said.

"Why not?" Defend Las Cosimas, your civic employer. Her mind was filled with sales slogans, phrases from glossy pamphlets.

"It's too dull—"

"Dull? We've got a killing spree going on and you say it's dull?"

He shook his head. "According to your local newscaster, the killer's behind bars."

"Alleged killer," she said. It had been on radio and TV, it had been talked about openly throughout Las Cosimas: Rezabek had a man suspected of "having information" about the murders. "Having information" seemed one of those phrases designed to console an unhappy populace. She felt it was somehow akin to taking junior aspirin when you had a blinding migraine.

"Alleged, whatever."

Silence. Even the sea, its tide drawing back, was a sudden mute force.

"You can't miss the fireworks," she said. "How can you walk out and be so unpatriotic?"

Daniel Romero shrugged. "This town's too small for me, is all."

It's growing, she thought. It's growing along with the whole microchip business. It's the Coming Place. More sales slogans. Jesus, she wanted this man to stay so badly, even if she knew him no better than she had at the very start. But a point would come, a place in time would arrive when she'd start to understand him. She was sure of that.

She looked at him curiously. "So. You just blow in and blow out of my life, Romero, huh? Just like that."

"I'm a wanderer," he answered.

"How romantic for you." She turned away huffily, facing the ocean. She tried to think good thoughts—that if this Carlos Ayala turned out to be the killer indeed, then Las Cosimas would no longer be terrifying; life would become normal.

But. But. But.

She was conscious of a great sighing absence inside herself.

"Look, Caroline . . ." Romero didn't finish his sentence. He rested his hands on her shoulders, then began to knead her flesh with his fingertips, slowly at first and then with more pressure and all at once the pressure turned to pain and she pulled herself free of him, walking a few paces forward across the sand.

"I have to leave," he said. "I don't think I can stay here, that's all."

"Okay." Just like that. Okay. Good-bye. Vaya con Dios. Fuck off.

"We had a time," Romero said.

Which you tell all the girls, Caroline thought.

What the hell. She could have a date for the fireworks display if she wanted one. After all, her Paul Manning had called, all she had to do was curl her little finger and voilà—she could have other men. Who needs Romero? (Me, she thought. I need Romero.)

"What are you running away from anyhow?" she asked.

"Who said I was running?"

"Who are you? I mean, what do you do? Where do you come from?"

"These are heavy questions," he said.

"Too heavy for you to lift, sweetie?"

Romero smiled. "Maybe."

She folded her arms against her breasts and felt the breeze slide through the thin material of her shirt. Ahead, the sands glistened in moonlight and the tide came and went like some slow, teasing spermal substance. She sniffed the night air. Overhead, on the wood boards of the pier, there was the sound of a movement. A creaking of wood. Somebody up there, digging the moon.

"Answer me this," she said. "Put my mind at rest over one thing at least, will you?"

"If I can."

"You made those calls, didn't you? Those creepy calls."

Romero looked at her with exasperation. "Look. You want a sworn affidavit?"

"It wasn't you?"

"It wasn't me, baby."

Why had she asked that question anyhow? There hadn't been any recent calls. Maybe the Caller had grown weary. There was a high attrition rate when it came to anonymous calls, she thought.

She turned to him and smiled. "This is our last night."

"Yes," he said.

"There's something I've never done, Danny."

"Tell me."

"I've never been screwed on sand."

"Oh, it's unhealthy, the grit gets everywhere, it becomes uncomfortable—"

"I should find out for myself, shouldn't I?"

She moved away from him, out from the shadows of the pier, and started to walk across the beach. Beyond the reach of lights from the Quarter, she stopped. He was coming toward her. She kicked off her sandals and let the tide lap her ankles. Barely seen, a jellyfish floated away from her, a bubble on the swell.

"The sand, huh," Romero said, He gripped her wrists.

"Yeah."

He pulled her down and lay alongside her.

As she turned her face toward him, closing her eyes, waiting for him to touch her, waiting for the old electricity to go off inside her head, she was conscious, as if in a pale dream, of a solitary figure passing under the lamp at the end of the pier.

And then it was gone and all she could feel were Romero's hands on her body and the tide rushing back and forth between her toes.

What Tobias had been unable to take was the smirk on Rezabek's military face, the curl of triumph on his mouth, the expression of victory. He thinks he's solved it all. Thinks he's got his man in the slammer. Tobias gazed at the kid through the bars. From the outer office he could hear Rezabek on the telephone to J M Dunbar, and the tone in the voice was that of a man who has conquered heathen territories and brought Gideon Bibles to the savages.

Carlos Ayala was one scared kid.

Tobias watched him a moment, his hands raised to the bars of the cage, as Rezabek's voice came floating down the hallway. "A whole box of . . . right there, sir, in his suitcase. . . ."

Tobias tuned out the sheriff's voice, rolled a cigarette, then stepped inside the cell and gave it to the kid. Carlos took it gratefully and Tobias sat down beside him on the bunk. The stud undone, Tobias thought.

For a long time Tobias was silent, studying the tiny high window of the cell. According to Rezabek, the kid had been picked up trying to hitch a ride. Grabbed him right there on the ramp, Manning. Plucked the sonofabitch right off the ramp like a cherry from a goddamn tree!

A cherry from a goddamn tree. This phrase rattled around inside Tobias's head. He listened to Carlos take long pulls on the cigarette and then he was thinking of the cheap suitcase and its contents—the box of jewels. The rewards of studdom. He turned to the kid, smiled, rolled a cigarette for himself. When he had it lit he said, "Tell me about Maude Logan—"

"I already told the sheriff—"

"Tell me, Carlos."

Carlos spread his hands. "What can I say? I go up there

to see her. I find her body in the what do you call the thing—"

"Gazebo—"

"Right. I find it lying there and I know she'd dead and I split because I'm scared shitless—"

"I don't need to know why you went up there, do I?"

"She liked me. She wanted me. Like weird, though. I always had to come up behind her and take her by surprise. Some surprise for me, huh?"

"Some surprise," Tobias said. "You service any other women in Las Cosimas?" Service, he thought. The sexual mechanic. Why did Romero cross his mind suddenly just then?

"Now and again," and the kid shrugged.

"All those jewels, they come from Maude Logan?"

"Sure. She liked to give me things."

"Emma Hamlett," Tobias said. "What about her?"

"Hey, her I never knew! And I'll tell you another thing, I never knew the Sharp woman either."

Tobias dropped his cigarette, stepped on it. He stared at Carlos. "So you went up to her gazebo regularly—"

"Yeah, pretty regular, it depended on if her old man was drunk. He was sober, I didn't go. I used to call her. Sometimes she'd call me." Carlos smoked his cigarette right down to the butt and beyond. "I swear this, Officer, I swear before God, I never killed Maude Logan. I found her body, but I never killed her. Hey, why would I kill this woman who's so good to me, presents and money, huh?"

Tobias stood up, listening to the creak of the bunk as he rose.

Rezabek's voice still echoed down the corridor. Tobias leaned against the bars, folding his arms. The kid stared down at the floor. Presumably old man Dunbar would be happy tonight. Presumably vindicated in his racist belief that the killer would be found in the Quarter. Presumably breaking open a little expensive brandy in his lonesome San Diego mansion tonight, his mood cheerful, his beloved Las Cosimas safe and secure and bolted down against the possibilities of further savagery. Tobias shuffled his feet, cleared his throat.

Daniel Romero, he was thinking again.

Andrew Conturas, knee-deep in a dying girl's blood.

And now Carlos Ayala.

He was juggling balls through the air and they were spinning faster than he could hope to keep up with. It was as if he'd lost the knack of keeping things in the air, keeping them all clear in sight at the same time, the way an old man would lose the ability to bite into an apple without leaving his dentures attached to the flesh of the fruit.

The juggler.

The ringmaster.

Hell, why wasn't he convinced that this kid Ayala was the killer?

Why didn't that jell in his brain?

It was too goddamn easy. A Mexican kid, no money for a good lawyer, an easy guy to railroad straight into the fucking gas chamber. Too neat. It didn't have the complexity, the mazelike core of the mystery.

Or was this just another personal grudge on his part? Envious that Rezabek, and not himself, had picked up the killer? He wiped his forehead. It had been a long, awful day.

Why doesn't it sit right in my skull? he wondered.

Coincidences. Goddamn coincidences.

Three dead women, all patients of one peculiar physician, whose concept of truth left something to be desired.

Okay. Suppose you came across a bunch of sticks in a

forest and they were arranged in such a way that they spelled out the word JOE or something, would you call it coincidence, some random occurrence, or would you think instead that a human agent had been at work?

You'd be disinclined to believe in the randomness of the arrangement, no? Some whim of nature? No, God, you'd think that somebody called Joe had passed that way and left his name shape from twigs, that's what you'd do—

So why three women who happened to be patients of Conturas, a man with a somewhat murky past? Why those three? And why the same MO every time?

Juggling again, faster and faster.

Romero Ayala Conturas

They were balls and they were all of different colors and they were running into blurs as he studied them and tried to keep them spinning.

romeroayalaconturas

Tobias yawned.

Go home, he told himself.

Sleep a little.

Maybe this kid is the killer.

He closed the cell door and walked slowly down the corridor to the front office, where Rezabek was hanging up the telephone.

"Dunbar delighted, huh?" Tobias said.

"Pissing his pants," Rezabek said. On the desk lay Ayala's suitcase, its lid open. Tobias looked at the collection of clothes and the box of expensive trinkets. It struck him as pathetic. A young boy's life stuffed in a suitcase.

"What makes you so sure, Sheriff?" he asked.

Rezabek allowed himself a laugh. It wasn't the kind of sound one might imagine issuing from that missile-shaped head. It had a certain delicacy to it, a high-pitched quality.

"Manning," and Karl Rezabek rose, stretching his arms. "An innocent man doesn't run away."

"If he's a scared young Mexican kid, he might."

"What is that supposed to mean?"

"It means he can't go out and get F. Lee Bailey to defend him, is what it means."

Rezabek waved the suggestion away, as if it were a fly that was bothering him. "Plus, just check his treasure trove, Manning."

"Okay. So you've got him linked to Maude Logan. I emphasize 'linked', Sheriff. You haven't got him connected in any way with Hamlett or Sharp, have you?"

Rezabek said, "You're miffed, aren't you?"

"Miffed?" Tobias stared at the guy a moment. He could feel a terrific tension behind his eyes, as if some force was exerting itself from within his brain, pushing at the sockets. "I like your use of langage, Sheriff. Miffed. Let me put it another way. I'm pissed off because I don't believe you've got the right man in there—"

Rezabek shrugged. "When I have his signed confession, you'll have to believe me then, right?"

"What are you going to use to get it, Rezabek? A crowbar?"

Tobias stepped out into the darkened street. He walked quickly across Hermosillo Square, pausing—as if by force of habit—to look up at Caroline's windows. Dark. Dark windows. A sense of emptiness.

Go home, he told himself again.

Go home.

Sleep.

Wake on a better day.

A day when you won't be humiliated by somebody like Romero. When you won't be pissed off by an asshole like Rezabek.

* * *

When he returned to the apartment there was no sign of Paul. The emptiness of the place assailed him. He went inside the bedroom and unlaced his shoes and lay down. Inadvertently, he let his eye stray to the collection of photographs that sat on the small circular table by the window. (Edie's antique table, picked up for a song at a barn auction one summer in Sterling, New York, salvaged from among the busted iceboxes and unstrung dulcimers and broken banjoes and boxes of shapeless, rusted-out tools—and what he suddenly remembered was the way Edie had turned to him and said, "The only thing they don't have here is a secondhand coffin.")

The photographs.

Edith's face.

A lovely oval shape, rather high cheekbones, wide intelligent eyes.

He looked up at the ceiling and he was filled with a terrible restlessness. That kid Carlos in the cell—it was wrong, all wrong. For starters, the kid had a good thing going with Maude Logan. The goose-and-the-golden-egg routine. For services rendered, he received his just rewards. Why knock her off? It didn't make a whole bunch of sense.

He rose, paced the room.

Okay, Art. What next? Who would you put your money on if this was Aqueduct?

And Art would chew his cigar and then, disgusted with a habit he couldn't ever seem to kick, lay it down in an ashtray and rip open a pack of Juicy Fruit, stabbing a stick into his mouth.

You got your doctor, he says, counting on his fingers. You got your young scared stud. And you got your mysterious stranger who might have been a suspect one time on a murder rap.

Right, Art, but you haven't shown me the color of your money yet.

If I was you, Art says, his jaws going so quickly around the chewing gum that his whole face seems to revolve, I would take a little time out and check this doctor guy again. For one thing, coincidence sucks. For another, he don't care much for the human race. And when a guy lies once, he's gonna lie again.

Tobias sat on the edge of the bed and Art Frye dissolved in front of his eyes.

He lay back, tried to relax by sending messages to his blood to slow down.

He shut his eyes and he slipped into a dream where he was going through some leafy glade with Edie and they were holding hands as they went across some slippery rocks that forded a stream. Edie lost her balance. Leaned against him, laughing.

He woke, his throat parched, the room still dark, when he heard Paul come in. And then he drifted back into sleep, a dreamless condition this time.

"Why are you whispering, Paul?" the voice asked.

"It's late, I don't want to wake my father, Streicher."

The man on the other end of the line was quiet a moment. "Paul, you were supposed to see me three nights ago. I don't understand why you missed the appointment. I explained my policy concerning appointments, the value of my time . . ."

Paul sighed. "I wanted to drive down here, that's all."

"Sudden urge to see father. Be with family."

"Maybe."

"Crawling back into what's left of the shell. Refuge from grief."

"Go fuck yourself, Streicher."

"Is that your favorite response to the world, Paul?"

Paul laughed. He took off his glasses. He noticed streaks of sand adhering to the sides of his sneakers and he brushed them with his fingertips.

"When are you coming back to L.A.?"

"Maybe tomorrow. Day after. I don't know yet."

"Staying for the Fourth of July, mmm? Patriotism. Another refuge."

"Jesus, Streicher, do you deliberately want to needle the hell out of me?"

"Worth a shot," Streicher said.

"You don't reach me. Okay? I'll see you when I see you."

Streicher was silent a second and when he next spoke there was a restrained anger in his voice. "You need me, Paul. You really need my help."

"I need your prescriptions," and Paul hung up.

He turned on the TV and checked the time on one of the cable channels that did nothing except display time and temperature and local news. It was 12:54. The temperature was 74 degrees.

He lay down on the sofa a moment. From the bedroom, he could hear the sound of his father gently snoring.

Then he saw words form on the screen, white words against a blue background.

A MAN HAS BEEN TAKEN INTO CUSTODY IN CONNECTION WITH THE SLAYING OF MAUDE LOGAN EARLIER TODAY IN LAS COSIMAS. THE MAN, TWENTY-YEAR-OLD CARLOS AYALA, IS A LOCAL RESIDENT.

A local resident, Paul thought.

He shut his eyes.

He snapped them open quickly remembering the man and woman he'd seen make love tonight on the beach. He'd watched from the pier, invisbile to them. The woman had screamed, although in a muffled way, as if maybe she had stuffed a handerchief inside her mouth or pushed her fist between her lips.

For a moment, he'd imagined the woman was Caroline.

The lovely Caroline.

Something in the way the couple had groaned together had made him uneasy, accentuated his solitude, and he'd driven around for hours in his VW, trying to think of nothing, trying to make his mind empty of everything.

Especially grief.

Caroline lit a joint and stuck her feet up on the coffee table. There was some small sense of triumph to be gained from the fact that she'd made Romero promise to stay for at least one more day and accompany her to the fireworks display. A small triumph, if a little hollow, because he was going, definitely going, the day after. No two questions about it. He was shaking the dust of Las Cosimas from his heels and going to wherever he pointed his Lincoln.

But there was a deeper void inside her than the realization of his impending departure.

She covered her eyes with her hands and the joint crackled in her fingers.

Boy, oh boy, oh boy.

The sonofabitch was married.

And she'd traipsed down that clichéd old pathway, the Rusty Brick Road, of falling for a goddamn married man.

She tried to think only of the sand. The experience on the sand. The way everything had fused together, moon and water and flesh and wind—but there was a gothic hysteria to this that made her want to laugh aloud. They'd left the beach and gone to Enrico's tavern in the Quarter and when he'd gone to the bathroom at one point, leaving his wallet on the table, she'd opened it slyly, seeing some business cards that said

Daniel Romero
Fine Porcelain
1800 Lincoln
Racine
Tel: 555-6780 (Office)
555-1844 (Home)

and she'd smuggled one of them out—then, behind the credit cards in the little glassine enveolpes, the pictures had flashed at her, wife and kids, lovely shining faces that accused her of housewrecking, of trying a demolition job on the old home fortress.

When Daniel Romero had come back, she was still leafing through the wallet. He seized it from her and she looked at him absently, trying to smile even if what she felt inside was a gastric flipflop, a missile launched into her solar plexus.

"Wife and kids?" she said.

"Wife and kids."

"You're going back to them?"

He had nodded his head.

"Why did you leave them?" Biting back tears then, overwhelmed by her own stupidity, her carelessness of the heart.

"To think things over. Take stock."

"I hope you took everything into account, Dannyboy," she had said. "At least give me the fireworks."

He'd smiled then, a little sadly.

Hell, she wasn't even sure of that smile.

He was still an enigma.

Her telephone was ringing.

She fumbled for it and, saying nothing, held it to her ear.

The voice on the other end of the line said, "You can't get well, Caroline. You know you can't get well, you can't ever get well again," and then the connection was dead, ruptured like something vital, and she tossed the receiver across the room, conscious of somebody out there in the dark of Las Cosimas, somebody who had her name and number as well as a purpose she couldn't begin to understand.

# 16

If you ignored the Quarter, it was arguable that the worst house in Las Cosimas was the one owned by Andrew Conturas. Shabby, grim, it seemed to have erected around it a series of KEEP OUT warnings, as if its occupant wanted only the pristine beauty of sheer privacy. As Tobias parked the Honda and looked up at the place—made even more decrepit by the hard morning sun—he thought that the only things missing were the ringing bells that would warn you of a leper colony. He got out of the car, hitched his belt, stared at the joint.

What to say? he wondered. How to begin?

Let's run everything through again, shall we, old fellow?

Let's be chummy, Andy, you and me. Clear this little affair up once and for all. And do let us have no more fabricated nonsense concerning your misdemeanor in Boston, what do you say?

Halfway up the path, Tobias paused. He had an uneasy feeling: the prospect of talking with this cold guy again, that was part of it. But there was also this other sliver of memory, the number of times he'd pushed Edie up here in the wheelchair. And that wouldn't budge out of his mind for a time.

All those times, his own sense of life dying inside him even as her heart withered in her body, all those times when his moods would swing from bright optimism to the black crepe of hopelessness, all those god-awful times when he'd find himself searching Conturas's face for a sign that Edie might get better, when he'd hang on the physician's icy words or listen, as if with a stethoscope of his own, for nuances and hidden meanings in the cold phrases of the doctor's speeches, when he'd find terror in the man's silences or in the way he cleared his throat or how he positioned himself in his chair—digging for significance in every move, every posture. Now Tobias realized that his despair then had been bottomless, a pit without limits.

When he moved again, he realized that the front door of the house was halfway open, which meant that Conturas was obviously somewhere nearby—maybe puttering around in the garden (albeit an unlikely prospect, given the nature of the jungle). He rapped on the door, which swung open, and then he called the physician's name. There was no answer.

He walked around the house, still calling.

The doctor, though, wasn't taking any calls.

He certainly wasn't answering them.

Tobias reached the front door once again and this time stepped into the hallway.

"Conturas?"

Not a damn thing. He stopped, listened to the house, listened to the way it seemed to deaden sounds by absorption, and he wondered if Conturas had performed his unholy cesarean in a similar house, a place where the screams of the girl couldn't be heard, where they'd be muffled by drapes and trapped in furnishings.

He went into the room on his left, the same room in which he'd talked with Conturas before, but the place was empty.

Across the hallway, another room, this one stuffed with furniture that had been covered over with dust sheets, ghostly drapes that hung motionless, almost shapeless. Tobias had the feeling that if he whipped the sheets away there would be nothing beneath them and he'd be left to marvel at the nature of this illusion. Back to the hallway, then the kitchen. Empty.

The stairs. The mysterious stairs.

Tobias began to climb.

Halfway up, he heard an odd gurgling sound and for a moment he imagined it came from a human agency (Conturas having a coronary, the irony of that), but it was so regular that it had to be mechnical or electrical.

He reached the landing, where the sound was louder.

He pushed a door open.

The noise came from pumps attached to several glass fish tanks in which swam perhaps the strangest creatures Tobias had seen. They were attached to each other as they shimmied back and forth, smaller blue fish attached to the heads of larger ones, like aquatic Siamese twins.

Tobias studied these for a second. Then he noticed various glass jars which contained what appeared to be tissues of several kinds. At first he thought these might be human, but as he moved nearer to them he realized they were parts of fish. In one jar, an entire head was suspended motionlessly in clear liquid, the flat eyes staring at him. The jars were clearly labeled, and every label was in Latin.

Photocorynus: otoliths.

A little sickened, Tobias stepped away. He was abruptly conscious of the fact that he was trespassing, that if Conturas stepped into the room all of a sudden he wasn't going to take the fact of Tobias's presence too kindly.

There was a desk by the window and Tobias moved toward it.

Papers. Folders. Drawings of the skeletons of fish.

He glanced at them, flipping pages.

So. This was it.

This was the big mystery up here.

Conturas was a fish hobbyist, albeit of a peculiar kind.

No bodies. No human hearts. No lungs or spleens in vases of formaldehyde.

He laid his hands on the desk surface, gazing at the brown blind that was halfway drawn down the window. The sun beat against it, creating an effect of shiny rust. He looked down at the desk again. There was a box of the kind that held index cards, three-by-fives, and he pulled it toward him.

He snapped the hinged lid back and removed one of the cards.

He read:

ISADORA SHARP

Myocardial infarction. Generalized arteriosclerosis with senescent debility.

Essential hypertension.

Symptomatology

Weakness, debility.

Shortness of breath.

Nervousness.

Tobias stuck the card back, took out another, realizing that what he had here was, so to speak, the mother lode, an index of Conturas's patients and their problems.

He scanned a second card quickly.

It was that of Maude Logan.

Give or take a phrase or two, it was pretty similar to that of Isadora Sharp.

Nervousness.

Loss of memory.

Loss of goddamn life, Tobias thought.

He removed a third card. Something clawed at his heart then.

EDITH MANNING

And under her list of symptoms, under those bastard names that had killed her, under those clinical items of jargon that had taken her away from him, was the solitary word

Deceased

Tobias put the card back quickly.

He found Emma Hamlett's.

He read it, found it meaningless, returned it.

One more.

One more card.

He slipped it out, his fingers clammy in this warm room, and he gazed at it.

CAROLINE CASSIDY

Caroline?

Caroline had come here to see Conturas?

But that didn't make any sense, Caroline was healthy, Caroline couldn't have problems of the heart—

He stared at the card.

Under her name was a scribbled phrase.

N/accepted

Meaning Conturas hadn't taken her on as a patient, presumably.

But he'd kept, in his own meticulous way, an index card with her name on it.

Isadora.

Emma.

Maude.

All dead.

All murdered.

The alarms in his head were shrill.

If somebody was killing Conturas's patients, if Conturas himself were doing it, you didn't have to be a math whiz to see that there were three down and one to go.

And that one—

A pulse beat in his throat.

He stepped around the desk to see if there was a telephone, thinking he might call the girl, and then he stopped—

Stopped dead—

His eye traveled very slowly to the floor, the space between desk and wall.

Slowly, too, a shape took form, a lifeless thing that seemed to float up toward him from murky depths, rising from silt to limpid surface.

He moved closer to it.

Bent down.

The body had been slashed in the dead center of the chest.

Like all the others.

Slashed in the heart.

Tobias leaned against the desk, breathing hard.

He stared away from the corpse and gazed at the grubby blind and he heard the roar of the aquarium pumps pound in his head.

Rezabek had a sheet of paper in one hand and, as if in

celebration of something, a plump cigar in the other. He glanced over the paper and appeared satisfied with what he read and then he knocked the cell door open with his foot, gazing at the kid as he did so. Carlos Ayala, who had spent a sleepless night cursing his bad luck and his good looks, stared up at the sheriff of Las Cosimas.

"You understand the meaning of the word 'confession,' Ayala?" Rezabek asked.

"Sure," Carlos said.

"Then sign this."

"Sign what?"

Rezabek thrust the paper at the kid and sat down on the bunk, his head momentarily vanishing within a cloud of thick cigar smoke. Carlos read the paper and then let it fall from his fingers to the floor.

The words on the paper that Rezabek had drawn up would put him in the death camp at San Quentin: "I admit I killed Maude Logan." He stared down at the floor, watched as the sheriff picked up the paper. Rezabek was thinking how stubborn this kid was going to be.

"Don't take a bad attitude with me, Ayala. Sign the goddamn paper."

"No way." Carlos stood up. "I'm supposed to get myself a lawyer, right? That's the law here, right? I sign nothing until I talk with a lawyer."

Rezabek smiled. A lawyer. That was the problem with these United States today. Everybody and his grandmother assumed they had rights and all the civil-liberties assholes and all the so-called principled lawyers had made the Constitution soft, like a half-finished freeway through which anybody could drive a sixteen-wheeler. Too many lawyers. Ambulance chasers, nothing more.

"You like to give me your lawyer's name, son?"

Carlos looked confused. He'd never needed a lawyer before. He didn't know the name of one.

Rezabek left the cell, slamming the door behind him. "When you think of it, I mean when it comes back to you, let me know, okay?" And he wandered toward his office, where he sat down. He glanced once more at the sheet of paper and he told himself: Kid will sign sooner or later.

Preferably sooner.

He looked up from his paper as he heard the outer door open and saw Tobias come inside the room.

There was a certain expression on Manning's face that he didn't like.

Without knowing why, maybe out of simple curiosity, perhaps from some more complex desire to subject herself to a moment of punishment, Caroline picked up her telephone and called the home number inscribed on Daniel Romero's business card. As she listened to a series of clicks and whirs, she remembered the voice that had talked to her last night, if talked was the word.

Was this the kind of sickness he was referring to?

Sitting here, wanting to hear the voice of a woman you'd never met and were never likely to either.

She tapped one foot on the rug, impatiently.

Put the receiver back. Forget this crap. Get on with your life.

She closed her eyes.

You're sick, Caroline . . .

It struck her then for the very first time that there was, after all, something faintly familiar in that voice, as if it were the voice of someone she knew, only he was talking through a handkerchief or something.

Why am I doing this?

Maybe I should be calling Mistresses Anonymous.

Whir, Click. Clicketyclick.

Fourth of July. Fireworks. Big deal.

She lit a cigarette, noticed her hand was trembling slightly.

Ring ring ring.

Then, a child's voice. "Hi," followed by the number.

Caroline hesitated. This was a bad threshold to be lingering on, she thought. What do you need this for?

Maybe I'm crazy or something. You sometimes read about people who made phone calls for no apparent reason. Or those other kooks who, having been jilted or otherwise discarded, continued nevertheless to pursue unrequited love through the good offices of the Bell system.

The kid said, "Hi," a second time.

"Hello," Caroline said. She tried to imagine an adolescent girl standing in a gleaming kitchen, telephone in hand, Mommy perhaps sitting at the table with a coffee cup and a cigarette—and an absence of Daddy.

What now, Caro? Isn't this enough?

Heigh-ho. "Can I talk to Mrs. Romero?"

A pause.

Caroline repeated her question.

The silence was thicker, a stew into which Caroline felt herself sink. Hang up, she told herself. Do it now! Curiosity is a lethal thing. But maybe it was more than that, maybe she'd become demented enough to become one of those supercilious bitches who took an inordiante amount of pleasure in telling tales to betrayed wives. Sorry to be the bearer of bad tidings, dear, but I saw your hubby sitting tête-à-tête, all very cozy, with So-and-So in the back room at Max's Bar, thought you'd want to know.... She wanted nothing more than to drop the receiver from her fingers, but it adhered to her skin as if by the force of magnetic attraction.

"Are you talking about Mrs. Daniel Romero?" the kid asked.

"I believe so."

"Are you out of your mind? I mean, Jesus, what kind of call is this?"

Caroline said nothing. The kid either had a poor attitude toward callers or there was something else lurking in the background here.

"I don't think I understand," Caroline said.

"What's to understand?" the kid asked.

You touched a nerve, Caroline thought. Something raw.

"My mother's dead," the girl said. "Died last year."

"I never knew that," Caroline answered and her throat was dry all at once. This is a wrong number, that's all, this is another Daniel Romero.

Another silence.

Then the kid said, "If you want to talk to my dad, he's right here."

Caroline put the receiver down slowly and she stood up, walking toward the window and looking down at Hermosillo Square, seeing nothing down there but the sharp sunlight bounce off the leaves of the pomegranate trees and making silvery coins out of the eucalyptus leaves.

A wrong number in a distant city, she thought.

Faraway Racine. How many Daniel Romeros were there anyhow?

A dead woman and a business card that didn't make any sense.

Fine porcelain, indeed.

In her mind she took a mallet and she smashed all that fine porcelain into pieces too small to be measured by any known instrument.

Karl Rezabek rose from his desk and watched Manning

turn to the water cooler, from which he drew a glass and drank thirstily. The sheriff was aware of having heard some vital new information here, but for a moment he was unable to absorb it. He approached Manning, who, quite infuriatingly, kept his back to him.

"Again," Rezabek said. "Tell me again."

Tobias turned. He noticed little droplets of sweat on Rezabek's brow. "When did you pick up Carlos?"

"Five o'clock."

"Five o'clock," and Tobias nodded. "I'm no forensic artist, Sheriff, but I'd say that guy was killed around midnight. I'd guess he'd been dead for ten hours when I ran into him. So, unless Carlos picked the lock, slipped out, killed the guy, came back again and relocked his cell, which is pretty damn stupid, then we're still looking for a killer in our fair town."

Karl Rezabek looked at his wristwatch as if there he might find answers to this new perplexing turn of events. Nothing suggested itself. A second hand moved meaninglessly, sweeping the dial.

Looking for a killer, he thought.

"Maybe he was dead longer than that, Manning. Look, maybe Ayala killed him before I picked him up—"

Tobias shrugged. "Like I say, I'm no forensic genius, Sheriff."

Rezabek sat down glumly behind his desk and examined the paper on which he'd composed Carlos's confession. A physician. He had to get an ambulance out to the Conturas place immediately. But Manning was already on the telephone, calling the hospital.

Rezabek didn't listen to the man's voice because his head was already filled with the sounds of his own crumbling convictions. He tilted his chair back at the wall.

Tobias put the reciver down, leaned against the counter and gazed at Rezabek.

"At least we can strike Conturas off our list of suspects," he said. "Unless he committed suicide by stabbing himself once in the chest and then, prior to joining the heavenly host, contrived to get rid of the murder weapon."

Suicide?

A little bulb went off in Rezabek's head. A tiny light of hope.

But it faded as soon as he looked at Manning's face, where he saw only a sly, teasing expression.

# 17

Gus and Morton had patched up their artistic differences as they usually did in the hour before one of their presentations was about to be unveiled. They set aside their arguments concerning colors and the appropriate amounts of such esoteric substances as antimony and strontium salts and mercury chloride. Now, with twilight falling, and the crowds already sitting on the roofs of their cars or spread on blankets, both men felt the flush of adrenaline that they normally experienced before a display. Morton hung an arm loosely around Gus's shoulder and Gus smiled with nervous affection.

Caroline, who had watched the two men finish their labors, went inside the Piano Bar of the resort and ordered a dry martini. The place was crowded tonight. The Fourth of July festivities, the usual stoned conversations that floated out on cushions of booze and cocaine and whatever else these highly paid, upwardly mobile executives jammed into their nervous systems. Maybe the talk was more relaxed than it might have been before Carlos Ayala had been stuck in the slammer. Maybe there was relief in the high-pitched conversations, the cries, the outbreaks of laughter. Whatever: she herself felt a sense of depression. She found herself turning time and again toward the door, hoping to see Romero come in—but even if he did, what was she going to say to him? Hey, I discovered you're not who you say you are?

Hell, did it matter?

Maybe, if he arrived as he'd promised, she would just go with the sweetness of the moment and then, come morning, admit to the fact that he'd just blown in and out of her life with the casual quality that was the hallmark of contemporary relationships. She'd enroll in est or Primal Therapy or Eckankar or do yoga and try to divine some inner serenity. Sinking, she had a second martini. Then a third. She speared the obligatory olive and held it up in front of her face and thought of some tiny hollowed-out insect skewered on a stick.

Why did the sonofabitch lie to her anyhow?

What was he doing traipsing around the country on fake ID?

And if it wasn't fake ID, what the hell else could it be?

Confused, she kept watching the door. Each time it swung open she caught a glimpse of darkening sky beyond the foyer.

Somebody touched her elbow and she turned to see Paul Manning stand beside her. He was wearing a tweed jacket and gray slacks and he had his hair slicked down.

"No glasses tonight?" she asked. Horror—her words were coming out like slurry snow cones.

"I don't always wear them," he answered. "You going to watch the display?"

She indicated her martini and the crucified olive. "Either that or I might start my own."

Paul Manning smiled and put his elbow on the bar. "Can I join you?"

"I'm not a club." Jesus, why had she said that? Smarting off at the mouth was sometimes the problem between herself and alcohol. She watched Paul slide onto the stool next to her. Why was it suddenly so noisy in this dump? You couldn't even hear the piano player. She sipped her drink, lit a cigarette, and noticed faint threads coming undone in that network of brain which coordinated spatial relationships. For instance, she couldn't quite reach the ashtray even though she stretched her hand out. Paul, still smiling, looking like he was on some natural high such as the kind you saw on certain faces rattling begging bowls at airports, passed the vessel toward her.

"Allow me," he said.

"Why, thank you, kind sir." She thought: I better be careful about now. I better step back from the slipway. She twisted her face and looked carefully at the young man. "You know, you're pretty good-looking without your glasses."

He appeared to be embarrassed. He fiddled with the cuffs of his jacket for a time.

"Sometimes . . ." She touched his sleeve and quite forgot what she was going to say. A danger signal. Red-light time. A whole sentence had just vanished out of her mind, a whole locomotive of meaning completely derailed. She imagined little boxcars of logic going crashing one into another, creating a concertina effect.

"Sometimes what?"

"It doesn't matter," she mumbled. She looked at her glass, still half-filled with clear liquid. Where was Romero? Why wasn't he here right now? Explaining things to her. Smoothing out the creases and crimps in his story. Fine porcelain. Taking stock. Wife and kids. He had a hell of a lot of explaining to do.

Paul had ordered her another martini and she watched the fresh glass slide toward her as she shook her head and said, "I can't, Paul, really, I think I'm getting pretty loaded already . . ." But then she didn't want to hurt the kid's feelings, so she drew the glass across the bar with her hand. The pianist was playing an old tune of Donovan's. "Mellow Yellow."

"You know that tune, Paul?"

Before he could answer there was a roar from outside and the sound of thunder splitting the sky and then he had her by the elbow and was escorting her across the foyer. Beyond the foyer the darkening sky was filled with zigzagging flashes of lights. It might have been the landing of UFO's.

"We can't miss the display," Paul said.

She wanted to say that she was waiting for somebody but he had already drawn her outside and was marching her across the grass, through parked cars and past people picnicking on blankets, walking her over spilled potato chips and squashed dill pickles and tangled infants enthralled by the chariots of fire.

Daniel Romero.

Tobias thought: It's all I have left.

Only Daniel Romero. Or whatever his name is.

When he'd punched the name into the computer, he'd waited a long time for a response.

He even wondered if the electronic marvel had broken down or if it had taken the Fourth of July as a good reason for closing its own banks of data.

Daniel Romero, the computer said eventually.

No record.

And then it had flashed again.

ROMERO, DANIEL
STOLEN CREDIT CARDS. RACINE,
WISCONSIN
VISA
# 4128 123 456 789
DINERS CLUB
# 3812 345 678 0001

AMERICAN EXPRESS
# 3712 345678 95006

The list went on and on.

And then the final snippet of electronic gossip, the information that the MacterCard had been used June 30 in Madison to rent a Lincoln Continental from Avis. The cards themselves had not been reported stolen until July 3.

The man calling himself Daniel Romero was enjoying a free trip through the countryside in a Lincoln hired with a stolen credit card. Enjoying fine dining and good hotels.

And Caroline Cassidy too.

Tobias squeezed his car through the overstuffed parking lot of the country club just as the dark sky was filled with extraordinary shapes. Gigantic birds came clawing out of nowhere, bizarre parrots scavenged the night, starlike clusters of macaws rose in stunning flight and then scattered into millions of diamonds. A dragon then, for God's sake, a great explosive reptile that had the Fourth of July crowd applauding and whistling.

He saw the black Lincoln parked in the lot and he stopped the Honda, getting out. So many damn people. He pressed his way through the foyer of the resort and then found himself jammed close to the desk, surrounded by people balancing drinks. The sky outside just kept blazing and fizzing. It wasn't a fireworks display, it was an outrageous act of God.

Tobias pushed his way through to the elevator, pressed the button, waited and waited. When the car came, he got inside and was at once brutalized my Muzak. "Raindorps Keep Falling on My Head."

Daniel Romero, he thought again.

There was nothing left to juggle with.

He comes here, for some obscure reason he finds out the names of Conturas's patients, and for a reason even more obscure than that, he starts to kill them.

Why?

Okay, so he wasn't the Danny Romero from New York, but what the hell did that matter now?

Tobias was thinking of Caroline. He'd stopped by her apartment, found the place in darkness, then he'd come out here as quickly as traffic would allow.

The man calling himself Daniel Romero was her lover.

Perhaps also her killer.

The doors slid open. He moved along the corridor to Romero's room. He knocked.

Knocked again.

Nothing.

He tried the door handle. Locked.

Back to the elevator, the foyer, the drunken crowds, the exploding sky. He made it to the desk, crushed on all sides, and he looked at the receptionist, a woman who had the myopic appearance of someone accustomed to long hours over a microscope.

"Mr. Romero," he said.

"He just checked out," the woman answered.

"How long ago?"

"Five, ten minutes."

Checked out, Tobias thought.

Vanished into the starburst darkness.

Tobias pushed his way out. The sky was a work of art. Reds, golds, yellows, blues, they dripped down through the dark like colors spilled from a palette.

He hurried in the direction of the parking lot.

The Lincoln was still there.

But there was no sign of Danny.

Tobias moved toward the car. Maybe Romero had already picked up Caroline, maybe they were out there somewhere in the crowd that spilled over the grassy ridges and was strung out along the edges of the golf course. Then how the hell was he going to find them? He stared upward at the sky, blinking against the descent of fiery parachutes, sparks, precious stones, the smashed petals of gorgeous flowers.

He tried to relax. Tried to think.

Romero was a cool sonofabitch. The way he'd faced Tobias down in the hotel room, knowing all the time that he was a resident under false pretenses. A goddamn felon—and still he didn't lose a sliver of his cool.

Tobias stared through the crowds, across the parked cars, seeing featureless faces lit by the glow of the crazy explosions. The noise of cracking and bursting filled his ears. It's impossible. It's going to be impossible to find them here.

Daniel Romero saw Caroline and a young man just ahead of him. Caroline walked in a swaying fashion, now and then colliding with the guy, knocking elbow to elbow. The kid slid an arm around her shoulders, more a gesture of support than an expression of affection.

Romero paused. The fireworks burned up the air overhead.

Caroline and the kid were going along the edge of the fairway. Maybe they were searching out some isolated place.

Romero paused a moment.

It was a pity about the Lincoln because he'd started to like the beast.

What the hell.

You were always moving on.

Fireworks, noise, the sky falling in, the sloshing of martinis in her empty stomach. Caroline felt sick suddenly. She had to stop, lean against Paul, wait for the sensation to pass. Water, she thought. She wanted cold crystal water on her face.

"You okay?" he asked.

She shook her head.

"You sick, Caroline?"

Dizzying rockets turned the night into a cascade of madness. Gravity had lost its center, leaving the world topsy-turvy. A great orb spinning nowhere. Exactly like her head.

"You are sick, aren't you?" Paul asked.

She knew where there was a stream. It ran across the golf course somewhere. She needed to dunk her face in its dark waters and she'd be okay.

She'd be just fine then.

She collided with him.

Motor collapse.

Slump slump. She had the feeling that she was an engine operating on coagulated oil.

And the knocking sound she heard wasn't coming from the fireworks, it had its origin inside her head.

Yeah, yeah, I'm sick, she thought.

I'm sick all right.

A tiny voice in my own head is telling me so.

An echo.

But then Paul was telling her he'd take care of her, he'd look after her, and she remembered through the haze that he was a pre-med student, so she didn't feel so bad after all.

She was in good hands.

Tobias stopped. He'd run into a station wagon around which stood a gang of Budweiser freaks. Three ice chests filled with Bud cans, some of them afloat on melting chunks. Thick tattooed arms, tank tops, cut-off shorts. Hats with BUDWEISER written on them.

"Hey, man, have a brewsky," somebody said.

"Yeah, a cop on the Fourth of July deserves something."

A can was popped and shoved into his hand just as the sky went berserk again and this time it blew apart in the shape of a snake rearing its skull to strike, and venomous colors, bloody colors, came showering through the blackness.

"Be happy. It's the Fourth."

Tobias took the can and pressed forward again.

Cars, bodies, babies, kids, Frisbees even.

He was hauling himself through the celebratory detritus of Americana, looking—in the midst of all this partiotism—for a sick killer.

He threw the Bud away and started to move.

Which was when he thought he saw Romero far ahead of him, the silver hair catching the last reflection of the disintegrating serpent.

The kid would be no problem.

Romero gazed up at the sky.

The kid would just go away. Just be made to go away.

Then he'd have Caroline to himself.

Probably for the last time.

You had to keep moving on.

Caroline couldn't remember where the stream was located. She doubled over, dipped her face into a shrub, and she vomited once. The sky was spinning.

Paul touched the side of her face.

A gentle, considerate touch.

"You're not any better, are you?" he asked.

She shook her head and tried to smile at him weakly.

The fireworks appeared to be miles away now.

"Poor Caroline," the kid said.

Tobias thought he saw Romero again as the light show went on above him, a skyful of splinters and streamers and ribbons, floating earthward like silken garlands. Then there were fragments of dark between the explosions of light and he wasn't sure if he'd seen Romero after all. He skipped around the side of a pickup truck filled with people from the Quarter, making one of their rare forays into the territories of the rich. The Fourth of July. The Great Equalizer, next to death itself.

He hurried in the general direction of the man he'd seen, but the abrupt darkness, as shocking in its own way as the outbursts of light, made him uncertain. And nowhere, nowhere had he seen any sign of Caroline Cassidy. He was working on the assumption that Romero was making his way to an appointed place, a meeting spot, somewhere removed from the general rabble.

The last name on Conturas's index cards.

The last name.

More ribbons of flame broke overhead and came streaming down toward him as if they were confetti from some celestial wedding

The last name, he thought again. And what he wished for right then was a special kind of eyesight, ultraviolet, something that would enable him to pierce the darkness.

There.

Moving ahead.

Tobias was sure.

Daniel Romero. Whoever he was.

Passing between two parked campers, from the depths of which there was the sound of partying and a stoned voice screwing up the lyrics of "Country Roads."

Hurry, Tobias.
Hurry.

The stream was nothing more than a slash of murky water carved across the fairway and straddled by a wooden bridge of a humpbacked design. Caroline recognized the bridge and, assisted by Paul, moved down the incline toward the bank. There, crouching, she cupped cold water in her hands and threw it around her face and neck, letting it drip through her cotton shirt to her breasts. Paul was kneeling beside her, his voice like a crooning on some radio that wouldn't stop playing in the background.

"You're going to be fine, really, you're going to be fine, Caroline, believe me."

She closed her eyes. Damp lashes, skull pounding, world falling apart.

She whispered, "It's a little better."

And she vomited into the stream.

As she did so, she took an oath that she'd never drink again, not even if somebody threatened her with a pistol to her head. Her hand damp, she touched Paul's wrist—a tiny gesture of gratitude for the way he was looking out for her.

Daniel Romero reached the bridge. He stood in the dead center of it and stared down through the darkness, watching the kid lean over Caroline. He could hear the noise of the girl throwing up. And when that stopped he moved in the direction of the bank.

At first, he planned to just tell the kid to split.

If the kid didn't do that willingly, then he'd have to take other measures.

It was his last night in Las Cosimas, after all.

And Caroline Cassidy was just too good an opportunity to waste.

Tomorrow, he'd have to be far gone from this place, looking for fresh pastures and new credit cards and another identity. And Daniel Romero, who'd been a generous benefactor, would regrettably have to be laid to rest.

Tobias realized that the cars and trucks were thinning out, that he was moving beyond the outer reaches of the celebration. Ahead of him lay the impenetrable dark of the fairways. Behind, there seemed to be a lull in the display, some kind of holdup, because the sky was unlit and the moon a poor match for the fireworks. Give me something, he thought. Give me a flare. A rocket. Give me something so motherfucking bright that it's going to fill the sky because I need to find a killer out there who's got a girl with him, please, give me a little something—

"This fuse, love, is fucked," Gus said, trying to sound both cool and irritated at the same time.

"That fuse, love, was your responsibility," said Morton, turning on a flashlight.

"This is neither the time nor the place to discuss responsibility," Gus answered snappishly.

Morton sighed.

Gus recognized that sound. It was the breeze of accusation whining in the empty spaces of Morton's peanut brain.

"I am growing weary, Morton," Gus said.

"Don't take that foot-stamping tone with me, buster."

"Please, Morton, the natives grow restless. Be a dear. Rush over to the van. Find me a replacement."

Morton huffed and hummed and then swished around and went stomping toward the Day-Glo van, while Gus cursed the fuse, cursed the break in the action, cursed everything that happened to cross his mind while he waited for the return of his partner and listened, with despair, to the murmurs of an impatient crowd.

Tobias felt the darkness as though it were a collar around his neck. How could he find anyone in this light? He stumbled into a sandy bunker just as the feeble moon was sucked behind cloudbanks, and he couldn't see a damn thing.

He groped out of the sand, made out the slack flag in the center of the green, moved toward it. Somewhere around here was a stream, he recalled.

And then, wondrously, a prayer answered, the sky was alive again, roaring, rumbling, stardust, the flashing of lights.

Daniel Romero, fully lit, like a stage figure, an actor spotlighted at the end of a performance, was moving just ahead of him. Then, where the land dipped, he vanished out of sight.

Caroline could hear Romero's voice. It had the sound of a phonograph playing in an attic room. Miles away. She wiped cold water from her eyes and raised her head and made out the shape of Romero standing on the bank.

"Danny?" she said. And she was confused, her senses spinning at that vortex where reality and the dream converged.

Romero came closer. He seemed to be looking at Paul. He said, "Why don't you run along home, kid? I have to speak to Caroline here. And it's private. Understand?"

Paul didn't move.

Caroline said, "Paul, it's okay, really."

Still, Paul didn't move.

Romero smiled. He took a step closer to Paul. "Did you hear me?"

"I heard," Paul answered.

"Well?"

"Caroline's sick," Paul said. "She needs my help."

"I can give her all the help she needs, kid," Romero said and he reached down toward Caroline, gripping her by the waist, hauling her up to a standing position.

The sky blew apart again.

Caroline heard the thunder roll and roll inside her skull. And she was aware of how damp her clothes had become, linen sticking to her flesh.

And another echo.

Caroline's sick.

Echoes could deceive. Could make you imagine things.

Sick, she thought.

She looked at Paul's face, which had been made suddenly yellow by something exploding in the sky.

"Paul, this is a friend of mine, I'll be okay with him," she heard herself say. "Everything's fine. Everything's going to be all right. Believe me."

"Listen to the lady, kid," Romero said.

Paul didn't move.

He let his hands hang by his sides a moment and, in the skylight that changed from yellow to bronze to red, an expression of pain crossed his face.

And then he moved swiftly.

A freak show, a chamber of horrors, a stroboscopic nightmare.

Tobias stood perfectly still on the bank, as motionless as he'd ever been in his entire life enveloped by a silence more profound than any he'd ever experienced.

Lights flashed.

He didn't notice them.

The world cracked open.

He didn't hear.

Flash. Paul moved, as if in a dance of terror, and Romero stepped backward, holding his hands to the center of his chest, then down, down and down to the grassy bank, moaning as he dropped. He seemed to hang in the air for a second before he spun facefirst into the stream.

And Tobias couldn't move.

Everything is fine, he told himself.

Everything's okay.

But it wasn't. It was wrong.

All wrong.

Only he couldn't exactly figure out why because his senses were not his own suddenly. His feelings, responses, memories—all these were the attributes of some waxen figure frozen in a store window.

He could read his own report. "Faced with the killer, Paul Manning protected the life of Caroline Cassidy. He stabbed the killer once in the chest. . . ."

A report.

Words on paper.

Yes. Everything's fine now.

Even as he stepped toward his son, who was standing in front of Caroline Cassidy—her lovely face expressionless, numb, Novocained—he knew that the whole world was wrong, tilted in its orbit, adrift in a void.

The knife in Paul's hand.

The blade catching all the distant bursts of color.

Mirrors of the big celebration in the sky.

Tobias wanted to weep. He felt moisture press behind his eyes.

Make me blind, he thought.

Make me unseeing, unfeeling.

Take away the thoughts I'm thinking now, the realizations that are crowding me. Dear God.

"Give me the knife, Paul. Give it to me."

He held out one hand, his skin turned to a serpentine green by the sky.

The pain was buried deep, buried a long way down.

The pain was more than the scorching core of grief.

Paul's pain. It ran through the kid like a network of hollows left behind by some blind, burrowing animal, it turned from hollows into one large cave of sheer despair.

My poor son. My kid.

"Give me the knife."

The knife was turned toward Caroline's chest.

"Please, Paul," Tobias said.

"She shouldn't need to suffer," Paul said. "Nobody needs to suffer. The way David did. The way Mother did."

David. Mother. A whole family shellshocked, shattered. Hand grenades of grief. All the delayed reactions of pain. Shrapnel wounds at the center of the boy's being.

"Conturas wasn't suffering—"

"He was only prolonging pain for people, that's all he was capable of doing—"

Tobias could hear something go out of him, something with the soft swish of a bird's wing, and he understood that a quality had flown from him, a quality he could never recover. It was as if his skin had been stripped away and the bare bones covered by a hard shell. A surface that could never be penetrated again.

"Caroline isn't suffering, Paul," he said.

"She was on the list, dammit, she was on the fucking list, don't you know that, don't you know, her card was right next to Mother's, for Christ's sake—"

"Give me the knife, kid."

"She's in pain, can't I make you see that, Caroline's sick—"

"No," and Tobias shook his head.

How could you go on after this? How did you live out your life? He gazed at his own outstretched palm and let the questions drift through his mind and away, free in the darkness.

"I can help her," Paul said. "I can free her, that's what I know how to do—"

Dear Jesus.

Sweet Christ.

The boy was an angel of goddamn mercy, scalpeling hearts. Emma Hamlett and Isadora Sharp and Maude Logan.

"Let me help you, Paul. Okay? What do you say?"

Tobias glanced at the body of Romero, half-submerged in dark water. A cheap Romeo, a cheap thief. Not a killer.

He felt his stomach rise into his throat.

Paul moved the knife. The blade flashed.

It rose upward and hung over Caroline with the inevitability of a guillotine.

My gun, Tobias thought.

How do I use a gun on my own kid?

That poor, suffering child—

The knife was red now. Red, silver, then red again.

At first Tobias thought it was the red of blood. But it was only the reflected glare of the endless rocketry that zipped through the night.

"The knife, Paul."

The boy didn't move. In the terrifying light his eyes were like coins from a foreign country. A currency Tobias had never seen before.

"Don't hurt Caroline, Paul. Don't hurt her."

And Tobias felt his hand go toward his holster, the most unnatural act of his entire life. He imagined the passage of a single bullet through his son's chest, saw the kid blown backward toward the stream, and in this image there were a hundred others, mirrors reflecting a multitude of mirrors—two boys and himself standing outside a pup tent in the Adirondacks in 1969, Paul's face strained in concentration over a sheet of paper on which he was writing a poem, Paul and David playing basketball in the backyard and the big ball falling in slowed-down motion through the hoop attached to the wall of the house, hundreds of pictures just went tumbling through him.

Now this. This knife.

But it isn't in the hand of any stranger, is it?

It's in the fist of someone I love.

Paul moved, the knife rose a little, Tobias took out his pistol.

But he didn't have to fire.

The blade slipped from the boy's fingers, tumbled away in the dark. Tobias stepped forward and embraced the kid, holding him hard, holding him as if he might never release him again, feeling the kid's pain course through his own body, feeling a closeness he'd never felt before with any other human being, a nearness that drowned his senses.

"I didn't know what else to do," Paul said. "I didn't know what else to do, how to help, I was doing the best I could, Pops. . . ."

The kid's face was wet.

Tobias pulled himself away just as the last of the fireworks display sizzled in the sky, throwing down great streamers of dazzling color that, as they illuminated the scene on the bank, reminded Tobias of nothing more than impossible tears.

"The only thing I could do," Paul said again.

# *Epilogue*

There was an orange sun in the October sky and the wind that shuffled up Forty-second Street was cold, nipping at Tobias as if it were already winter. He crossed the street and entered the cafeteria on the corner of Third Avenue. Warm inside, good and cozy, a big room filled with smells of strong coffee and freshly baked bread and pickles.

He looked around and then he moved to a window table in the far corner, where Art Frye was poling at a saucer of coleslaw with a plastic fork.

"Goddamn plastic, would you look at it, Tobe," and Art brandished the tiny implement in disgust. "Used to have silverware in here. Back in seventy-eight. I remember when they went plastic." Art smiled, wiped a strand of cabbage from his plump lower lip, crumpled the napkin in his fat hand. His face was redder than Tobias remembered it and his eyes more watery, as if he were constantly staring into a bright light.

Tobias sat down and undid the buttons of the overcoat. He said, "I start January one."

"Great, great," Art said.

"I don't know if we'll be working together, but . . ." Tobias gazed at the menu, but he wasn't hungry. "McMullen said there was always a chance."

"McMullen. It was a minor miracle he made inspector, you know that? I figure he prayed so hard for the promo that God got bored and just gave the fucking opening to him." Art Frye opened a tiny container of nondairy creamer. "Would you look at the goddamn ingredients on this, Tobe? This shit's never been near a cow's udder."

Tobias realized that Art Frye wouldn't know a cow's udder if he collided with one. He liked to bitch, that was all. Bitching about the world changing was an essential prism through which his personality came.

"Department's changed a lot too, Tobe. We got more women these days than we ever used to have. A couple of lookers as well. Can't understand some broads wanting to be cops. Never could."

Art was silent and in his silence there was a strain, an awkwardness that was palpable.

"How's the kid, Tobe?" he asked eventually. The question had been on his mind all along, Tobias knew that. It had been submerged beneath the talk of nondairy creamers and female cops and Inspector McMullen.

Tobias put one hand in his overcoat pocket. The kid, he thought. There was a letter in the pocket from the hospital in L.A., but he hadn't opened it. Hospital, he thought. There was a euphemism. Wards with bars and combination locks and orderlies who looked like they knew jujitsu or could kick your face in with one karate chop.

Tobias shut his eyes a moment. "He's . . ." His voice faded away.

Art Frye put a hand on Tobias's arm. "It's good to have you back here. I mean that. This city's turned to scum since you went away. There're more criminals than cockroaches, I swear."

Tobias smiled. The last letter he'd received from Paul had been lucid, concise, done in a firm upright hand, a steady hand that suggested a sense of direction. The letter before that might have come from a different person altogether, filled with phrases redolent of intense pain, a work of grief. And the kid's mind had seemingly entered a time warp of sorts, because he'd referred to his family as if they were all alive, he'd written about David's upcoming birthday and some movie he wanted his mother to see—and Tobias, crying over that letter, understood that Paul's relationship with the world was a fragmented thing, as if he perceived events through frosted glass, seeing only shadows whose identities he couldn't grasp, whose purposes he couldn't understand.

He didn't know what to expect in the one he hadn't yet opened.

Recovery was a long road when you didn't have maps or compasses. He stared at the menu, which blurred in front of his eyes. Suddenly, he was back in Paul's mind, back at the point when he'd last seen the kid after the trial, after the jury recommendation of "psychiatric treatment for an indefinite period"—he was back in the kid's nightmare of pain, his wild confusions, his conviction that he could heal the suffering.

Recovery.

The word felt slippery in his mind, an eel he couldn't quite grasp, something that kept slithering and slipping away from him.

He blinked.

"When the crooks heard you were back in town, Tobe, they started to batten down the hatches, you know that?"

Tobias smiled.

"Swear to God, I could hear sighing and feel trembling."

"Those were subway vibrations," Tobias said.

"My ass," Art Frye said, and patted the back of Tobias's hand. The he rose and looked down at Tobias. "Want to ride around the old precinct with me?" he asked.

Tobias nodded and stood up.

"Sure," was all he said.

## ABOUT THE AUTHOR

THOMAS ALTMAN is a writer who lives in Arizona. His first novel for Bantam was the very successful *Kiss Daddy Goodbye*, published in 1980. It was followed by *The True Bride*, *Black Christmas*, and then by *Dark Places*.